W0037652

COPPER RAVENS

JENNIFER ALLIS PROVOST

SPENCE
CITY

© 2014 Jennifer Allis Provost

Sale of the paperback edition of this book without its
cover is unauthorized.

Spencer Hill Press

This book is a work of fiction. Names, characters, places,
and incidents are products of the author's imagination or
are used fictitiously. Any resemblance to actual events,
locales, or persons, living or dead, is entirely coincidental.

All rights reserved, including the right to reproduce this
book or portions thereof in any form whatsoever.
Contact: Spence City, an imprint of Spencer Hill Press, PO
Box 247, Contoocook, NH 03229, USA

Please visit our website at www.spencecity.com

First Edition: May 2014.
Jennifer Allis Provost
Copper Ravens: a novel / by Jennifer Allis Provost – 1st
ed.
p. cm.
Summary:
In a strange land whose customs she doesn't understand,
Sara struggles to find her place in Micah's world.

Cover design by Lisa Amowitz
Interior layout by Jennifer Carson and Marie Romero

978-1-939392-85-5 (paperback)
978-1-939392-89-3 (e-book)

Printed in the United States of America

For those who never lost sight of their goals

1

My name is Sara Elizabeth Corbeau, and I'm an Elemental.

I'm also a fugitive.

For most of my life, I did everything I could to appear ordinary. I avoided magic like I avoided large spiders and stepping on cracks, and not just so I wouldn't break my mother's back. After the Magic Wars had ended, in which magic had been the definitive loser, it was just too dangerous to be caught using. That was how my brother, Max, got arrested and turned into a science experiment at the Institute for Elemental Research. That, coupled with the fact that my father had gone missing during the wars, meant that I went through life claiming a total and complete ignorance of magic.

Then Micah appeared in my life (technically, he first appeared in my car, even though I was dreaming at the time), and everything changed. And I mean *everything*. Micah is a metal Elemental like me, although he's of silver whereas I'm a copper girl. Together, we rescued Max, destroyed the Iron Queen, and put a serious dent in the military branch of the Mundane government's (the inappropriately-named Peacekeepers) operation. So, yeah, that would be how I became a fugitive, along with the rest of the Corbeaus.

All of that had happened about three months ago. Micah, kind soul that he is, had offered my entire remaining family—Mom, Sadie, Max, and even the Raven—sanctuary at his home in the Whispering Dell. So far, no one had died, though a few of the silverkin had come perilously close. Officially, we all understand that the silverkin are manifestations of the massive vein of silver that runs below the Whispering Dell and only exist to serve Micah, the reigning Lord of Silver; I had called Micah a king once and had been rewarded with one of his rare frowns.

While not truly sentient, the silverkin are the most well-meaning of creatures. However, the critters do come up short in the common sense department. A prime example of their lack of self-preservation skills was when they had insisted upon bringing Mom a few snacks and a cushion while she was meditating in the garden, despite her many refusals.

Luckily, Micah was able to mend the dented 'kin, and, after a stern lecture, the silverkin agreed to only speak to Mom when spoken to, and Mom—amazingly—agreed to not damage any more of the servants. For now.

Destruction of the help notwithstanding, Mom was having a far easier time adjusting to our new life in the Otherworld than Sadie or Max were. Now, I could understand Sadie's issues, being that she had been ripped from her safe, boring life as a college student (studying to be a librarian, of all things), informed that she was the Inheritor of Metal, and thrust headlong into the magical reality that was now our lives. Yep, I understood how that could be a bit disconcerting.

Max, on the other hand, had no such excuses. He'd lived in the Otherworld for more than ten years now, and all of this strangeness should have been old hat to him. Yeah, so what if most of his time here had been spent in the Institute? He was still *here*. He should know *something*.

I wish I could say that I was gracefully taking on my new role as Micah's consort, but that would be a lie. And fey don't lie, you know? Not that I'm a fairy. Well, not completely, and only on my mother's side.

Anyway, it turned out that politics in the Otherworld were just as maddening as politics in the Mundane realm; if anything, the addition of magic and factions of perpetually bickering Elementals made it more so. Not that anyone cared what I had to say, mind you. I was expected to appear on Micah's arm at these varied events, perfectly coiffed and perfectly silent, since, as a mere consort, I was viewed as little more than a decoration. A mute, compliant decoration.

Yeah. I'm about as mute and compliant as a howler monkey.

I didn't blame any of those misconceptions on Micah. He had never treated me as anything other than his lover and his equal, but the fact remained that I was not Lady Silverstrand, nor would I be until I bore him a child. Which I hoped wouldn't happen for a long, long time.

What's worse, these events that demanded our presence were becoming all too frequent, since the sudden death of the Iron Queen had left a gaping void in the Elemental power structure. Being that we were responsible for said royal demise (technically, I'd cashed in a favor owed to me by the Bright Lady of the Clear Pool), Micah's attendance was required at each and every Gathering of the Heavies, as Sadie had so eloquently termed these functions. His opinion was sought out in all matters, while I was only expected to stand there and nod. Couple that with the strange and varied formalities that I was required to commit to memory, and it was enough to drive one mad.

"How was I supposed to know that Old Stoney couldn't drink wine?" I grumbled after one such gathering. Old Stoney was the *de facto* ruler of the earth Elementals, at least until the as yet unknown

Inheritor of Earth surfaced. Speaking of surfaces, Old Stoney was of granite, specifically. Apparently, those of earth—or granite, at least—do not ingest liquid refreshment, since it rolls right on out of them like so much rain on asphalt. Little things like those were what I was expected to know, and I managed to come up short more often than not. Exasperated, I flopped down on Micah's bed. I was still a little weirded out calling it *our* bed.

"Old Stoney?" Micah repeated, quirking a silver brow.

"I can't remember all these foolish names," I muttered. Old Stoney's actual name was Something Greymalkin, or maybe it was Something Greymountain. "Why isn't anyone named Todd or Jim?"

"Because we are not denizens of the Mundane World." Micah crawled onto the bed beside me and smoothed the hair back from my face. It had been done up in one of those elaborate confections that were a silverkin specialty, but by now it looked less like sleek waves and more like a bird's nest. A ratty, lopsided bird's nest. "You think those of the Otherworld do not have trouble with Mundane names?"

"There are no Mundanes here, besides me and my family." I snuggled up to Micah, enjoying a moment's peace. "I really screwed things up, didn't I?"

"Between me and Old Stoney?" Micah asked. I laughed, hiding my face against his throat. "Not likely. Remember, we of metal still have the upper hand." Micah wrapped his arms around me; as I moved to encircle his waist, my hand bumped his sword belt.

"Can you really use a sword?" I asked. I'd seen Micah perform a few incredible feats—such as ripping the head off an iron warrior with his bare hands—but I'd never seen him in a swordfight.

"I can," he replied.

"I bet you'd look pretty hot chopping someone's head off," I murmured. Micah, who struggled with Mundane idioms as much as I struggled with Elemental names, rolled me onto my back.

"Hot is good?"

"Very good," I affirmed. Micah laughed, the gentle rumbles in his chest once again making everything right in the world. After a fair bit of snuggling, I asked, "Have you heard anything new about the queen?"

Oriana, the Gold Queen, had been captured by Ferra, the Iron Queen (the one we had, um, *rusted*), and had spent the past few years as a prisoner in the Iron Court. After Ferra's demise, Oriana had been promptly rescued, but her health was hanging on by a thread.

"She is convalescing," Micah said, to my relief. If Oriana died, my life would become immensely more complicated. You see, next in line for the metal throne is Micah Silverstrand, the man whose bed I sleep in. And I do *not* want to be a queen.

2

Once I'd extricated myself from the rest of my formal attire and dragged a brush through my copper-colored hair, I made my way downstairs, intent upon visiting with my family. All these formal events Micah and I had attended of late had really only served to remind me that I was a stranger in this very strange land. Not to mention, very few of the Elementals that I had so far encountered welcomed me as one of their own. Most saw me as a weak mortal, an outsider who should have stayed in her home realm.

And *you're welcome* for getting rid of the Iron Queen.

What these haughty Elementals don't know is that my mother, Maeve Connor Corbeau, was once the Queen of Connacht and had gone on to become

Queen of the Seelie Court. Since Mom gave up her fairy ways when she married Dad, we've been trying to keep her Irish heritage quiet. Still, I wonder how those snooty jerks would react to learning of my own royal lineage.

As I passed a large window, I spied Mom in the garden, leaning against one of the apple trees. It was in full bloom as well as heavily laden with fruit, as only an Otherworldly tree can be. I debated joining her, but she was wearing that wistful expression that had begun appearing often after Dad disappeared. Mom had originally fought with the government for information about Dad's fate; she'd screamed at them so loud and often that my ears rang for years. Then the Peacekeepers had arrested Max, and the loss of her husband and her son was just too much for Mom. Within a few weeks of Max's arrest, she had given up her weekly—sometimes daily—shouting matches with the local Peacekeepers and had taken up vegetable gardening. She doesn't even like vegetables.

Well, we'd managed to find Max, so finding Dad couldn't be too difficult. Not that we had any idea of where to look for him, or any leads, but we hadn't had those with Max, either. Our big break had come when I'd decided to dreamwalk to Max, all by myself. Yeah, that wasn't the brightest plan. Still, I had found him. Not bad, for my first solo dreamwalk.

Both Max and I had since tried dreamwalking to Dad, but we both came up short. We'd been terrified at first, thinking our lack of success meant that Dad was gone, but Micah had assured us that this wasn't necessarily the case. Most likely, Dad was being held somewhere that was warded against dreamwalking.

"Or perhaps," Micah had amended, seeing my horrified face, "he has made himself unreachable." Well, that was certainly a more attractive concept than Dad being surrounded by wardsmiths strong enough to keep out Dreamwalkers.

When Mom had first heard the news that her husband was probably alive and possibly being held by evil sorcerers, she tried every trick she knew to find him—charmed maps, locator spells, you name it, she conjured it. And, none of them worked.

After her hundredth failure, she had started these daily meditations in the orchard; at first, we thought she was trying to come up with a new spell. When Max had offered to help her with said spell, she confirmed that she was merely trying to clear her head, along with my worst fears. Just like she'd done in the Mundane world, Mom was withdrawing into herself rather than admitting that she needed help. It was a supreme irony that the individual most capable of freeing Dad from any sort of evil magic was the one hiding in the back yard.

I sighed, and decided that leaving Mom alone with her memories was the best course of action, for now at least. I continued on to the ground floor of the manor and found Sadie in one of the many empty rooms.

My kid sister was seated on the floor, smack in the middle of the room, intently staring at a few lumps of metal. Mustering all my stealthiness, I hung back and watched as she coaxed the metal into long ribbons, up and up and over her head, stretching and curling before her in a serpentine dance. They curled into and out of spirals, perfectly symmetrical, like tiny metal clouds bouncing across the sky. I was impressed; she had excellent control of the metal, but then again, she'd been practicing. Give Sadie a structured lesson plan, and she could move mountains.

"Very good," I murmured, only to watch the ribbons fall to the floor and shatter.

"Sorry," I offered as I plopped down beside her. "That was really cool, though."

"Yeah." Sadie fingered the broken metal; she'd stretched it so thin it was translucent, like a fine china teacup. "How was the Gathering?"

"Long and frustrating. Where's Max?"

"Out." She didn't elaborate, and I didn't ask. Not having specific knowledge of Max's extracurricular activities had always served us well.

"You know, as the Inheritor you should really be going to these Gatherings with me and Micah," I said.

"And do what? Show off my party tricks?" Sadie's head drooped, and she covered her face with her hands. "I'm useless."

"You're not. You're just new at it." Sadie nodded but remained silent. I idly poked at the bits of metal scattered across the ground; she'd been working not only with copper but with a few hunks of silver, too. I squinted and probably screwed up my mouth in the way that always makes Micah laugh. Since working with metal was also new to me, I tended to overcompensate.

Slowly, the copper and silver pieces worked themselves into segregated piles, then they morphed and melted and stretched into long wires. After wiggling them this way and that, I willed them toward each other and twisted them together in a single fluid motion. A moment later, a heart formed of the two metals floated onto my lap.

"Thinking of Micah again?" Sadie said with an eyeroll. I shoved her in retaliation, but it was playful. Undeterred, Sadie took the heart and ran a finger along its curves. "You really love him?"

"Yeah." My belly warmed just thinking about him. "I do."

"So, what's all this heir business?"

I sighed and took the heart back. I remembered one of the first talks Micah and I had had about heirs—children, I mean children. His and my potential children. Babies.

My hands trembled just thinking about it.

We hadn't started out discussing babies, though. It had been two days after Micah had rescued me from the Institute where Max was held, the morning after the first night I'd spent in the manor. I was wearing the silverkin's first attempt at jeans—a noble effort on their part, but so very, very wrong. The pockets were too low on the sides of my legs, so I couldn't stuff my hands in them, and they were way too loose. Still, I had appreciated that they had tried, so I had worn them.

We won't discuss the monstrosity of a sneaker they produced.

Baggy denim notwithstanding, I was on cloud nine. Micah was all warm and snuggly in the morning; I'd worried that our first morning together would be awkward, all bed head and bad breath, but it wasn't. Micah had asked the silverkin to serve us breakfast in bed, and we had lazed around, getting crumbs and tea stains on the sheets, for the better part of the morning. We had decided to get up shortly before noon, really only so someone else could deal with all those crumbs and tea stains, and Micah had taken me on a tour of the manor's gardens. They were vast, lush, and colorful, packed with flowers and herbs and beautiful vine-covered nooks where we could while away the day.

And the orchards! The gardens were surrounded by trees bearing every sort of fruit, from standard apples and pears to fruits that I hadn't even known grew on trees, such as mangoes and star fruit. I'd never even known that something called star fruit existed, which is further evidence of the Peacekeepers' stellar nutrition policies.

We'd been walking through one of the orchards—plum, I think—when I asked, "When do you think it will be safe for me to go home?"

Micah's brows quirked. "Love, you *are* home."

I stared at him for a moment, wondering where my voice had gone. "You want me to live here? With you?" I whispered at last.

"Of course. You are my consort." He brushed his warm fingers across my cheek, neck, shoulders, his hands coming to rest at the small of my back. "Do you not wish to stay?"

"I do," I whispered, leaving off the part about this all being so sudden.

"Good," he murmured, kissing me lightly. "I'd be lost without you." I wrapped my arms around his waist, happy and content and more than a bit elated about my new home. Then, to my utter horror, he brought up babies.

"I hope that you'll soon be with child," he said, his fingers coming around to caress my belly.

"Your heir," I murmured, pressing my face to his chest so he couldn't see its bloodless state. "An heir is very important to you, isn't it?"

"Heirs are important to every house, but more so here. I am the last Silverstrand."

I hadn't even considered this. I knew that Micah didn't have any siblings (and thus will never know the joys of an elder brother covering him with shaving cream while he slept, or a younger sister crawling into bed with him when she's sick, only to puke on his favorite pillow), but I'd thought there were more Silverstrands somewhere. Maybe a few cousins, or a wacky aunt, even. But no, it was just Micah, lording over all the silver, all alone.

"And, you want *me* to produce this heir?" I pressed. Micah laughed and tightened his arms about me.

"I can think of no one better than the woman I love," he said. I couldn't really argue with that—not that I'd wanted to, anyway—and we'd left it for a time. Then there had been the business of rescuing Max, bringing Mom and Sadie safely out of the Mundane realm, and dealing with the Iron Queen. Life had been moving at a pretty fast pace, and we hadn't had time to discuss such details as babies and inheritance.

Then Oriana was rescued from the Iron Queen's oubliette, and as she struggled with her long recovery, the Heavies began discussing things like succession. You see, if childless Oriana were to perish, the rulership of metal would be passed to Micah, but he was also childless. Couple that with the lingering animosity between those of metal and those of stone, and it was a most precarious situation indeed.

Naturally, Micah and I had resumed our discussions about children. No, discussion was too strong a word; Micah had gushed about how much he loved me, and how happy he would be once we had our first child. First, as in he expected me to do this multiple times. Me, I just sat there, smiling and nodding, hoping he didn't notice my sweaty palms. It seemed that, as long as I was a part of Micah's life, the threat of babies was a part of mine as well.

I glanced at Sadie and sighed again. "Heirs. That's what he wants."

"Is that what *you* want?" she pressed.

"I guess." Sadie raised her eyebrows; if she had been wearing glasses, it would have been the perfect "quiet, this is a library" look. "I mean, he needs an heir. And I don't want him having them with anybody else. Besides, once I'm pregnant, I get to be Lady Silverstrand."

Sadie pursed her lips and asked, "You're already his consort, and you keep saying that you don't want anything to do with politics. Do you really need to be Lady Silverstrand?"

Leave it to the little one to ask the tough questions. "I want to be his wife."

"You mean you have to pop out a kid first?" Sadie demanded.

"No, I just have to be pregnant. Then, *poof*," I flicked out my fingers, miming a small explosion, "we're married."

"That's ridiculous. What if you were pregnant with someone else's baby?" I glared at her, so she amended, "I know you wouldn't do that. But still, this custom doesn't seem very well thought out."

"Tell me about it." I sighed and pinched the bridge of my nose. "Stupid customs or not, it's what's done around here. And, since I want to be his wife, babies are definitely in my future."

"You love him that much?"

"I love him that much."

"Well, then." Sadie looked around the room. "Do you think Micah will let me set up a library?"

"With what books?" I countered.

"I'm sure the silverkin can get some." She got to her feet, holding her hands together as if she were framing a scene. "All good aunts read to their nieces and nephews. Just sayin'."

I threw the heart at her.

3

Since setting up a library was the first thing Sadie had shown any interest in here in the Otherworld, I went ahead and summoned the silverkin in order to get things started. After all, in addition to lots and lots of books, we would need shelves, tables, chairs, and a few lamps. Sadie even wanted a card catalog to keep everything organized. As if anyone besides her would be able to make heads or tails of *that* system.

Before long, Sadie was discussing her new library with the silverkin; she'd even made a few book wish lists, along with some fairly detailed schematics. *How long has she been planning this library, anyway?* While the little guys were normally quite attentive, today they were so aflutter they could hardly pay attention. After a bit of questioning, I learned why the silverkin were so agitated—Max had returned to the manor while Micah and I were at the Gathering of the Heavies and had brought his typical path of destruction home with him. Since we had entered via the garden door and taken the back stairs to our chamber, we'd avoided the mess Max had created.

The mess in question did not sit well with the silverkin's leader, an energetic little fellow I called Shep, short for Shepherd. He's forever inciting his flock of 'kin to scrub harder, faster, and more efficiently. He has no qualms about kneeling down to clean off the soles of your shoes while you're still wearing them. He'd scrub under my toenails if I let him.

Shep and the rest of the silverkin had truly met their match in my brother, the epitome of slovenliness. Max typically trudged home in the dark of night, tracking mud, branches, and other filthy things across Shep's shining floors. Once, he'd even brought home a clutch of boggarts, easily the ickiest creatures in the Otherworld. They ranged in size from chihuahua to bull terrier, though boggarts walked upright, and tended toward mud-brown pelts, long pointy snouts and ears, and enormous bellies; that last bit was because they ate everything in sight, regardless of whether it was actually food. And, they stank something fierce.

Shep had barred the doors to the kitchens and the larder, which didn't go over too well with the clutch. In retaliation, the boggarts had immediately claimed the front sitting room as their own. They were a pain in every sense of the word, from their insistence that Max had won them, fair and square, and that they needed to stay close to their leader, to the skinned knee I'd suffered as we herded them into the garden. Boggarts are not indoor pets.

It turned out that Max hadn't actually won the boggarts. In reality, he'd lost a rather epic bout of gambling and, unable to pay his debts (again), had been cursed. It was Mom who had detected the curse, and Mom who had known the proper way to reverse it. Then she had to re-curse the boggarts with short-term amnesia, since we couldn't very well have a band of scruffy beasts trolling about the Otherworld, claiming that they had seen a Fairy Queen living in the Whispering Dell, and one who should have been long since dead, at that.

With a sigh, I eyed the evidence of Max's latest revels. The front door had several long scrapes in it, the atrium was trashed, and there was mud on the ceiling. *The ceiling.* At least we hadn't found any boggarts, or other beasties, hiding in the corners or under a chair. Yet.

And where was the one responsible for this mess? Max, true to form, was snoring away on the couch, muddy boots propped up on the cushions, while Shep directed the silvery cleanup crew. I looked on in awe, amazed that my brother was such a jerk. A filthy, inconsiderate jerk. I mean, he could at least have the common decency to look ashamed. *Awake* and ashamed.

Although the way Mom had described Dad's younger days, I was fathered by the very same sort of jerk. Intrigued, I left Sadie with the silverkin and went in search of Mom. She'd come in from the gardens and was taking her tea in the kitchen, oblivious to the chaos in the front of the manor. I sat beside her and grabbed a scone.

"Was Dad ever as bad as Max?" I began. Mom nearly blew out her tea.

"Oh, Beau was much worse," Mom replied. "Give Max time, though. He's still new at raising hell." I smiled as I worried at my scone, reducing its tasty goodness to a heap of crumbs.

"What if…what if you find a man who isn't so fiery?" I asked.

"Like Micah?" Mom asked. Okay, I know I was being obvious, but she could have let me beat around the bush a little. "I think Micah is a fine man. Don't you?"

"I do."

"Then, what's troubling you about him?"

"*He's* not troubling me," I clarified. "He wants a baby. I don't—not yet, anyway—but I want to be more than a useless consort."

"Do not make the mistake of seeing consorts as useless," Mom said. "Many have shaped our world from the bedchamber."

"I don't want to shape a world! I just…" I shoved the plate away and sent crumbs flying. A silverkin was there in an instant to sweep them up. "Why do

I have to be obviously pregnant before I'm Lady Silverstrand?"

"Ah. You don't feel that consorts are useless; you feel useless *as* one."

"Of course I do," I grumbled, now pouring my own cup of tea. "No one pays any attention to me; no one cares what I do or say."

"Micah does."

"All they do is stare at my stomach, looking for bulges." I dumped too much sugar in my tea, stirred it a few times, and pushed it away. "So? Why do I have to be pregnant?"

"To prove that your relationship has been consummated," Mom replied. "In the old days, a bride was held in a tower from her wedding night until she was heavy with child. That way, no one could dispute who'd fathered the babe."

Well, that was pragmatic. "I hope Micah doesn't stick me in a tower," I mumbled.

"Come, now. It wouldn't be *so* bad."

"Mom!"

"That was the original intent of the honeymoon," she continued, undeterred. "To drink sweet mead and come away with a babe for your troubles."

"Is that what you and Dad did?" I sneered.

"Careful, or I'll tell you," she warned. She watched me squirm for a few moments before she continued. "As to your first question, Max will be fine. For all that he's of metal, there's fire in his blood, and he's never gotten a chance to feel it. Let him burn a bit."

I nodded, gazing past my mother to the heavy mantel above the kitchen hearth. Since the kitchen was always the heart of the home, it's where we'd put the one of the few mementos we had from the Raven Compound—the picture of Max, Sadie, and me in the backyard beneath the fairy tree, taken when we were kids. As I looked at the sweet-faced boy crammed between his sisters, I tried to reconcile the brother of my memory with the man of today. "If he burns any more, Micah may extinguish him."

"That he may," Mom murmured. "That, he may."

4

The next morning dawned bright and clear, complete with fluffy clouds and a soft breeze. I should have known that something bizarre was going to happen from the deceptively calm way the day began.

I'd spent the bulk of the morning shuffling around the manor, bored out of my mind. Micah had been summoned to some sort of a meeting that had to do with the Gold Queen, and, being that I'd insulted Old Stoney only the day prior, we both thought it best to give the old rock a bit of time to cool down. So I had helped Micah back into his formal attire and handed him his sword, and, after a lingering goodbye, he went off to hear about what I hoped was the Gold Queen's most excellent recovery.

And really, it's not that I minded being left to my own devices. I liked having free time to explore the manor and its surrounding gardens and orchards, since it was now, and probably always would be, my home, too. It was a far cry from the tiny two-room apartment I had rented in the Mundane realm, not to mention the gaudy opulence of the Raven Compound. Just like the girl in the fairy tale, I'd found myself a charming prince and moved right on in to his castle.

However, spending the last few weeks surrounded by this never-ending luxury had left me feeling more than a bit jaded. The Otherworld is an amazing land, filled with untold wonders and beauty, yes, but sometimes I just wanted to play a game on my phone. My poor, trusty, old phone, which by now had probably been confiscated and dissected by Peacekeepers, who were now very aware of how often I had called for takeout.

Speaking of takeout, I missed eating it in front of my elderly Picture Vision while I watched bad postwar movies and good prewar movies. Not to mention all the types of takeout I, um, took out— pizza, grinders, rubbery Chinese. Yeah, the silverkin could whip up anything I asked for, but they couldn't quite manage the proper containers. Yes, I missed the little white cartons, and paper coffee cups with their badly fitting plastic lids, and my car, and...

I scrubbed my face with my hands; this trip down memory lane wasn't going to accomplish much, other than feed my misguided nostalgia for the less fine things in life. Searching for a distraction, I left my rooms and prowled the manor's silver hallways. Eventually, I found Sadie on the second level, standing alongside a heap of scrolls and books while she attempted to explain to Shep the basic concept of a library; I don't think it ever occurred to her that the silverkin don't read and therefore have little use for books.

Come to think of it, I wondered if they *could* read. They didn't technically have eyes, and they were constantly bumping into things, but something was helping them navigate. Sonar? I made a mental note to ask Micah, and a second mental note to ask Sadie if she'd like to teach remedial reading to a bunch of metal critters. A class full of silverkin would sure keep her occupied.

Not wanting to get involved in any library-related hubbub, I continued down the hall to the large windows that looked out over the gardens. I saw Mom in her usual spot, meditating yet again; at this rate, she was on track to become an honorary Buddhist.

Really, I understood why Mom was behaving the way she was. It had been obvious how much she and Dad loved each other, even to us kids. Once, I'd tried imagining what I'd do if Micah disappeared, and the mere imagining was terrible.

"You went into hiding?" I'd asked her, back when she was still working locator spells. Luckily, Mom had been in the rare mood to share some of her history. It seemed that she had made quite a few enemies while she was queen of Connacht, back in her mortal days, and a fair few during her later days as the queen of the Seelie Court. "And that was how you ended up in Fairy?"

"Not exactly," she replied. "My mortal enemies grew to be more than my court could handle, so I retreated to a *brugh*." A *brugh*, I then learned, was a fairy hill. A single night's revelry under the hill could be as short as a day, or as long as a century in the Mundane realm's timekeeping.

Mom didn't just party there. She became their queen.

"Drink enough of their wine, and one's mortality burns away," she had explained. "Then the prior Seelie Queen, Eleanore, was killed, and I took up the throne." I'd learned long ago that when Mom uttered innocent-sounding phrases such as "took up the throne," she actually meant something along the lines of "I fought a long and bloody battle and killed all who opposed me." My mom's badass that way.

"So when did you decide to leave?" asked Sadie, who had literally been on the edge of her seat. Not that I blamed her, since a story about Mom's past was a rare treat indeed.

"I never decided, not one way or the other. Beau did that for me." Mom smiled, gazing at a far-off memory. "He'd managed to infiltrate his way into the *brugh*, all yells and kicks. He was a scrappy boy, Beau was." Sadie and I had laughed at that; around us, at least, Dad was anything but scrappy. "Once my guard captured him, he was dragged before my throne, this impertinent mortal with the greenest eyes I'd ever seen."

"Love at first sight!" Sadie squealed.

"More like love after his next bath," Mom said. "After a few days of having your dear father around, I realized that my court's magic would eventually overpower Beau's, leaving him more fey than Elemental. I couldn't let him lose his identity, so we slipped away."

"And your court never looked for you?" I asked. If Micah went missing, I had no doubt that all those of metal would overturn every rock and twig in the Otherworld in order to find him. Shep would follow, straightening things up in their wake.

"I imagine they were too busy naming my successor," Mom replied, in that way of hers that meant something a bit more involved had happened.

"You gave up being a queen for Dad?" Sadie asked, a bit awed.

"Oh, it wasn't such a sacrifice," Mom said. "I left behind a lonely life as a monarch for a husband and three wonderful babes. I'd make the same choice again a thousand times over, and I wouldn't change a thing."

"Even though he's gone now?" I ventured.

"Aye," Mom murmured, tucking a length of hair behind my ear. "Even so."

As I remembered that short discussion, I wondered if I should go down to the gardens and try to talk with her. I mean, all of this moping disguised as meditating was getting us nowhere. In the midst of my internal debate, Max emerged from his room.

"Hey," I greeted. All I got was a grunt in reply. "What's up?"

"Nothing, yet." Max shoved past me and made his way toward the kitchen. Not having anything better to do, I followed, then watched in utter amazement as he ate four bowls of oatmeal in the space of a few minutes, drained two truly enormous mugs of coffee, and then asked for a plate of eggs. It was like he was fattening up for hibernation.

"Where's Micah?" he asked as he shoveled eggs into his mouth.

"With the bigwigs." I picked at some bread. "And Sadie's trying to build a library with the silverkin, and Mom is doing the strong and silent thing again, which means that I'm bored out of my mind."

Max took another swig of coffee and wiped his mouth on the shoulder of his shirt. Classy. "Want to come to the village with me?"

I eyed him dubiously, remembering his return the prior evening. "Depends. What's going on there?"

He set down his tankard with a thud and scowled. "What's Micah told you I do?" he countered.

"We're all wondering what you do," I snapped. "You come home in the dead of night, looking like you were dragged through the woods with these things chasing you... What *are* you doing?"

"I used to hang out at the market, but after the boggarts—"

"Wait." I put my palms flat on the table and stared at my idiot brother. "Do you mean the Goblin Market?"

By the look on Max's face, that was exactly what he meant. The Goblin Market was where the true evil congregated; the creatures that called the market home made the Iron Court look like a petting zoo. We'd been warned to stay away from the Goblin Market for as long as I could remember. Well, Dad had warned us. Mom had threatened us with eternal grounding.

"You are not," I said. "If Mom finds out—"

"I haven't been there since—"

"What good reason could you have for going there anyway?" I demanded.

"I was looking for Dad." Max exhaled heavily, drank some more coffee, and worried at the edge of the table. "I figure if I go out in public, raise a little hell, word will get around. Eventually, it'll get around to Dad."

I stared at my big brother, shocked and amazed for reasons he would not like to hear about. Yeah, I suppose that Dad would eventually hear about these antics, and if the creatures Max was hanging around with didn't kill him, Dad sure would once he found out. This was the stupidest, most irresponsible plan I'd ever heard, and I'd grown up with Max's stupid plans.

And yet, that didn't stop the guilt that stabbed at my heart. Here I'd been, mooning over having to get dressed up and attend court functions and worrying about the possibility of babies, and forgetting what we were all supposed to be doing—looking for Dad.

I'd just turned seven when my father got the call to war; I was eight and a half when the war, and the reports on him, abruptly ceased. To this day, we had no idea what had happened to him, not even if he was alive or dead. The Iron Queen had led me to believe that Dad was still alive; she'd insinuated that she'd known him, and said that she couldn't imagine death taking him. Still, I didn't think it was wise to put my faith in a known liar.

After Micah and I had freed Max from the Institute, he'd revealed that Dad had remained in contact with him for a few years after the wars ended, though the rest of the family had been unaware of this. To Mom, Sadie and me, Dad was just gone; I don't know what hurt more, the fact that Dad hadn't come by, or Max's revelation that, two years after the wars ended, all contact abruptly stopped. I could only think of two things that would have kept Dad from us for that long, and if he'd been imprisoned, he'd have probably escaped by now. The other option, I just refused to consider.

But Max seemed to think our father was alive, and, being that he'd apparently once been headquartered in the Goblin Market, near enough to the Whispering Dell to hear about these drunken escapades. Mind you, getting in fights in the village square was not the proper way to locate a missing man. One should organize a search, complete with maps and compasses and things. However, I didn't have any of those things, or the resources to put together a search party, or any desire to hear Sadie talk about the fricken' Dewey Decimal System ever again.

"So," Max said, "want to come with me?"

"When do we leave?" Really, what could go wrong?

Call me naïve, but I'd always assumed that the seedy underbelly, whether in the Otherworld or the Mundane realm, was only out at night. I mean, how could such ne'er-do-wells prosper in the full light of day? While the sun watched from above, respectable shopkeepers and artisans went about their business, making quality products and earning a fair wage for their honest work. Once the mats were rolled up and the stalls were shuttered, and the sun's watchful eye was asleep, the bad guys emerged to cheat and pilfer what was left.

Yeah, naïve.

On this day the sun was blazing hot, though it was long before noon, and there I was with my brother in what we from the Mundane world would call a dive bar, complete with battered chairs and a sticky floor. All that was needed to complete the trashy ensemble were a jukebox and a mechanical bull. Oh, and some off-key karaoke wouldn't hurt.

As I pried my shoe off the floor, I was hit with a pang of homesickness for The Room, the dive where I used to hang out with my coworkers at Real Estate Evaluation Services, though they weren't actually my coworkers. It was a sham job, set up by Peacekeepers to spy on my family. You would think that the government would find other ways to spend our tax dollars.

Anyway, The Room's floor had never been washed, at least not in the year and a half I'd frequented it, and for a long time before that. But, the beer had been cheap and cold, the pretzels salty and crisp, and the music wasn't completely horrible, so I kept going back. I wondered if this place, aptly named The Dell's Alehouse, had any good beers on tap.

Oddly, at least to me, a stream ran through the center of the common room. Was this their version of running water? No, I'd seen a well outside the building, so this was…decorative? For fishing? I sighed and took a seat at the bar next to Max; for all I knew, the stream kept evil from crossing sides.

Hey, that just might be it.

"You come here a lot?" I asked. Max signaled the bartender, and two brightly colored concoctions that reminded me of unset gelatin were delivered a moment later. So much for beer.

"I've been a time or two." He drank from his glass, the contents leaving a ring of orange slime around his mouth. Nice.

"Too bad we didn't invite Sadie," I murmured, now tilting my glass from side to side. It seemed that, the more the liquid moved, the more it solidified. Weird.

"Like she would have come," Max said, annoyed, and I could hardly blame him. Sadie hadn't left the manor since the Iron Queen's death; in fact, she hardly even left the main house to walk the grounds, lovely as they were. I get antsy if I'm holed up at the manor for a day or so, even with my morning walks around the orchards, but Sadie seemed content to haunt the silver halls until the end of time.

"What's she hiding from?" I wondered, not expecting an answer. Max, true to form, did the unexpected.

"This," he replied, gesturing to encompass the bar. "All of this." I squinted into the dark corners and saw a few orcs embroiled in a drinking game, some horse-faced beings arguing over their bill, and a pixie, roughly half the size of a human, slowly gyrating for a table full of human men. It was an odd sort of chaos, kept to a dull roar by the constant threat of the bartender, who was the largest, ugliest man I'd ever seen. And, since his head was covered in bulging eyes, he saw everything all the time.

Which came in pretty handy when Max signaled for a refill. "She's terrified," I murmured. Max nodded as he sipped his second drink, intent on watching the pixie. "She's got to realize that it's not all bad here."

"How are we gonna make her realize that when we can't even get her out the door?" Max asked. The pixie had slipped her gown off her shoulder, leaving the men at the table, and my brother, fully enthralled. *By all that is holy, please don't let Max start drooling.*

"There's something else we need to talk about," Max murmured. "Mike Armstrong. He's making a bid for the Presidency."

"Mike Armstrong?" The name was familiar, but I couldn't recall a politician named Armstrong. The only person I had ever known with the surname Armstrong was…

Oh, crap. Juliana.

I had met Juliana in middle school, a few years after Max had been arrested by the Peacekeepers. She and I had become fast friends; for much of my life, she had been the only friend I had. School and the teen years are tough enough, but having an M.I.A. father *and* brother and a surname synonymous with Elemental power, not to mention living in a mansion when most others resided in government shacks, doesn't exactly ingratiate oneself to one's peers. Without Juliana, I don't know what would have become of me.

Fast forward a few years: I'm an adult, living in my own government-issued apartment, and working with Juliana at Real Estate Evaluation Services. I meet Micah and learn that I'm a Dreamwalker and that my father and brother are (probably) still alive. Despite being a *supposedly* responsible adult and somewhat intelligent, I decide to dreamwalk to Max. Alone. Without even Micah's help.

Yeah. I know.

Anyway, I'd found Max, trussed up like a science experiment gone wrong, in the Institute for Elemental Research. In the control room, with all the other lab coats, was Juliana.

She was a Peacekeeper. My lifelong best friend not only turned out to be a Peacekeeper, but *she had known where my missing brother was all along*. Frickin' bitch. I hope she got fired after we rescued Max.

"Who's Mike Armstrong?" I asked, hoping against hope that he was someone I'd never heard of.

"Juliana's uncle," Max replied. "The head of the Institute for Elemental Research."

"The who of the what?" Feigning ignorance, I took a long pull on my drink, both surprised and disappointed to learn that it was the Otherworld's version of Kool-Aid. Based on the direction this conversation was heading, I wanted something eye-wateringly alcoholic.

Almost ten years ago, Peacekeepers had stormed into the Raven Compound and arrested Max for his so-called crimes against humanity. That was political speak for the fact that he wouldn't stop practicing magic, which was his birthright as a metal Elemental. There was a sham trial that we, his family, weren't even invited to, and then Max was hauled off to prison. At least, that's what we were told.

What had really happened was that Max had made a deal with the Peacekeepers. They were methodically eliminating the Inheritors, those gifted souls who came along once a generation that had a more intense affinity with their Element, or so it seemed. In reality, the Peacekeepers were capturing and attempting to study them, but the Inheritors were decidedly against being lab rats. Ultimately, they all perished, all save one—the Inheritor of Metal.

After the last Metal Inheritor, Olquin, died, no one knew the identity of his replacement; no one, save my parents and Max, knew that Sadie, the youngest Corbeau, was the new Inheritor. That fact was one of the main reasons Dad had so readily gone off to fight in the Magic Wars; for all we knew, he was still fighting today. Before Dad left, Max had promised our father that he would protect the family by any means necessary, so once Dad disappeared, and Olquin was dead, Max felt like he was out of options. He'd contacted the Peacekeepers, represented himself as the Metal Inheritor, and went willingly to the Institute.

According to Max, all had gone as well as could be expected for the first few years, until he'd found a bit of metal out in the exercise yard, shaped it into a lily, and had given it to a girl as a love token. Things went downhill from there, and by the time Micah and I had rescued him, Max was nothing more than skin and bones, held in a plastic coffin with wires and tubes stuck all over him, his days spent in a drug-induced stupor.

And now he tells me that Juliana's uncle was the man responsible for all of it.

"You didn't know?" he asked.

"Of course not," I snapped. "Juliana lied to me about everything."

"She didn't have much of a choice," Max said, surprisingly without rancor. "Sometimes, I think she was way worse off than I was."

"Yeah. I'm sure her cushy job as a Peacekeeper kept her up late at night." Max gave me a sidelong glance but dropped the subject of my former friend.

"Anyway, her uncle runs the Institute," he reiterated. "And now, he wants to run the world. His platform is that his research on Elementals gives him an edge to keep the Mundanes safe."

"You mean his research on you," I grumbled.

"There were others," Max said, tracing the edge of his glass.

"There were?" I recalled my own brief forays into the Institute. There had been lots and lots of Mundanes, guards and lab coats and such, but the only Elemental I ever saw was Max. Then again, I'd only been concerned with finding my brother. "Are they still there? Should we help them?"

Max shook his head. "I outlived them. All of them."

"Oh." I shuddered, the specter of dead Elementals I'd never even known chilling me. Desperate for a subject change, I continued, "So what if this Mike Armstrong wants to be president? What's the difference—" Recognition hit me like a ton of bricks, so hard I almost fell off my stool. "Wait. *Uncle Mike*?"

Max's eyes slid back to mine. "You *do* know him."

Uncle Mike was a fat, jolly man, a lot like Santa without the beard. Or much other hair, for that matter. He was the patriarch of the Armstrong clan, being that his brother, Juliana's dad, had died while she and her little brother, Corey, were very young. He was the man who had looked out for Juliana and Corey and their mom, making sure that Corey got to attend music school and that Juliana and her mother were always well cared for. I remembered the Armstrong summer get-togethers, with Uncle Mike manning the grill, burning hot dogs, and slipping us beers when we were way underage.

I also remembered Juliana's warnings to not drink those beers and to never let myself be alone with her uncle. At the time, I'd thought he was just a dirty old man. Now, I wonder if his plan was to bag me and start a whole different batch of experiments.

I grabbed my drink and swirled it. "Yeah. I remember him."

Max nodded. "He's the bad guy, Sara. He's high up in the Peacekeeper ranks. If he becomes President, there's no telling what he'll do."

"I still don't see what difference it makes. Life already sucks for human Elementals."

"Yeah, but at least they're kinda free," Max said, once again distracted by the dancing pixie. "Don't practice, don't show your mark, and you can live a normal life. You know that; hell, Sadie wishes she could go back to that. Trust me, if anyone can make things worse, it's him. He was the one in with Ferra."

Max let the implication hang in the air. Evil Peacekeepers united with evil Elementals would make life worse for everyone, but would that really happen? I mean, surely Elementals would rise up against that. Surely we of the Otherworld would band together and—

And I remembered that we had done just that, during the Magic Wars. We'd lost an entire dimension to those righteous lunatics. Maybe Max was right, and we should do something about Uncle Mike. I mean, if I had to choose a new president of Pacifica, my first choice would not be the mad scientist who'd been in with the evil queen.

"You know all this, but how?" I asked.

He shrugged. "People talk to me."

I tugged on Max's sleeve, wanting to discuss this Uncle Mike situation a bit further, but the pixie's gown was now off both shoulders, held to her breasts by a delicate hand. I sighed and left Max to his fantasies while I looked around at the patrons. People-watching had always been one of my favorite pastimes, and the Otherworld certainly didn't disappoint. And, the bartender notwithstanding, residents of the Otherworld tended to be uncannily beautiful.

I was watching a seal maiden, what Mom would call a selkie, unceremoniously shed her clothes, ignoring the chorus of catcalls as she slipped on her seal skin, when I spied one of the reasons for Sadie's fears. As the selkie flopped into the stream and swam away (so *that's* what it was for!), I saw that the table behind the seal maiden was occupied by an iron warrior.

"Max!" I whispered. When he didn't respond, I followed his gaze; the pixie's gown was down around her waist and, based on the pile of offerings before her, it would be going lower.

"Max!" I grabbed his arm. "One of Ferra's warriors is in the corner!"

"So?"

"So!" I squeaked. "So what if he's mad? What if—"

"All right," Max said. "Act cool, and we'll leave." Max dropped a few coins on the bar alongside our empty glasses, spared a longing look at the pixie, and we casually moved toward the exit. And yes, the metal man followed us.

"Max—"

"Just follow me." We walked down the middle of the wide avenue, past alleyways and shops as we headed toward the central open air market. "We'll lose him in the stalls."

I nodded, desperately trying not to look over my shoulder. You know, like how you specifically didn't peek out from under the covers to see if the monster was in your room? Unless it was the sort of monster that always disappeared when you looked. Then, you had to stick your head out, at least once.

After a panicked yet slow stroll about the market, I stopped at a booth that sold cloaks made from raptor feathers. I don't know what aspect amazed me more—that some fool had actually gone out and gathered all these feathers or that people wanted to dress up like overgrown parakeets. As I examined a gaudy pink creation, I hazarded a look down the street. "Hey," I called to Max. "I think it worked."

Max smirked the "I'm the oldest, of course it worked" smirk. Before I could comment, the iron warrior—the very same iron warrior that Max had assured me wasn't a threat—launched himself out from behind the stalls and tackled Max.

Now Max is no slouch with his abilities, but he was taken completely by surprise. They rolled around on the dusty ground, and in a heartbeat's time the iron warrior had Max pinned. That left me, still new to my Elemental nature, to save my brother.

The warrior had his full weight on Max's chest, crushing his lungs. I squinted, concentrating on pulling the warrior off Max. He moved enough for Max to breathe, but only just. I spied a metal door across the square, and I increased the affinity between the door and warrior, hoping the larger door would help me drag him away. I was shocked when it actually worked, and the warrior inched off Max's body.

Not only did it work, it also made the warrior mad. No longer content to kill Max slowly, he raised an iron fist and aimed right at Max's chest. Max threw up his hand, and the warrior's own hand began melting, dripping away before his eyes; if Max hadn't had the weight of the warrior on his lungs, he would have been screaming in pain. As it was, he could hardly draw breath. Then the warrior bellowed, a rusty, grating sound, and moved enough for Max to roll out from under him. Wheezing and wincing in pain, Max finally found the breath to speak.

"Sara!" he rasped. "His head!"

"What about his head?" I didn't get an answer, since the warrior had gotten to his knees and was raising his other, non-melty arm to strike. I screamed, Max bellowed, and assorted patrons and shopkeepers ran for cover. Then, the warrior clunked over sideways, as lifeless as a car without its engine. Behind him was the dancing pixie from the bar.

"You are safe now," she said. "I've taken the spark that allows him to be." She opened her hand, and nestled upon her palm was a small, glowing orb.

"Thank you," I said; Max was too battered and burnt to do more than nod. "But, why risk yourself for us?"

"Do you not remember? Not so long ago, you saved me." I took in her appearance, her long, silky hair and glimmering wings, and noted the two gaping holes in her wings.

"You're the pixie from Ferra's camp," I said, and she nodded. "Will your wings heal?"

"They've healed as much as they will," she replied, waving her hand as if the disfigured state of her wings hardly mattered.

"Why were they torturing you?" I remembered how she had been chained to a wooden plank, manacles around her wrists and metal spikes through her wings, and how I had used my ability to loosen her restraints. She had leapt into the air and flown away, and I hadn't seen her since, not that I'd expected to, especially not dancing in a bar. Or rescuing us from yet another iron warrior.

"They did it because they are beasts," she replied. "Filthy, reprehensible beasts. Iron warriors have taken many of my kind. I'm one of the few who ever returned home."

Just when I thought the Iron Court couldn't be any more terrible, I learned that they were trapping pixies like lightning bugs. "I'm glad you're okay."

She inclined her head. "Since you freed me, I've learned the metal warriors' weakness, and how to exploit it. They'll not trap me again. And I've told all I've encountered to spread the word of how the new Inheritor of Metal saved me, and how she will be the one to restore order amongst the Elementals."

"I'm not the Inheritor," I protested. "My sister, Sadie, is."

Her brows furrowed. "But it was you who freed me, you who destroyed Ferra. Surely—"

"She's right," Max interrupted, levering himself to a sitting position. "Sadie, not Sara, is the Metal Inheritor."

"No matter," the pixie said. "I have owed you a favor since you freed me. We are now even."

"I feel like I owe you now," I said, but she shook her head furiously.

"In our world, it does not do to owe another," she said. "If it pleases you, I will call on you if I am ever in need. But do not think that you are obliged to answer."

"It does please me." With that, the pixie smiled and flew away, leaving me and a slightly battered Max in the square. Since his burns had been caused by hot metal rather than fire, his chest was already healing.

"Well, that was interesting," I said, watching her fly away. "Do you think anyone else feels like they should be doing us favors?"

"Us? No—*you*." I looked quizzically at Max, so he continued, "I'm here every day, getting beat on, shoved in the dirt, and no one has ever offered me anything. Not once, not ever." He made an awful noise in the back of his throat, then spat. "Yet they all talk about you, the copper girl that lives in a house of silver."

"Huh." I took this in for a moment. "But—"

"But nothing." Max stood, wobbled a bit, then dusted himself off. "C'mon, it's not even lunchtime. Let's see how much more trouble we can get into."

As it turned out, Max and I had already reached our quota of trouble for the day. After an uneventful afternoon and evening spent in the village, mostly in taverns (all devoid, to Max's disappointment, of barely clad pixies), we returned to the manor. I'd just gotten myself washed up and into bed when Micah returned, shedding articles of clothing as he neared the bed; I suppose, when you've grown up with an army of silver critters constantly picking up after you, it's an unavoidable habit. Then he was beside me, wrapping his arms around my waist as he kissed the back of my neck.

"I missed you," he murmured. I didn't roll over just yet; the feel of his warm belly against my mark was amazing, and I think he knew it. "Tell me about your day."

"I went to the village with Max." Micah withdrew my hands from underneath the blankets and made a show of counting my fingers. "What are you doing?"

"Ensuring that he returned you to me in one piece. Toes next." Micah dove under the blankets and proceeded to count my very sensitive toes. He was lucky I didn't kick him in the head. When he emerged, after much shrieking on my part and laughter from both of us, he was serious again. "If you travel with Max again, take the silverkin to guard you."

"Max wouldn't let anything hurt me," I protested. I left out how, if it hadn't been for the pixie, that would have been a moot point.

"He does not have to let them," Micah replied. Then he gathered me close in that way of his that made it nearly impossible for me to remain angry with him. "I cannot bear the thought of you harmed. Please, for my sake, take them along."

"Micah…" I looked into those silver eyes, so wide and accepting of me and my wackadoo family. "I can't."

"Why?" he asked softly, tracing my cheekbone. "Why can my Sara not promise to be safe?"

"Max is looking for Dad." Micah's brow furrowed, and I misinterpreted his expression as anger. "I'd have told you, if I knew before today," I babbled. "It's what Max has been doing, raising hell and—"

"Hell?" Micah repeated, alarmed.

"Not real hell," I soothed. "When Max started brawls or gambled all night or—"

"Or destroyed parts of my home?"

"He was looking for Dad," I finished in a small voice. "He…he thinks that if he makes a spectacle of himself, word will get to Dad, and that Dad'll come find us." As I said it out loud, I realized how stupid Max's plan really was. Of course I'd known it was a foolish endeavor from the get-go, but I'd ignored my misgivings, hoping that Max was right. He wasn't, and we were just two stupid, stupid kids.

"You think this plan is sound?" Micah inquired, and his soft, nonjudgmental tone made me break down in tears. After much holding me close and stroking of my hair, I was calm enough for him to ask, "So, not sound, then?"

"No," I snuffled. "Not sound." I didn't offer any more, and Micah didn't press. I stroked Micah's mark, and in the process found hard knots in his neck and shoulders; he always carried his tension there. "How was your meeting?'

"Curious," he replied, rolling onto his back. "I saw Oriana."

"She's well, then?" I asked. The last time I'd seen the Gold Queen she'd just been lifted out of the Iron Court's oubliette and was little more than a cadaver. A screaming, filthy, furious cadaver.

"Well? No." He brought my hand before him, playing with my fingers. "I suspect her captivity has driven her to madness."

"She can hardly be blamed for that," I murmured, shuddering as I recalled the stinking hole of darkness she'd been hauled from; Micah and I had the honor of attending, being that we'd caused the Iron Queen's demise and had thus inadvertently restored Oriana to the throne. Ha. Some honor. "What did she do?"

"First, she proclaimed that we were all sent to kill her. Then, she announced that she suspected one of us of sewing poison into her clothing, so she stripped naked. Then, she danced and laughed, quite pleased with herself that she'd thwarted her poisoner."

Can you sew poison? I kept my musings to myself and prompted him to continue. "Then she demanded that we all expose our marks to her, to prove that we are, indeed, Elementals. Shapeshifters cannot duplicate Elemental marks, you know," Micah added, then laughed mirthlessly. "She went so far as to touch each mark, to prove our authenticity."

"She touched your mark?" Jealousy rose like bile in my throat. Micah was mine, his beautiful silver mark off-limits to everyone but me.

"For the barest moment," Micah replied. "She was far more interested in the Inheritor of Fire."

Ayla was the Inheritor of Fire's name; I'd made a point of meeting her, since she was human like me. She was tall and lean, with a head of hair such a bright shade of red she made me look like a mere brunette. "Why was Ayla there?"

"Oriana requested her." Micah rolled again, now onto his side as he pulled me into his cocoon of Micahness. "I do not know how we of metal should proceed, if our queen proves mad. Our queen is meant to symbolize wisdom, not weakness." He fell silent, his fingers caressing my back in long strokes.

"She doesn't sound mad," I said. "So she's a little shell-shocked from her ordeal. That's to be expected. And, after what the iron warriors did to her, I'm not surprised that she'd prefer a woman's company.

Maybe…maybe she just needs a little more time," I suggested.

"Time. Yes, perhaps time is the proper balm for her ills." Micah considered my words for another moment, then he drew my face to his. "My wise consort," he murmured, his gentle caresses becoming a bit more urgent. "Truly, your words soothe my mind. Now, let me soothe you."

I bit my lip; I'd taken my last contraband Mundane birth control pill yesterday. Since I couldn't exactly tell Micah that, mostly because I'd never told him about them in the first place, I let him roll me beneath him and concentrated on loving him.

5

Micah had learned pretty early on in our relationship that I was liable to say anything at any moment, regardless of present company or future consequences. Much to my well-mannered consort's chagrin, he had witnessed me unintentionally insult everyone from Shep right on up to Old Stoney, though neither of us had really minded pissing off the old rock. Shep, though, that was another story; all I had said was that the stairs weren't as shiny as the main floors, and Shep took that as an insult against his housekeeping skills. I hadn't meant anything like that—in fact, I liked that the stairs were a bit duller, especially for those occasions when I was wearing a dress—and I'd felt so guilty I'd ended up helping clean the manor for weeks. However, what I asked

Micah the morning after my trip to the village with Max surprised even me.

"Can you teach me to fight?" By the time I'd gotten up the nerve to ask that, we'd been up for almost an hour, lounging away in bed. Micah hated mornings nearly as much as I did.

"Fight?" he repeated, one silver brow halfway up his forehead.

"Yeah. With a sword," I added. For the past few weeks, Micah had been offering me and Sadie instruction on how to better utilize our power over metal. He had also offered his services to Max, who had snorted and stomped out of the room. Nothing like being an ungrateful ass to the man who fed and housed you.

Micah took my hands, examining my knuckles before carefully turning them over. "Have you ever used an edged weapon in the past?" he asked, grazing his thumbs over my palms.

"No," I admitted, "but I'd like to learn."

"You are able to halt any foe with your Elemental abilities."

"But what if something happens, and I can't use my awesome Elemental powers?" Micah began protesting, but I kept going, "What if I'm out somewhere, without you, without any silverkin to protect me? What if I'm captured and put in a place like Max was, and all that's nearby is concrete and plastic? Then I'd be helpless."

Brows now deeply furrowed, Micah mulled this over. "I do not like that my consort may need to fight."

"Neither does your consort, but if I'm forced to defend myself, I'd at least like to know what I'm doing." For a few heartbeats Micah just looked at me, and I thought I'd have to appeal to Max for help, or worse, to Shep. Then Micah sprang upward, leaping out of bed as he threw the blankets over my head.

"Your first lesson is to never, ever drop your guard," he said while I clawed my way to the surface. "Not even in our home, where I personally guarantee your safety. Always remember, love, that a foe's best hiding place is in plain sight." Undaunted, I climbed out of bed and affected my best fighter's stance. Okay, it was a yoga pose, but whatever. I was learning. Amused, Micah dropped into a stance that looked slightly more effective, and we began circling each other.

"Got it. What's my next lesson?" I'd asked a perfectly reasonable question, and wouldn't you know it, that elf responded by throwing a silver teacup at my head. Arms flailing, I knocked it away just as Micah tackled me. We landed on the bed in a heap of limbs, the teacup lodged under my back.

"That anything—*everything*—is a weapon," he answered. "Never think you are helpless, my Sara. Always use your surroundings to your advantage."

"What if there's no tea service nearby?" I yanked the teacup free and tossed it behind my head. "Will a plate do?"

"Certainly," he murmured. "You have passed your second lesson," he said, nuzzling my neck. I laughed, as much from the absurdly simple lessons as his ticklish breath.

"Did I pass the first one, too?"

"You did," he murmured.

"So, when do I get a sword?" Okay, I hadn't meant that as a joke, but from Micah's laughter you'd have thought I was the headline act on a comedy tour.

"Love, one does not begin with a sword," he said once he'd calmed himself. "One begins with simple hand-to-hand techniques."

"You just showed me hand-to-hand," I pointed out.

"No, I put a blanket over your head, then I threw a teacup at you," he corrected. "You do not know how to disarm another, or how to incapacitate an attacker."

"Then teach me."

"Very well." He sat up, and I followed suit. "Hit me."

"What?"

"Assume that I am an attacker. Hit me." I moved to whack him with the back of my hand, and I would have if Micah hadn't snatched my wrist from midair. "Sara, assume your life is in danger. At least make a fist."

"I—I don't want to hurt you."

"You won't." I don't know if it was his smug words or his even smuggier grin, but one or the other or both got my dander up. I clenched my fist and swung at Micah with all my might, convinced that he'd be the one apologizing from behind his swollen lip.

And then I was beneath him, pinned immobile to the bed.

"That wasn't fair!" I shouted.

"Wasn't it?" His silver eyes danced, but I'd had enough.

"Why can't you take me seriously?" I burst out. "This isn't some kind of joke!"

Instantly, he relaxed his hold. "My Sara," he murmured, "I am not treating it as one. But you must understand, lo—"

Using what I'd just learned, I took advantage of Micah's distracted state and bucked my hips upward. As Micah fell forward and tried to steady himself with his left arm, I pushed his right shoulder and flipped him onto his back. I don't know who was more amazed: me, because that little move had worked, or Micah, for the exact same reason. As I looked down at him, his confused expression quickly gave way to indignation. Not trusting those sinewy arms, I set my knee close to his throat. "Understand what, love?" I purred. Micah didn't reply and man, did he look peeved. I leaned down and kissed him, at first just as an apology, but I didn't protest when he had me beneath him again. I considered it a well-earned reward for showing up the teacher.

Later, we snuggled while my fingertips sketched patterns on his chest. "So, I can have a sword?"

"You may have a sword," Micah replied, pressing a kiss to my temple. "We shall visit the smith in the village and order one."

"Can't you just magic one up?"

"I could, but if you are to be armed, I would rather it be with a sword made by one with an intimate understanding of weaponry."

"A special sword, then? Just for me?" Before Micah could reply, there was a knock at the door. Micah called for them to enter; it was a group of silverkin, of course, greeting their master and informing him of his impending day. As Shep chattered away, I noticed some of the other 'kin readying Micah's fancy clothes. "Are we going somewhere?"

"I must meet with the Elemental lords," he replied, without meeting my eyes. I understood why he was uncomfortable; this was obviously a meeting of some import, and as a mere consort, I wasn't invited. Little did Micah realize, I liked not being invited to over half of these boring events. I much preferred being bored at the manor.

"Is it about the Gold Queen?" I asked, trying to distract Micah from the fact that I wasn't going. Or from him getting the bright idea to take me along anyway.

"Yes," he replied. "Oriana's well-being is at the forefront of all our thoughts."

"Oriana, what?"

Micah looked up, his head tilted to the side.

"Oriana has only one name? No family name?" I asked.

"Monarchs are usually only known by a single name," Micah replied.

"But, you're a Silverstrand," I pointed out.

"And, as you may have noticed, I am not a queen," he replied with a wink. I blushed at that and forced a laugh to hide it. "Raintree. Oriana's family name is Raintree."

"Oh," I murmured. "That's a pretty name."

"Oriana's situation illustrates why heirs are so important among Elementals," Micah continued. Great. Back to babies, and before breakfast, at that. "A large family can help one gain and hold the throne."

"I thought all those of metal would stand together," I said. "Or at least, wouldn't all those of gold support Oriana?"

"One can turn upon their own nature to support another, such as what occurred when Ferra captured Oriana," Micah explained. "I don't know if I've ever told you, but none of Oriana's children survived to adulthood. That tragedy was one of the many reasons Ferra, along with her supporters, sought to overwhelm the Golden Court. If Oriana and Eurwynn had had any living heirs, those of their bloodline would have defended them. Eurwynn might not have been executed; perhaps they wouldn't have been dethroned at all."

"Why didn't anyone support you?" I asked, since, as silver, he was next in line. Micah sighed, pain creasing his features. I began apologizing, but he waved it away.

"No. You should know." He sent the silverkin away with a look, then he perched on the bed. After he took another deep breath, he stared at the floor as he told me how Ferra had committed the ultimate betrayal.

"Those of earth, specifically the greater stones, were always the ruling element." He shook his head. "No, not always, but for many generations. Then we of metal had the grand idea that we were somehow more suited to rule than those of stone, and we plotted a coup." I sat beside him and slipped my fingers against his palm. Micah smiled at that, but it didn't reach his eyes. "While we plotted against stone, Ferra plotted against gold. She gained the support of not only the lesser metals, such as wolfram and zinc—"

"What is wolfram?" I interrupted. I had never heard of such a substance. "Metal used by wolves?" Micah smiled again, a bit wider this time.

"No, love," he replied, kissing my hair. "In the Mundane realm, you refer to it as tungsten."

"Tungsten," I repeated. I wondered how many other metals went by stage names in the Otherworld. "Are there a lot of…of wolframs?"

"Many of them, far more than can claim to be of gold, or silver or copper for that matter," Micah replied. "Ferra was never picky in choosing her minions."

"Huh." In the midst of wondering if a tungsten-wolfram Elemental looked, um, wolfish, I realized that Micah was looking at me expectantly. "I'm sorry. Go on."

"So the lesser metals joined with Ferra," Micah continued, "as did other beings not of the Elements." I remembered the pervading chill of the Iron Queen's court, dark and dank and populated with the creatures of nightmares. Those lesser metals must have been pretty desperate to have their voices heard, to hang out with those monsters. "Once her army had been raised, Ferra invaded the Golden Court and beheaded Eurwynn herself. After seeing her beloved husband's head rolling away from his body, Oriana was easily captured. Once the Gold King was dead, and the Gold Queen was bound in iron chains, Ferra became our queen."

"Shouldn't the next rulers have been your parents?" I asked. Micah squeezed his eyes shut, his voice little more than a rasp when he answered.

"My father died while I was still very young," he said with the detached grief of one who could hardly remember the person he grieved for. "I am their only child."

"Then, your mother should have been the Silver Queen."

"She was killed," Micah whispered. "We were caught unawares, just she and I, in the far orchard. My mother summoned the silverkin, but only a few were able to reach us in time. She ordered them to shield me, and then she drew the attackers away from me. That was the last time I saw her alive, heard her voice." He went on to describe the protective cairn the silverkin had formed as a shield above him, how he had heard his mother's cries, her killer's laugh deep and terrifying, like boulders breaking in an avalanche. True to their orders, the silverkin hadn't dispersed until they were certain that Micah was safe, and by then it was too late. Selene Silverstrand was dead.

Micah went on, explaining that he had been so distraught that after he buried his mother he'd destroyed the family home, unable to bear so many memories. In his mother's honor, he'd built a new house, the solid silver manor we now lived in, directly on top of the old. While he was drowning in his grief, the Elemental power struggle played out without him.

"Oh, Micah," I murmured, wrapping my arms around him. "I'm so sorry."

"It was war," he mumbled. "Casualties happen in war. That is to be expected, but no one ever expects the ones they love to fall." Micah tightened his arms around me, holding on to me as if I was a lifeline. I silently vowed to never, ever complain when he sent the silverkin to guard me. Maybe I'd start sending them to guard *him*.

"Ironically, the strife in this world is what led to the Magic Wars in your world," Micah said, his lips against my neck. "We couldn't support your war mages, since we were so busy fighting amongst ourselves."

"And you were all alone," I mumbled, remembering the first time Micah had brought me to his home. I'd found a lavish estate, so beautiful I'd had to squint to see it all, filled with luxuries I'd never imagined, and not a living soul in it, other than Micah.

"Alone no more." Micah shifted so he could see my face; now, his smile was genuine. "Now, I have my copper girl. Soon, our family will fill these halls, and we won't be alone ever again."

I ignored the flutters in my belly and returned his smile. "Soon."

6

A short time later, Micah departed for the latest Gathering of the Heavies, this time without his loyal consort. He was apologetic and reassured me yet again that once I was Lady Silverstrand, my burgeoning belly and I would be welcome at any and all functions.

Great. So by the time people paid attention to me, I'd be fat.

I stayed in bed for a while after he left, my hand resting on my flat stomach, wondering how much longer it would stay flat. I had no reason to not want a child with Micah; he was kind, and gentle, and loved me completely. And I loved him.

And yet…A few short months ago, I was an office worker at Real Estate Evaluation Systems. I lived in a small apartment, ate only (okay, *mostly*) government-sanctioned food, and avoided magic like the plague. I went so far as to dye my copper-colored hair dirt brown and wore long shirts to cover my mark, which manifested as a copper raven emblazoned across my lower back. It signified my Elemental status, and it also told whoever was looking that I'm a member of the Raven clan, one of the most powerful magical bloodlines in history. By so thoroughly hiding my heritage, I was, for all intents and purposes, living the life of a Mundane.

Then Micah had appeared in my life—in my car, to be exact, while I was napping away my lunch hour—and everything had changed, almost immediately. In many ways, Micah wandering into my dream was the best thing that had ever happened to me, and many good things have happened since our first, somewhat scandalous, meeting. There was Micah, for one, the man who I loved more than I had ever thought possible. Together we freed my brother from the Institute for Elemental Research, a prison disguised as a medical/research facility.

It still amazed me that Max had gone there willingly. I mean, his intentions were sound, being that he had only wanted to distract the Peacekeepers from Sadie, and he was following Dad's instructions. However, when Dad told Max to keep the family safe at any cost, I don't think he meant for his son to sacrifice himself for the greater good.

Boys. So literal.

I also learned that my lifelong best friend, Juliana H. Armstrong, was a government spy, and that my job at REES, which was actually run by Peacekeepers, not real estate moguls, was a carefully constructed maze in which I was the rat. And, just yesterday Max had informed me that Juliana's uncle, Mike Armstrong, was some sort of mad scientist-politician, and that he had now decided to campaign for President of Pacifica.

So, no, not only good things had happened.

All these changes in just a few weeks…Was I a bad person for wanting things to just stay as they were for a little while?

There was also my complete and utter lack of maternal instincts to contend with. When I had mentioned this deficit to Micah, he merely shrugged and assured me that motherhood was natural, as if the knowledge of how to care and feed a tiny person would magically appear inside my brain. This, coming from an only child who lived with metal servants. It's not like *he* knew anything about parenting.

I sighed and kicked my way free of the bedclothes. These ruminations were getting me nothing but a headache. Besides, Micah was so, um, *attentive*, I'd likely be pregnant soon enough anyway, and I'd yet to find an Otherworldly form of birth control. However, it wasn't like I'd really looked…

After I got dressed and asked Shep for the location of the nearest apothecary, I made my way downstairs. When I saw the heap of parcels in the atrium, I asked a nearby silverkin if Santa had arrived. He didn't get the joke, but he did tell me that others of copper had begun sending me gifts.

"For me?" I approached the heap, full of items in all sorts of shapes and sizes, wrapped in crisp brown and white papers, and secured with trailing vines in lieu of strings. A few were decorated with brightly colored flowers, and some of the larger ones had shiny copper baubles dangling from silky ribbons. "Why me?"

The 'kin chittered away, informing me in his high-pitched cadence that the gifts had begun arriving yesterday, shortly after I'd been seen in the village with Max. That pixie must have had a pretty big mouth.

Anyway, the news was that I had single-handedly held off the iron warrior; the fact that the pixie was the one who'd immobilized the brute was a little detail that the rumor mill had failed to mention. Well, since there was no current leader for those of copper, at least no one local, and I'd done such an awesome job of fighting off the enemy, others of my Element were now looking to me for guidance.

"We can't accept these!" My outburst scared the 'kin, whose only real fear was of displeasing me or Micah, and he scuttled off for reinforcements. Another heartbeat later, Shep was kneeling before me, proffering his shiny hide as penance for whatever offense had been committed. Once I'd calmed them down, and assured them that no one had done anything wrong, I attempted to reason with Shep.

"Don't you see?" I said. "They think I'm going to be their leader, but I'm not. I don't lead anything." Shep hung his head, so I crouched down to his level. "You didn't do anything wrong when you accepted these, because you didn't know. But if anyone else comes with a gift, can you explain—nicely—to the people that we can't keep them?"

The silverkin both nodded vigorously, excited to have a new task, and the three of us set about opening the parcels. Even though I fully intended to return these gifts, I was itching to see what was inside the cute, little packages. Most of the items were perishable, food and flowers and such, so I couldn't really have sent them back to the givers. Well, that and the fact that I didn't know who had given them to me in the first place. The Otherworld wasn't big on using return addresses.

The few nonperishable gifts were a sight to behold, comprising such varied items as candlesticks, jewelry, and ornate mirrors, all of highly polished copper. After we'd found the third such mirror, I asked Shep if it was customary to send gifts to one's leader. To my utter horror, he replied that it was only done when two or more were vying for the position, and the gifts were used as a show of support.

"Support against who?" I demanded. When Shep claimed that he didn't know (though I'm not so sure I believed him), I yelped, "But I don't want any support!" Who did these people think I wanted support against? Another of copper? Whoever that person was, they could have the job. I did *not* want it. The silverkin freaked at my outburst, but I calmed them down...again. After we had opened the bazillionth package, I left Shep and his flock to sort out the gifts on their own. As for me, I continued on my quest for breakfast. This "support the ruler" fiasco wasn't going to get resolved any time soon, at least not before I talked to Micah, and I had other fish to fry. Before I got to the kitchens, I found Sadie in the parlor, sipping something warm from a delicate silver cup.

"How do the silverkin manage espresso?" she murmured. I pictured the manor's rustic kitchen with its large, open ovens and well-worn surfaces, and had to admit that I hadn't the foggiest. "And the foamed milk?"

"Magic?" I offered with a shrug. I took a seat beside her and was promptly presented with my own frothy concoction. Really, I didn't care what steps were necessary to create cappuccinos in a medieval kitchen, so long as those steps worked.

"And the muffins," Sadie continued, now enamored of a basket of baked goods that had appeared alongside my cappuccino. Maybe the silverkin were really angels, sent to earth in order to watch over dry throats and empty bellies. "I never knew something this bready could be so delicious."

I laughed and recalled that Sadie had spent her last few years subsisting on school food, which was little more than cardboard compared to what I had been getting from the Promenade Market and Mom's garden, and had likely forgotten what real food tasted like. It was amazing that she had been able to complete two-thirds of her master's degree while eating only government rations.

Sadie and I sat together for a while, sipping our drinks and talking about nothing, before I got up enough courage to ask, "Want to come to the village with me?"

"I—" she began, then she clamped her mouth shut. She knew that I knew she didn't have anything better to do. "What for?"

"I need to hit the apothecary."

"For what? To replenish your cauldron?"

"Something like that." She pursed her lips and turned away. "Listen, I know it's freaky out there, but you have to get used to it. It looks like we're going to be here a while, and you're the Inheritor. The *Metal Inheritor*. You can't be seen as weak." I left off the rest of my thought, that if Sadie was deemed incompetent, others of metal were likely to murder her, in the hopes that their own offspring would take her place. Her blanched face told me that she already knew that.

"Just the apothecary?"

"Just the apothecary." I tossed back the rest of my cappuccino and stood, just as Shep appeared bearing our walking shoes. These silverkin do think of everything.

Whispering Dell, the village, was located at the opposite end of the valley from the Silverstrand manor. It was a short enough walk, though I hadn't planned on walking. Under Micah's tutelage, I'd gotten pretty good at traveling along the vein of silver that runs the length of the dell, just underneath the grassy surface. The vein was how Max and I had gotten to the village and back yesterday, but since Sadie had never traveled by leaping from metal to metal, I didn't even bring it up. I was just happy she'd agreed to set foot outside the manor.

Gods, but I missed my car.

Still, it was a lovely day and a lovely walk. I'd worried that Sadie would invent reasons to run back to the manor, such as a possibility of rain or a woodland creature looking her way in a menacing fashion, but she seemed to enjoy being out in the fresh air as much as I did. If only I could manage to repeat this experiment at a later date and enjoy similar results.

She wasn't even that weirded out once we arrived in the clearing before the village, though weirdness certainly abounded. The clearing was innocuous enough, though it bustled with people, Elemental and otherwise, going about their day. A harried woman who reminded me of the Old Woman in the

Shoe was herding a group of young fauns toward the schoolhouse, without much success. Carts and deliverymen sped across the clearing, narrowly avoiding collisions. Off to the side, a hawker peddled cold drinks and parasols to shield our delicate skin from the sun. Being that I never managed to tan, I thought his stand was brilliant.

Beyond the clearing were the village gates, the first official—well, for the village, anyway—station of weird. They were towering masses of organic, living silver, constantly twining together and apart, depending on whether or not you were allowed entry. Footmen stood on either side of the gates, clad in bright silver mail and armed to the teeth. While I'd never seen anyone be refused entry, I sure didn't want to be on the business end of their spears.

The footmen immediately recognized my oak leaf and acorn token and bowed. They frickin' bowed! Sadie was as shocked as I was, but before I could stammer out a "hey, stand up straight!"-themed comment, a doorway swirled into being before us. Sadie eyed the silver walls dubiously but followed me through, anyway. Good for her. Once we'd passed the gate and she saw the village proper, her eyes nearly fell out of her head.

As with most centers of habitation, there are good parts and bad parts of the Whispering Dell. Unlike most Mundane cities, these two halves are very easily discernible to the naked eye. To our right lay row upon row of brothels, badly-lit pubs, and more than a few criminals masquerading as magicians for hire. The entire path was swathed in a thick, palpable darkness akin to the dense smoke generated by burning soggy leaves, which was just as well. This wasn't the sort of vista you wanted to see all that clearly.

In stark, sunny contrast, the path that snaked to our left was carpeted in daisies and bluebells. No, really; as you walked along, inevitably crushing flowers as you meandered down the path, a lovely perfume rose up for your enjoyment. Birds sang, dew sparkled, and the street was lined with maidens seated before the shop fronts, combing out their shining tresses, while minstrels plucked away at their lutes. Truly, the left path seemed like a veritable heaven, and, to my jaded eyes, just a bit too perfect. Give me an honest thief over a simpering two-face any day.

Having taken a good, long look at our options, my sweet, innocent sister asked, her voice wavering only a bit, about which way Max and I had gone yesterday. "To the right, of course," I replied. And we were headed to the right today.

"This must be the wrong way," Sadie said, clutching my arm as I stepped toward the mass of smoky, stinky fog. "It has to be."

"Shep said that the apothecary was this way," I said. "It's just a few doors in."

"There isn't one that way?" she asked, hopefully eyeing the path to the left.

"Shep said that the one to the right has a better selection of herbs and stuff." I tugged at her arm, but she remained rooted in place. "C'mon. We've come all this way. We'll leave as soon as we're done."

At that she relented, and we walked confidently into the darkness. Okay, I walked confidently; Sadie had her fingers wound so tightly around my arm I lost circulation.

True to Shep's directions, the apothecary was the fourth shop on the left, situated right along the main way. We stepped—well, I stepped, Sadie was dragged—inside the modest building, which hardly had space for the two of us. Once my eyes adjusted to the dim interior, I sucked in a breath at the towering heaps of clutter, then the coughing started. The place was blanketed in filth, and I'd just inhaled a vacuum's worth of dust.

Once my hacking subsided, and I could see again, I took a good look at all that junk. The shop was packed from floor to ceiling with jars containing murky liquids and dull-colored powders. From the rafters, various things, some animal, some vegetable, and some unidentifiable, were hung up to dry. In the space not occupied by hanging and jarred dead things, rolls of parchment and dusty, cracked leather tomes were stacked in teetering piles. In short, if Shep were to ever visit the apothecary, he would have his work cut out for him.

Behind all the clutter, magical and otherwise, sat a hunchbacked crone. She was straight out of a fairy tale, complete with gray, stringy hair, skin crisscrossed with wrinkles as deep as chasms, and a shapeless robe in varied shades of used bathwater. She sat behind a wooden table, upon which lay a stack of pelts.

"Help you?" she croaked, glancing up from the pelts she was sorting. A few were still bloody, and one of them wiggled.

"I'm looking for something," I said, my voice mostly holding steady. Now that I was really there, really doing this, I almost completely lost my nerve. "Something to keep me from having a baby."

The crone cackled, the sound filling the tiny space of the shop and rattling my bones. "So, you like him well enough, but not too much?" I opened my mouth, whether to protest or explain how much I really did like him I didn't know, but she waved it away. "I've some extract of Queen's Lace in the back," she said, creakily unfolding herself from her chair. "I'll be but a moment."

"What is Queen's Lace?" Sadie demanded, once the crone was out of sight.

"It keeps you from getting pregnant," I whispered. Sadie drew back, shaking her head.

"Micah won't like this," she warned.

"What makes you think I haven't told him?"

"If you had, you'd be here with him instead of me." Good point. Thankfully, before Sadie pointed out the rest of the holes in my argument, the crone reappeared bearing a blue glass bottle.

She set the bottle on the counter, and for a moment I just stared at it. I was surprised at how small it was, based on how drastically the contents could—would—alter my relationship with Micah.

I touched the cork stopper, and then the glass itself, unable to suppress a shiver. It was nothing to be scared of, nothing to be intimidated by. I mean, it was only an herbal extract, just like the vanilla I would add to cookies, or the peppermint oil that kept away pantry moths. Still, if I took this innocent little bottle back to the manor, my life would take a decidedly different turn.

I swallowed and made my choice. "How much?" I asked.

"For Lady Silverstrand?" the crone sneered. Obviously, if I used the extract I'd never be Lady Silverstrand. All I would ever be was a freeloader in Micah's home. "Take it, with my compliments."

Despite her words, I was still fumbling with my purse. "I'd rather pay—"

"And I would rather a friend in my lord's home," she finished.

"I'll be your friend," I said, firmly placing a few coins on the pile of stinking pelts, "but I'd rather not owe anyone."

The crone cackled again, this time with her head thrown back and spittle flying. "How quickly you've learned our ways!" She swept the coins into a fold of her robe. "But do me this, dearie—don't tell my lord where you obtained this."

"And you, dearie, won't tell anyone that I purchased it." She nodded, and with that Sadie and

I exited the shop. My hands were shaking, and I was coated in a cold, clammy sweat; though he wasn't even here, I felt like I'd just lied to Micah.

7

Just as I'd promised, once my business at the apothecary was done, Sadie and I immediately left the village and returned to the manor. She didn't even give us time to walk through the nicer side of the village, not even to visit the bakery. And here I'd thought that cookies make every day better.

Still, Sadie was in a surprisingly adventurous mood after surviving our sojourn to the village, not to mention our encounter with the crone, and she agreed to return to the manor by way of the metal pathway, instead walking on the much safer, and much longer, road. She must have realized that I only suggested traveling by metal because I was trying to distract her (I am a firm believer in the Shiny Object Theory), but whatever. I would take what I could get.

We landed, if that's what you want to call it, in the gardens that stretched behind the manor. No matter how many times I had set foot in the gardens, the lush beauty never failed to take my breath away; every flower and shrub always seemed to be in full leaf and covered in flowers, and, more often than not, also laden with ripe, juicy fruit. Surrounding the gardens were acres and acres of orchards, the trees carefully maintained in orderly rows like so many wooden soldiers. Beyond the orchards was a deep, dark forest.

As beautiful as I'd initially found the manor's grounds to be, once I'd ventured into the forest, aptly named the Great Wood, that bordered the far edge of Micah's land, I was truly amazed, and more than a bit terrified. At first glance, this Otherworldly forest was similar to the woods I'd played in as a child, complete with oak groves, gurgling streams, and the occasional furry critter scuttling by. However, the deeper one went into the Great Wood, the denser it became, and it wasn't only packed with trees.

There were carnivorous plants large enough to capture and digest a horse, as evidenced by the piles of bleached bones heaped before their stalks. There were also raptors nesting in the canopy that were strong enough, and hungry enough, to pluck that horse right out of a leafy maw and gobble it down themselves. Flowers clad in jeweled hues might spit a fine, paralyzing nectar on a passerby, thus rendering you immobile for hours, or maybe even days or weeks. The first time Micah had taken me into the

Great Wood, a length of strangleweed had reared up and tried to grab me. If not for Micah's quick reflexes, I might have ended up as some animal's, or plant's, afternoon snack.

The Great Wood wasn't only populated with death traps. It also sheltered the loveliest flowers I had ever seen, some so delicate they reminded me of blown glass, as well as a multitude of critters, both magical and otherwise. Micah had warned me to stay away from the northern quadrant, being that it was populated by a herd of trolls that got a bit grumpy around strangers, and that the eastern side was home to a tribe of elves. When I had asked if he was related to the elves, Micah gave me such a look of revulsion you would have thought I'd asked if he was descended from dung beetles. Apparently wood elves are somewhat beneath Lord Silverstrand.

Micah also told me about a woman who lived at the heart of the Great Wood; her hair was a fall of flowers, her clothing made up of vines and thorns. She and one of Micah's ancestors had quarreled long ago, back when the orchards were first planted. Somehow a truce had been brokered between the forest queen and the Silverstrand house, but she occasionally got testy and threatened to swallow the whole of the manor with her vines.

"Shouldn't we find a way to get rid of her?" I'd squeaked; this bit of information had been casually revealed shortly after the strangleweed incident. Micah had laughed at my terrified face and assured me that she was only strong within the Great Wood, and that his will was stronger yet. After all, he had that giant vein of silver from which he drew strength, and surely silver was stronger than any leaf or bit of vine. I'd murmured in agreement, since I'd never doubted Micah for one moment. Still, as Sadie and I leisurely made our way past the flower beds with the Great Wood visible in the distance, I was glad that Micah was able to keep the Wood's influence at bay.

We took a roundabout path to the manor, one that was both far from the Great Wood and close to the Bright Lady's pool. I always made time to speak with her, since without her help, the Iron Queen would have likely killed me, along with Micah and the rest of my family. The Bright Lady had never acted as if I owed her anything—in fact, she'd all but given me leave to call upon her—but my gratitude to her remained enormous.

Unfortunately, a visit with my watery friend would have to wait. As soon as Sadie and I entered the formal knot garden, we found Micah, despairing over a heap of unmoving silverkin.

"What happened?" I asked, sinking to my knees beside him. I touched a little silver arm; it was cold and lifeless, just a piece of ordinary metal. "Are they sick?"

"Your mother," he bit off. "She's destroyed them. All of them."

"All of them?" I squeaked. "Even Shep?"

Micah nodded, looking more distraught than I'd ever seen him. The silverkin weren't truly alive, being that they didn't breathe, or have beating hearts, or need to keep their bellies full. What they were was the embodiment of that vein of silver that lies beneath the Whispering Dell. Nevertheless, they had served Micah's family since long before he was born, and Micah treated them as members of his family. Since his mother's death, they were all the family he had left.

And my mother had just reduced them to a heap of scrap metal.

"Sadie, find Mom," I said, over my shoulder.

"But—"

"Find her!" Sadie ran toward the house, and I rested my hands on Micah's shoulders. Gently, I rubbed his mark through his leather shirt, calming him as best I could. "Do you know what happened?"

"She unmade them," he replied.

"Unmade?" I repeated. I glanced at the pile; they still looked pretty made to me.

"I turned them back into normal metal, which is what they should have been all along," Mom explained, coming up behind us, with Sadie cowering behind her. "As they were, they were little more than meddling nuisances."

"Mom, you can't do that!" I said, standing to face her.

"Oh?" she countered, raising a brow. "It appears that I did."

"Well, undo it!" Mom crossed her arms and lifted her chin, defiance written across her face. Good grief, the ageless Queen of the Seelie Court was acting like a two year old.

"Fine!" I spun around, turning my back to my lunatic mother. Micah hadn't moved, his eyes still fixed on the lifeless silverkin. I crouched beside him, and asked, "Is there any way we save them?"

"We need to replace their sparks," Micah murmured. "Now that she's taken them, they cannot be reanimated, much as if you or I were to die, no one could install another soul in our bodies." I shivered, imagining a horde of tiny metal zombies. "That is the problem we now face."

"Oh, Micah," I murmured, lacing my fingers with his. "Can you make more?"

"I can, but they won't be the same." Micah reached out and traced an immobile silver limb. "My mother created them, all of them...so long ago, she made them...their sparks were born from her. They are all a part of her. Now that their sparks are gone, they are as good as dead."

Gods, I'd had no idea that the silverkin were created by Micah's long-deceased, yet still very much beloved, mother. This situation needed to be fixed, and quickly. But how?

Sparks...Micah had said that Mom had taken their sparks. Yesterday, when Max and I were in the village, the pixie had taken the iron warrior's spark, held it in her hand like it was a regular old tchotchke, then she'd flown away with it. Which meant that Mom probably still had the silverkins' sparks, in her hand or in a pocket or—or somewhere. Which also meant that I should be able to get them back. Well, assuming that my mother decided to act like an adult.

I glared at my mother over my shoulder; I'd read somewhere that you always wanted to confront a wild animal head-on and look it directly in the eye. Probably so the animal knew what it was about to munch on. "You see what you've done?" I demanded. "You've destroyed a part of Micah's family. What did they do to you, anyway?"

"They…they are annoying," she said, waving her hand in a dismissive gesture.

"Annoying?" I was on my feet again, standing directly in front of Mom and yelling in her face. "Listen, this isn't the Raven Compound. You can't just dispose of servants because your bath's too hot or your tea's too cold. The silverkin are Micah's; they're all he has left of his mother, and you are a guest in his house, and…and you need to behave!"

Mom's eyes widened; I bet she forgot that I knew exactly why we'd had a mansion and no maids, not even someone to fold the laundry. Oh, we used to have maids, back when Dad was around to protect them from Mom's wrath. By the time Dad had been gone for a full year, Mom had hired and fired six maids and ten cooks; by the time Max got arrested, word had gotten out and no one even applied. What was the point of a job that would only last a few weeks, and one working for a crazy lady to boot?

I missed the cooks the most.

Mom just stood there, her face a mask of shock and anger, and for a moment, I thought I was going to end up permanently immobile, just like the 'kin. Then her gaze fell on Micah's hunched shoulders and softened a bit. Not much, but a bit. "He feels their loss so deeply?"

"Yes. He does." I held out my hand. "Please, give them back their sparks. I'll tell them to leave you alone. Promise."

My mother is a lot of things—haughty, indignant, and even a bit bloodthirsty at times—but she's not cruel. Being that she's not a metal Elemental, she couldn't even be blamed for how she felt; she saw the silverkin as nothing more than bits of moving furniture, certainly not as the only companions a lonely orphan once had. Even so, something about Micah's despair spoke to her, and she placed her hand on mine. In another moment, I held a double handful of glowing orbs, but they weren't all that similar to what the pixie had held after she had stopped the iron warrior from attacking Max. The iron warrior's spark had been a dull gray and had lain in the pixie's palm like a dumb lump. The silverkin's sparks were white, and they wiggled back and forth as I held them. I couldn't say why their sparks were so much more active, save perhaps that their sparks were a reflection of their makers—one dull and uninteresting, the other happy and full of life. And, they tickled! One adventurous spark tried climbing up my arm, but I corralled it in the crook of my elbow. I couldn't risk losing one, not now that I'd just gotten them back.

"Thank you," I murmured, flashing her a quick smile before I returned to Micah's side. His face was hidden by his hands, and, since mine were full, I bumped his shoulder with my hip. "I have them," I said.

He looked up, his silver eyes reflecting the sparks nestled in my palms. "So you do. Thank you," he said, with a nod to Mom over his shoulder.

"Um, I don't know how to return them."

"Let me." Micah stood and placed his hands upon mine. A heartbeat later, the sparks, now glowing with a coppery tinge, erupted from our hands and flitted across the heap of inanimate metal as the orbs searched for their owners. Once the orbs had settled into the nooks and crannies around the bodies, Micah and I stood breathless, gripping each other's hands.

"Why is it taking so long?" I whispered.

"Patience, love," Micah replied, patting my hand. "Give them time to remember who they are."

If there's anything I don't have, it's patience, and those long, silent moments nearly drove me crazy. Just as I was about to ask Micah if this spark application always took so frickin' long, I heard a noise. A weird noise, one that you don't hear every day, except maybe if you're an Elemental.

Silver scraping against silver.

My breath caught in my throat, my fingers wound around Micah's so tightly they ached, then went numb. Slowly, creakily, the silverkin shook their heads, then they stretched their limbs. Then a silver head poked free of the mass, and I recognized him at once.

"Shep!" I cried as the little guy pulled himself free from the rest. I snatched him up in a bear hug, which clearly embarrassed him. Luckily for him, metal doesn't blush. "I'm so glad you're back!"

"My Sara, look," Micah said, tracing a pattern on Shep's arm. It was faint, but there was an undeniable swirl of copper, where there had previously been nothing but pure silver. I looked at the rest of the 'kin, all of whom now had graceful copper sigils across their arms and legs. "They all have copper marks now."

"How is that possible?" I murmured, tracing the elegant pattern on Shep's arm.

"You restored them," Micah murmured, pressing his lips against my temple. "Now, they are more than just silver."

I smiled, though I didn't think we'd start calling them the copperkin anytime soon. "You see, Mom?" I asked, carrying Shep over to her, and displaying his newly decorated arms. "There's part of me in them now, too. You can't hurt them without hurting me."

Her mouth was twisted up in an unflattering way, but she relented. "Fine. If they bother me, I'll just send for their mistress."

I cuddled Shep at that, as much as one can cuddle a metal being. He swatted my arm with his tiny hand, but made no attempt to escape. "Good."

8

It didn't take all that much longer for the silverkin to sort themselves out and, wouldn't you know it, they were immediately back to their energetic little selves. Instead of taking time to recover, they were off sweeping floors, straightening drapes, and making tea by the gallon. Despite their recent adventure in slumberland, they were apparently none the worse for wear. About the only thing the little guys were doing differently was giving my mother a wide, respectful berth. That was a very, very smart move on their part.

As for me, I couldn't stop staring at them. Each and every 'kin, from Shep on down to the littlest sweeper, now bore flowing copper spirals across their arms and legs. The calm, rational portion of my brain understood that these new copper sigils had only appeared because of my exposure to their sparks, nothing more. Still, I took it as a sign that I finally belonged in the Otherworld.

"Of course you belong," Micah said, when I shared why I was smiling. We had remained in the garden long after Mom and Sadie had gone inside, and we were contentedly watching the silverkin harvest fruit. After all the hubbub of this afternoon, there needed to be pie in my future. "My Sara, the Whispering Dell is your home as much as mine."

"It's not." I hadn't meant to sound so whiney. "You were born here. I'm from another world— *literally*, another world. It's not like I fit in."

Micah laughed, a warm, rumbling sound. "Does anyone 'fit' in the Otherworld?" he asked, while his arm made a sweeping gesture, encompassing both the manor and the lands beyond. "I have servants of metal rather than flesh and blood, and a nymph resides in my pool. Beyond the pool is a wood witch, who would strangle me as soon as greet me good morning. My village is populated with all manner of Elementals and beasts, and more than a few Mundanes. We are none of us alike."

I smiled and leaned against his shoulder. "I suppose you have a point." He accepted his win gracefully and kissed my hair. "I just like seeing something of me here. Everything's so silver."

"What would you like?" Micah asked. "To be copper, that is."

"Anything?"

"For my Sara, anything."

"Hmm." I considered my request carefully, not wanting to waste what might be my only redecorating opportunity on something frivolous. Maybe a spiral staircase of polished copper would enhance the place, or that roof I'd once coveted? Before I came up with any good ideas, we heard yet another commotion, this one coming from the opposite side of the garden. I really needed to start chucking salt over my shoulder to ward off these sorts of days.

Micah leapt up and ran toward the noise. I followed close behind, but we both halted when we saw the source of this latest uproar. Of course, it was Max, who was fending off a gang of iron warriors.

"Max!" I shrieked.

"They followed me!" he yelled, ducking to avoid a punch. There were four—no, make that *five*—iron warriors surrounding my brother, with the remains of two others lying nearby. The warriors were huge, monstrous creations, each one of them tall and broad, with a mouthful of teeth like broken saw blades. Not to mention, all of their punches were death blows.

Max, by comparison, was positively puny. I'd like to say that my brother was holding his own against the mob, but, well-honed as his abilities might be, he could only disable one iron man at a time. The warriors had apparently caught on to his weakness, for while one attacked him head-on, the others closed in from behind, harrying him and getting in those cheap shots that added up to blood loss and exhaustion.

I had no idea what to do or how to help my brother, when all at once, the iron warriors stopped moving and became little more than metal sculptures decorating the garden. Max's confused face let me know that he hadn't engineered this turn of events. Since I knew that I hadn't done anything but jump up and down and flap my arms, I glanced to the side. I flinched when I saw Micah's outstretched hand, his silver eyes boiling in fury.

"They followed you?" Micah said, his voice rumbling like a volcano moments before the eruption. "Where did they follow you from?"

"The village," Max said. I realized that he couldn't move either, also thanks to my consort. I'd never seen Micah so angry, and I was amazed that he could hold all six individuals completely immobile. I was awed by his control, his strength, and more than a bit frightened. "Sara and I saw one the other day—"

"The one whose spark was taken by the pixie," I interjected.

"And you went looking for more," Micah deduced. When Max remained silent, Micah continued, "You sought out the henchmen of my greatest enemy, and *led them to my home*?"

"I wanted to know who they work for now!" Max shouted. "I thought—"

"No, Max, you did not think." Micah approached the warriors, and their heads creaked around to face him. "Whom do you serve?" he demanded of the iron men.

"The Iron Queen," they answered in unison.

"Are you aware that she is dead?"

"It does not matter," replied the one who'd lunged at Max. "She created us, and we will carry out her will."

"Will anything deter you from this course?"

"Nothing, unless we are remade."

Micah nodded, then squeezed his hand closed. The warrior's mouth clamped inward on itself, his jaw crushed and dented so badly that he might never speak again.

"As he stated," Micah continued, as he turned to face my brother, "any metal creatures created by Ferra are honor bound to carry out their mistress' commands. Do you know anything of honor, Max?" Max opened his mouth, but Micah didn't give him the chance to reply. "No, of course you don't. Otherwise, you would not have acted so foolishly. You would not have acted so *recklessly* and brought danger to your family's doorstep." Micah stepped before Max, using his advantage of height to stare down at him. "Had you bothered to ask me, I would have told you that, like as not, any iron warrior would attempt to kill a Raven on sight. *Any* Raven, your sisters and mother included. I do know more of the ways of metal than you, boy."

I could see Max fuming, but he knew he was wrong. The evidence lay heaped up around him like a supernatural scrap yard. "I just thought—"

"We have already established that you do not think," Micah spoke over him. "I do understand. You wanted to prove yourself the hero. You failed." Now Micah leaned into Max's face, not stopping until he was a hair's breadth away from him. "My patience with you grows thin. Take care that it doesn't grow thinner."

With that, Micah turned and walked toward the manor, with me following. Of course, Max couldn't just let us go.

"You think you're big, bad Micah, and want us all to bow down to you," my idiot brother shouted. "Well, you're not so powerful!"

Micah halted, but he didn't turn around. Instead, he raised his hand. Amazingly, all seven of the iron warriors lifted into the air, screaming as they were crushed together like a giant wad of aluminum foil, the sound like a thousand rusty grates being dragged shut. Micah flicked his wrist, and, like a corrupted shooting star, the iron blob sped away across the sky.

"Where did you send them?" I asked, my voice and hands shaking. Each warrior must have weighed as much as a small car, and Micah had just flung seven of them away without even breaking a sweat.

"Ferra's castle," Micah replied, "where they belong."

The Iron Court was miles away from the Whispering Dell. Miles and miles...I wrapped my arm around Micah's waist and coaxed him inside the manor. I glanced over my shoulder and saw

Max standing among the huge ruts in the lawn, the carefully tended flowers that had been trampled down to nothing. With wide eyes and a bloodless face, he stared at the destruction he'd caused. Maybe Micah's lesson in humility had taught him a thing or two.

Then again, this was Max.

However Max had taken it, I wanted him and Micah as far apart as possible; while I didn't think Micah would do anything that would harm Max, I understood how close Max had just come to being thrown out on his ear. Who knows what kind of trouble Max would stir up as a homeless derelict in the Otherworld? I led Micah across the atrium, where we passed the newly reminted silverkin as they polished the stairs, and up to our rooms. Once the door was shut, Micah's hard exterior crumbled away and he sat heavily, his head in his hands.

"I'm sorry," I murmured, perching on the arm of his chair. For the second time that day, I rubbed his mark. "I'll talk to Max."

"How could he have led them here, to our home?" Micah mumbled. "Why did he go looking for them?"

"Max probably didn't mean to bring them here," I said. "I'm sure he just got in way over his head and needed help." The image of the iron warriors flying across the sky bubbled up in my mind, and I couldn't help but smile. "I had no idea you were so strong."

"I'm not," he replied. "I was furious."

I slid around, balancing myself before him on the arms of the chair. "Max is pretty lucky he's my brother, huh?"

At that, Micah laughed. "He is. Which makes the message I received this morning all the more perplexing."

"Message?" I let go of the arms and slid onto Micah's lap.

"Our queen has decided to make a formal appearance," Micah replied. "All of the Inheritors should be present, and we of metal shall formally pledge ourselves to her."

"Everyone of metal?" I asked.

"Not every last being. Your sister will, yes, as will all the rulers."

"So, not me, then." Once more, everyone was interested in Sadie and Micah, not poor, pathetic, "just a consort" Sara.

"Yes, you." Micah smoothed back my hair, his hand coming to rest on the nape of my neck. "You and I are as one."

"I don't rule anything," I whined, but Micah silenced me with a kiss. I think he was tired of hearing that same old complaint.

"Hush. We are going, you and I and your sister." I noticed that he omitted Max's name. Smart.

"Will those of iron be there?"

"That is not likely. They are somewhat disgraced at the moment. When a new iron ruler emerges, they will first need to make reparations to Oriana, if such reparations are even possible." Micah tightened his arms around me. "You will be quite safe in the Gold Court, my love, of that I am certain."

I laid my head on his shoulder, not voicing my thoughts. Safe from iron, yes, but what about all the other Elementals?

9

Micah and I remained in our rooms for the rest of that day and into the evening, though he balked when I described us as hiding from my family. He claimed that the true reason for our seclusion was that he had missed me, and how could I argue with that? Besides, I did like having him all to myself.

Of course, I couldn't just enjoy our time alone. "So, did you see all of that junk in the atrium?" I ventured. We'd been sitting at the table before the window, playing chess. He was even letting me win.

"You mean the gifts from others of copper, supporting you as their ruler?" Micah countered, without even looking up from the board.

"Um. Yeah." I stared at the chess pieces, wishing one of the bishops or rooks would offer some advice. They didn't. "Can we make the gifts stop?"

"In my experience, love, gifts are given according to the giver's preference, not the recipient's." Micah moved a pawn, then he grabbed my hands. "Do you think you'd not rule well?"

"I think random fake office work doesn't qualify me to do anything but alphabetize reports," I mumbled, being that I'd only ever been given busy work in my position at REES. "Can't they support someone who knows what she's doing?" I looked at him, my next words almost as desperate as I felt. "What should I do?"

Micah rose and scooped me into his arms, settling us onto the window seat. I loved it when he carried me, but I always told him I'd rather he didn't. If he knew how much I enjoyed it, my feet would never touch the ground again. "You truly do not wish to rule?" he asked.

"I truly do not."

"Then we shall learn who else wishes to be leader of copper, and we shall support them."

I blew out a breath I hadn't realized I was holding. "We can do that? It's that simple?"

"Yes and yes."

I laid my head on Micah's shoulder, relieved beyond words. "You're brilliant. I love you."

"Only for my mind?"

I glanced at his face; there was that grin, the one that only made appearances when we were alone. I'd move mountains for that grin. "Maybe for a few other things, too."

The next morning found Micah still in full-on Corbeau avoidance mode. He had instructed the silverkin to deliver breakfast to our rooms, and while I enjoy having my coffee in bed as much as the next gal, all this sulking was getting a little old. I tried to distract Micah out of his funk by asking him about Oriana's impending appearance and trying to learn a few details about what would surely be quite the event. I only asked for basic information, like who was expected to attend, what we should be wearing, would anyone be handing out pronunciation guides for all those multi-syllable names, things like that. My Micah had other ideas and suggested that instead of spending the day inside discussing such dry matters, we head on down to the village and visit the smithy.

"For your sword," Micah said when I asked why.

"Oh. You're really going to teach me?"

"Didn't I already agree to it?" he countered. "What with your brother's exceedingly bad judgment, and your mother's tendency to destroy those who can guard you from whatever follows Max home, I now see the need for you to be armed."

"A sword can help me against iron warriors?" Maybe Micah was going to get me a super sword. Cool.

"It would not," Micah clarified, "but it could be useful against other creatures who are displeased with your brother. He accumulates enemies the way a squirrel gathers acorns."

I smiled, grateful he wasn't holding a grudge over Mom's and Max's bad behavior; well, at least he wasn't holding one against me. After a leisurely breakfast involving all three major food groups—caffeine, heavily buttered toast, and extra caffeine—we were on our way. I, in turn, surprised Micah by suggesting that we walk, instead of taking the metal pathway.

"Sadie and I walked to the village yesterday," I explained, "and it's such a nice, sunny day. It would be a shame to miss it by hopping around from metal to metal."

"Why did you and Sadie decide to visit the village?" Micah asked.

"I had to get her out of the manor," I said in a rush. The little blue vial I'd purchased at the apothecary was still wrapped up in plain brown paper on my dressing table. "She needs to, you know, acclimate herself."

"Did you bring a silverkin?"

"I thought I only needed one when I was with Max." Micah blinked, so I amended, "Actually, I didn't think about it."

"You didn't think about being safe?"

"I was intent on getting Sadie to act like an adult." Not to mention that I was worried that a silverkin would rat me out. I leaned up and kissed Micah's cheek. "I'll remember next time. I promise."

"Mmm." Micah accepted my response, lame as it was, and my elf and I enjoyed a leisurely stroll to the village proper.

What's really interesting about the village of Whispering Dell, and Micah's rulership of it, is that he does almost all of it from afar. He rarely sets foot in the village, today being only the second time he'd passed its gates since I'd lived at the manor. Instead, he preferred to have his magistrates or tax collectors or whoever come to the manor for any matters that required the magic Silverstrand touch. I supposed having one's business affairs handled by one's minions was a fringe benefit of being royalty.

Despite his lack of regular appearances, every living soul in that village was well aware of Micah's status as their lord, both by name and by sight. What's more, each and every one of his subjects positively adored him, and as soon as we'd passed through the liquid silver gates, Lord Silverstrand was surrounded by a good-sized mob of well-wishers. Content to be overlooked, for once, I stepped back and gave his fan club a wide berth.

"You just let them attack me," Micah grumbled once he extricated himself.

"It was a loving attack," I said as I took his arm. I noticed that two exceptionally beautiful women were waving goodbye to their lord, gazing after him with something akin to unrequited love. Before I could muster the proper outrage, and to my utter amazement, both of the women morphed into exact copies of Micah, right down to his leather clothes and poufy hair.

"They are shapeshifters," Micah explained, once I'd gotten my jaw off the ground.

"Like werewolves?"

Micah laughed. "Not at all. Lycanthropy is a strictly human affliction. True shapeshifters can take on the appearance of any being they gaze upon."

"So, they're just going to wander around the village, pretending to be you?" Call me old-fashioned, but wasn't that identity theft?

"No shapeshifter may hold a false shape for much longer than a day; what's more, a shapeshifter cannot replicate an Elemental's mark. And a great crowd watched them shift, while I walked away with my lovely consort." He leaned closer and kissed my hair. "Fear not, they will do nothing to tarnish my good name. I can manage that quite well on my own."

"How? By hopping into sleeping women's cars?" I teased.

"Yes," he murmured, pressing a kiss to my temple. "Exactly like that."

I leaned against his shoulder and let my dishonorable man lead me through the intricate maze of streets and alleys. I realized that, while the good and, um, less good sides of the village were clearly separated at the gate, the lines blurred the further we descended into the warren. I saw a prime example of these shades of gray at a tailor's shop, which was presided over by a plump gentleman wearing a smart green waistcoat and holding a pocket watch. He was so jovial he could have modeled for holiday cards. I don't know precisely what the shop next door to the tailor's traded in, but several species of animal, both furred and feathered, hung upside down in the front window, their blood draining into a carved trough below. Before my eyes, the tailor whipped out a silver dipper and scooped up a healthy swig of blood.

"How do you know who the good people are?" I murmured, clutching Micah's arm as my eyes searched for a safer scene. I settled on a woman, who was reaching up to pick a shiny red fruit from a low-hanging branch. It turned out that the tree didn't care to be robbed and struck her with a leafy limb.

"Good?" Micah asked. "Good in what way?"

"You know. Who are the good guys, and who are the bad guys?"

"Ah. I forget, you humans like to make such simple distinctions." Micah hugged me closer and kissed my hair. To our left, the tree screamed as the fruit thief struck its trunk with a heavy satchel, sending chunks of bark scattering across the street.

"They are all my people," he continued, gesturing to encompass the whole of the Whispering Dell, both the village and the valley beyond. "That means that I accept them, all of them, for their good attributes as well as their flaws. After all, even the best of men may occasionally commit a less than honorable act."

"Like Max?"

Micah's eyes darkened. "Yes, much like your foolish brother. For all his flaws—of which there are many—his intentions are sound."

"But what about those who really are dishonorable?" I pressed, raising my voice above the fruit thief's shrieks; the tree had grabbed her by the hair and was demanding that its property be returned. Must be some apple. "You know, like the ones who are really evil? You don't keep them around, do you?"

"Those who are truly beyond the pale I banish, but I've not been called on to do that in a long, long time." Micah took a long look up and down the street, blood-drinking tailor and murderous tree included, and smiled. "Yes, my people are good to me, and I, in turn, am good to them."

Micah fell silent then, and I was left contemplating the many shades of gray present in the Otherworld. I remembered Ferra's court, stuffed full with some of the scariest creatures I'd ever seen in the flesh. Now, that court had been evil, beginning right at the front door that had looked suspiciously like a gaping maw. Ready to have swallowed me whole and gnaw me to bits.

But then, Ferra had been an evil woman, no doubt about that, and Micah was her opposite in every way. Perhaps the demeanor of the ruler influenced their people, or maybe evil just attracted evil, and good did the same. Before I got the chance to ask Micah for his thoughts on the matter, we arrived at our destination.

The smithy turned out to be a lean-to that stank like burning rocks and belched thick, black smoke. The blacksmith, a burly Satyr called Ash, seemed to have earned his name from the substance he was smeared with. It coated him like a second, flaky skin, save where rivulets of sweat had worn away little valleys, his skin starkly pale against the soot. That crumbly layer, and his leather apron, served as his only garments.

Once Micah had explained the purpose of our visit, Ash grunted and set about examining my form with a level of scrutiny I hadn't experienced since my college entrance exams. At least he only used his eyes.

"What sort, eh?" I blinked when I realized that Ash was directing his question at me.

"What sort of what?"

"Sword, lassie," he replied gruffly. "Ain't that what yer here for, eh?"

"Sword. Um…" I spread my hands and looked hopefully at Micah. The only sword types whose names I knew were claymores and rapiers, and I didn't think either would be a good answer.

"Perhaps a short sword?" Micah offered.

Ash grunted again, which was evidently his all-purpose response. "Probably best. She's a wee lassie, don't want 'er to topple over, eh?" Before I could decide if I should be flattered or outraged at being called a wee lassie, Ash turned his back and rooted around for something in his shop, thus revealing his bare Satyr bottom and fluffy little Satyr tail.

"Like a little goat," I murmured, a few lines from *Three Billy Goats Gruff* struggling to burst forth from my tongue. Micah, always one to sense my distress, decided to be unhelpful and quirked an eyebrow. That was way, way too much, and I nearly burst out laughing, right there in front of the blacksmith's forge. I turned to face the street and became intensely interested in a butcher hacking up something. Then the something squirmed a bit, and I decided I'd be better off studying the shop's awning. Yes, a fine awning it was, all green and shady and not at all blood-spattered…

"'Ere, lass, 'ave a go at these." Biting my lip, I turned around and saw that Ash held out a few plain swords in varying lengths. I tried the largest first, which was so heavy I almost dislocated my shoulder. That's what I got for laughing at the blacksmith's behind.

Just as Ash had predicted, the short sword won out, with the second smallest and lightest sword feeling the best in my hand. The actual smallest probably would have been better, but I wasn't about to give Ash the satisfaction of being *that* right. Once Micah and Ash had agreed on a price, and Micah gave the smith a small purse as a down payment, we left the smith to work his magic.

"That was fast," I murmured. I'd imagined that ordering a sword would take all day, though I was a bit disappointed that I'd have to wait a week or more for it to be done. I do hate waiting. "So, why don't you come down to the village more often?" I asked. The village was nothing if not exciting, with better live entertainment than anything on my old Picture Vision, and it wasn't even noon. I couldn't wait to witness the nightlife firsthand.

"I've no need to," he replied. "I prefer the solitude of the manor."

"Don't you get lonely?"

"I have you to fend off loneliness," he replied, his mouth quirking in that half-smile of his.

"You've had me for only a few months," I pressed. "What about before?"

Micah began his reply, but for the life of me I couldn't pay attention to what he was saying. We had turned a corner and there, right in front of us, was the apothecary. And, of course, the crone was standing in the doorway, staring right at me. "Love?" Micah said, and repeated before I swiveled around to look at him. "Is something the matter?"

"Do you...Do you think the apothecary has any tea?" I asked. "I mean, I know the silverkin can brew up anything, but sometimes I just want to make a cup without bothering with them."

"It may, but there is an excellent tea shop next to the cobbler." He slipped his arm around my waist and tugged me away from the crone. "Come, love, I'll take you there now."

With that, we made another turn and left the apothecary behind. Before we were out of sight, I dared to glance over my shoulder and saw the crone mouth the words, "Thank you, dearie."

Ack. What had I gotten myself into?

10

The tea shop did indeed offer a vast selection of teas, along with eggshell-thin tea services nestled on hand-painted trays. Micah indulged me by purchasing a different blend for every day of the week and a set of pink and green teacups shaped like lotus flowers. That led to the agreeable problem of how we were going to transport this many awkward and breakable items, being that most shops in the Otherworld didn't stock those annoying plastic bags. Turned out we didn't need them, since the shop's proprietor readily agreed to have them delivered later that day. Actually, he practically begged for the privilege of bringing our purchases up to the manor himself, which gave me the impression that only a select few were allowed to visit Micah's home.

"Not so," Micah replied when I asked. We had left the village and were enjoying a leisurely walk home. "Any one of my people may approach me at the manor. All in the Whispering Dell are aware of this."

"Then why did he act like it was such a big deal?" I pressed.

"Perhaps because he has never been to the manor before?" Micah would have said more, or rather he would have answered more of my questions, but our attention was captured by a group milling about before the manor's front door. They were led by my favorite Elemental, Old Stoney.

"Farthing Greymalkin," Micah barked. "What misfortune has caused you to darken my door?"

"Lord Silverstrand," Old Stoney greeted with a mocking bow, completely ignoring me. Good. "I have been instructed to escort you to the Golden Court."

Micah eyed the assembled guards. "On whose authority?"

"Why, the Gold Queen's authority," Stoney replied. "Late yesterday evening, several iron warriors were found near Oriana's court. They had been attacked and were terribly maimed. One looks as if he will never speak again."

"Oriana bears no allegiance to iron," Micah stated.

"She does not," Old Stoney conceded. "However, she wishes to know if you were somehow involved in this event. It seems that vigilante acts disturb her most delicate constitution."

"Why would Oriana suspect me?" Micah demanded. Micah trusted the old rock about as far as he could throw him, and Old Stoney was made of granite. "And why has she sent her guard?"

"Oriana suspects you because very few Elementals possess the strength to defeat a single iron warrior, much less several. As for the guard, that was my suggestion. For the queen's safety, of course," he sneered.

Great. So in a lame attempt to suck up to the queen, Old Stoney had decided to play the hero and round up Micah like a common criminal. I was about to run inside and get Mom, to show Old Stoney how intimidation was really done, when Micah spoke.

"Allow me a moment, Farthing, to speak with my consort," Micah said. "Then I will accompany you to the Golden Court and explain my actions directly to our queen." With that, Micah ushered me inside the manor and shut the door, while I stared at him in disbelief.

"You're going to go somewhere with that maniac?" I demanded. "He could hurt you!"

"He will not," Micah replied. "Oriana's guard will not allow it, and Farthing is still begging her favors. I will simply explain what happened, and the queen will understand."

If only life really were that simple. Aloud, I only said, "Are you sure you'll be safe?"

"Of course. He is only of stone." With that, Micah kissed me goodbye, and I tried not to look too pathetic as I watched him walk off with Old Stoney and the goon squad. *Consorts need to be strong, you know.*

"Where's he going?" I turned and found Max standing behind me.

"A pile of mangled iron warriors turned up at the Golden Court, and Micah needs to go and explain himself to the queen." Max's face remained impassive, which was no surprise. In Max's world, his judgment was always correct, regardless of any unintended side effects. Understanding that continuing to discuss the iron warriors would only lead to an argument, I opted for a subject change.

"All that stuff you said about Juliana's uncle," I began, "how do you know what he's been up to?"

"Newspapers, mostly."

"Which you get how, exactly?" I pressed. I'd experienced a lot of weird happenings here in the Otherworld, but home delivery of the *Daily Bugle* wasn't one of them.

"The newsstand." I pulled back to smack him. "You know, the one where we used to buy slushies and ice cream."

My hand hung in midair, the threat of violence forgotten in light of my brother's apparent insanity. "You didn't."

"Why not? I like to know what's going on."

"Max! We're wanted! If they find you, it's back to the Institute!"

"Nah. You pretty much destroyed it, remember?"

And I wanted to hit him again. As if Micah and I—and Sadie and Mom, for that matter—hadn't risked *everything* to get him back. In the case of Sadie, she had lost almost everything, from her dream career to her sense of safety. Before I could well and truly give Max a piece of my mind, he brought me back to the one subject even I couldn't dispute.

"Listen, after the war ended, Armstrong was the engineer behind all the Elementals getting rounded up," he said. "I bet he's got some intel on Dad."

For a moment, I almost accused Max of having tunnel vision, being that his singular goal in life was creating foolish, not to mention "likely to get him killed super extra dead," plans in order to find out what had happened to Dad. He never acted with the tiniest bit of common sense or self-preservation, and I was sick and tired of his attitude.

Instead, I shut my mouth with a *clack*. Dammit, I wanted to know what happened to our father just as badly as he did.

And that was how Max and I ended up skulking around the Mundane realm about half an hour later. We'd hopped through the static portal at the wooded edge of the Whispering Dell, which had brought us right to my former employer's parking lot.

"You really worked in that monstrosity?"

I tore my eyes away from the Lovers' Pine and followed Max's gaze toward the concrete box that housed the sham company of Real Estate Evaluation

Services. "Yeah. I worked there with Juliana for a little more than a year."

Max shuddered. "Place looks like a cross between a mausoleum and a prison."

"I don't know," I said, scrutinizing the unopenable windows and badly maintained entrance. Someone should really trim the shrubbery. "It kinda reminds me of the Institute."

"Same thing."

Even though REES appeared to have been abandoned, Max and I knew better than to underestimate Peacekeepers. Well, I did; I think Max just wanted to play spy. Instead of walking across the parking lot to the sidewalk, we went to the back of the lot, scrambled over the fence (which, thankfully, wasn't electrified) and slunk around the abandoned office park. In no time, we were walking through the Promenade Market's main entrance.

"C'mon," Max said, turning up his jacket collar. My brother, the master of disguise. "Let's see what's up."

My heart raced and my palms sweated as we approached the wide entrance, and I imagined that our faces were plastered across those "most wanted" posters that decorate post offices. But there weren't any posters, at least not that I could see, and, being that it was still early, I didn't even see any armed Peacekeepers prowling among the stalls.

Then we were in the maze of crooked streets crammed full of booths and hawkers and a wave of homesickness hit me full-force. I missed the afternoons Juliana and I used to waste away, trolling this overgrown junk shop, searching for prewar books and movies, funky shoes that I never had the guts to wear in public, and, most often, lunch. The market had a whole section of booths that sold non-government sanctioned foods, like real cheese and hearty bread, as long as you knew who to ask. It was pricey, but so very worth it. While the government-run grocery stores were a lot cheaper, and legal, you could only buy processed crap that tasted like sawdust or rubber.

Max raised an eyebrow when he saw me eyeing a selection of aged cheddar. "Cheese?"

"I like cheese." I sighed; since I didn't have any Mundane money, I was doomed to admire the dairy from afar. Max shook his head and took off toward the newsstand. I, dutiful sister that I was, followed. What I saw on the racks shocked the hell out of me.

Each and every periodical bore an image of Mike Armstrong's face plastered across its cover. Some of the photographs were in profile, showcasing his bulbous nose and a hairline that had receded like the tide; some were full frontal shots, full of smiling, too-white teeth. There was even one of him holding a baby. I hoped it was a doll; I mean, what mother would be foolish enough to hand her baby over to that lunatic?

I glanced around; I was surrounded by people discussing Armstrong's excellent plans to restore

Pacifica to its former glory, mothers included. I guessed I had found the fools.

While the photographs differed, the headlines were nearly identical; over and over, Dr. Mike Armstrong was lauded as the human race's savior, the man who had effectively squashed the Elemental menace.

"Menace?" I mumbled. I hadn't meant to strike up a conversation, but a woman near me overhead my musings.

"Oh, yes," she gushed. "Before the wars, we were all subservient to those evildoers. Dr. Armstrong's research is what helped us win the war and put those freaks back where they belong." My initial reaction was to wonder at the usage of both subservient and evildoer in an impromptu conversation with a stranger, but then I spied the magazine tucked under her arm. She'd just quoted the cover blurb, nearly word for word.

"I don't really remember the time before the wars," I admitted. "I was young."

The woman patted my arm. "Be glad that you don't. And be sure you vote for Dr. Armstrong in the upcoming election. Mark my words, we need him as President."

I nodded, then I sidled toward the other end of the newsstand, searching for a magazine that hadn't devoted itself to politics. My choices were mostly limited to fashion and home and garden, although there was one about raising meat iguanas (chicken of the tree, you know), and another for gun hobbyists. Though, the gun magazine did feature a few action shots of Mike during some target practice with the Peacekeepers. We do want our president to be well-rounded.

And is iguana really all that tasty?

"So," I said, once again at Max's side. "All this." I indicated the magazines with my eyes.

"Yeah. Lucky for us, Dr. Armstrong came along." Max practically shouted that last bit and was the recipient of a few agreements and even a clap on the back from the newsstand's owner. He had quickly and effectively worked his audience, just like Dad used to do.

"Tell me about it," I mumbled. Max shot me a glare, but my sarcasm flew right over their heads. "So, what party is he running with?" I asked as I flipped through the pages.

"Dr. Armstrong doesn't have a party," Max said, affecting the patient tone one would use when explaining things to one's somewhat slow sibling. "He's running on his own."

Okay, now that shocked me. Since Pacifica had become, well, Pacifica, there had been two Mundane political parties—Mirlanders and Pacifists. The Mirlanders weren't so bad, though they did suck at winning elections. The Pacifists, in no small bit of irony, had become the military force we now call Peacekeepers.

How these two outwardly similar, yet ideologically different, groups came to inhabit the same country is one of the first history lessons I remember learning. Our country, Pacifica, is so vast that it stretches all the way from one ocean to another; eventually, two separate sets of colonists landed, one group on each shore. The set that arrived first made landfall close to what's now called Capitol City and had named it Portland in honor of the natural harbor. They named the surrounding land Mirland, which meant Peaceful Land in their native language; there's a rocky outcrop, called Sunpoint, where these newcomers had watched the sun rise over the ocean. According to the history books, that had been the site of their first meeting hall, a precursor to the government buildings that were raised much later. The Mirlanders were the first Elementals to set foot on Pacifica.

About a hundred or so years later, the people we now know as Peacekeepers landed on the opposite shore. They called themselves Pacifists because they were all about humans living together and avoiding bloodshed. Yeah, right.

Anyway, in no time, the Pacifists had made their way over to the Mirlanders, who had been quietly eking out a peaceful existence on their peaceful land. Not surprisingly, the two sets didn't get along.

It turned out that the Pacifists had basically fled their homeland under the guise of religious persecution. They hated all things magic and thought that by crossing such a large body of water they would be rid of it forever. Yeah, well, the whole running-water ploy only works on evil magic, and only on a specific kind of evil magic. Someone hadn't bothered to do their homework.

Also, Pacifists were banking on the land being devoid of magic and hadn't planned on bumping into a full-fledged colony of Elementals in the midst of their paradise. The Mirlanders didn't mind sharing space with the Peacekeepers, being that they weren't fleeing their homeland in the first place, and the land was more than big enough for everyone. However, the Pacifists didn't trust Elementals, not even then, and this led to lengthy negotiations and the eventual signing of the Compacts.

As for the people that lived here before the Mirlanders arrived, no one much cared what they thought. But that's a different story altogether.

The native population notwithstanding, the Pacifists and Mirlanders—Mundanes and Elementals—worked together to write the Compacts, which were intended to ensure justice and equality for all. Basically, the Mundanes worried that the Elementals would run the whole show, both magically and politically. In the first of many mistakes, the Elementals let the Mundanes get away with more than they should have, because they viewed the Mundanes as weak and deserving of protection. Little did they realize that even a weakened snake retains its venom, and it really only needs one opportunity to strike.

In time, the Mirlander party evolved from one populated by Elementals to Mundanes with a slightly less conservative agenda, such as those who thought that funding schools and road work were just as important as funding the military. And, while everyone agreed that roads without potholes are nice, and wouldn't it just be grand if that school could be un-condemned, no one running on the Mirlander ticket had won anything since long before the Magic Wars. No matter how good their platform was, or how charismatic the speaker, they were forever tainted by magic.

We Elementals had gotten out of politics altogether. We had been content to sit back and watch the Peacekeepers and Mirlanders argue away, keeping our own counsel, assuming nothing those puny Mundanes could cook up would ever have any kind of lasting impact. We were so arrogant, so complacent in our own strength, that we effectively hobbled ourselves. While we were busy ignoring those we thought were weak, they gathered strength and took us out. Hindsight does tend to be the clearest sort of vision.

And now, Dr. Armstrong seemed to be the political forerunner, and he didn't have the backing of either party. Everyone, responsible citizen and loony conspiracy theorist alike, was buying what he was selling.

Things were so much worse than Max had let on.

I turned back to the glossy covers, at once entranced and repulsed by the repetitive images, and noticed that Dr. Armstrong was frequently pictured alongside a rail-thin, oily-looking, little man.

"Who's the creepy sidekick?" I asked, grabbing a copy of *Politics and Poetry*. Max glanced at the cover, his jaw tensing.

"Langston Phillips," Max ground out. "He's Armstrong's right-hand man." I was amazed at the animosity in Max's voice, the hatred in his eyes. When Max had talked about Dr. Armstrong, he had just relayed the facts and let me make my own conclusions. But, by the way he was staring at the magazine in my hands, it looked like he wanted to rip Langston's throat out.

"I take it you two have met?" I ventured.

"Yeah. A time or two."

Max turned back to the display, and I flipped through the magazine. It was filled with the requisite political commentary, as well as essays and poems—*poems*—written by popular politicians. I guess that explained the title.

I scanned the table of contents, then replaced the magazine on the rack. I was certain that I would not ever want to read poetry written by any animal control officer, current or retired. Instead, I picked out one of the home and garden magazines, a fashion magazine to help explain my wardrobe requirements to the silverkin, and a literary review for Sadie. Max nodded, adding the daily paper and a few comics to our haul, then he slipped the seller a few bills. Once our reading material was bagged, we were on our way.

I specifically did not ask how Max had come by Mundane money.

As we walked down the Promenade's main aisle, I was struck by how the market was just the same as it had ever been. I know, I'd only been gone from the Mundane realm for a couple months, but I had expected to see more of a change, more signs of humanity slipping into the chaos wrought by our uncaring government. It was kind of irritating to find out that life had just gone on without me.

Then I spied a familiar face up ahead, and my mood lifted. It was the jeweler from whom I'd purchased spools of copper wire and shiny beads, along with some of the tiniest pliers in existence. Ultimately, those ingredients had become a copper cuff studded with malachite and amber, the token that proclaimed that Micah was mine. It felt like I'd last stopped at the jeweler's booth centuries ago, not just a few short weeks.

The shopkeeper, a woman who only looked middle-aged because of her silvered temples, smiled when she saw me. And well she should recognize me; the last time I was here, I'd spent a small fortune on the supplies for that cuff. "How did your last project turn out?" she asked brightly.

"Perfectly," I replied, smiling as I remembered the first time I'd seen Micah wearing the cuff. To think I'd worried that it wouldn't be good enough for him. "He wears it every day."

"Of course he does," she said, as if that had never been in question. "Looking for a new project?"

"Umm, yeah." I really wasn't, but I needed something to do at the manor. I bet Max would buy me a few things, if for no other reason than to keep Micah from throwing him out. "Do you have any more copper?"

The shopkeeper gave me her most dazzling "I'm about to make a sale" smile, then she turned around to gather up the more expensive items—lengths of chain, polished stones, and even a tray of pearls. While I waited, I looked over a few of her finished pieces, trying to decide if I'd like to try my hand at a necklace or maybe some earrings.

"What's all this?" Max asked, plunking his comics onto a tray of bracelets.

"Be careful," I hissed. Couldn't he be a little considerate, just once? While I rearranged the display, Max, bored with all this girly stuff, turned around and scanned the area.

"Sis." I looked up, then followed Max's stare. Peacekeepers, a whole company of them, were making their way down the aisle. And they were coming right toward us.

What's worse, they were led by Peacekeeper Jerome.

I'd had the misfortune of meeting Peacekeeper Jerome the morning after I had completed Micah's copper cuff. I'd meant for the cuff to be a quality token, to replace the pennies I'd given him in the spur of the moment. Once it was done, I'd left it on my windowsill and fell asleep; when I woke, the cuff was gone, and Micah wasn't there. Fearing the worst, I'd sped toward my then-employer, Real Estate Evaluation Services, intending to jump through the portal in the parking lot and find Micah. I'd been waylaid by Peacekeeper Jerome, who had proceeded to check my identification, hit on me, and order someone's death, all in the space of five minutes.

And if his big grin and hearty wave were any indicators, he totally recognized me.

"You know what, I have to get to work," I said in a rush. The shopkeeper peeked over her shoulder and smiled wanly. Since it wasn't her fault she was losing a sale, I grabbed a nearby pendant, glared at Max, and watched as he threw some money on the counter. "I'll just take this for now. Have a good day!"

"But your change," she protested.

"Put it toward my next purchase!" I called over my shoulder. Then Max and I were off, calmly wending our way around the booths and tents. The Peacekeepers gave no sign that they were pursuing us, or even that any of them, other than Jerome, had seen us. Still, after the recent run-ins we'd had with the iron warriors, I wasn't taking any chances. Surprisingly, neither was Max.

"This way," he murmured, grabbing me by the elbow and steering me toward the food vendors. It was the busiest aisle in the Promenade, by far the easiest place to lose a pursuer. Which explained why we rounded the first corner and practically walked right into Jerome.

"Sara!" His grin got even wider and became a bit smirky. I bet he thought I was looking for him. Jerk. "Remember me, from that morning at Real Estate Row?"

"Y-Yeah," I stammered. "I'm surprised you remember me."

"I never forget a pretty lady. Though your hair was brown then." Before I could think of anything not too damning to say, Max started in.

"Who's this?" he asked. "Old flame?"

"Max!" I hissed, but Jerome was nonplussed.

"I wish," he said. "In fact, I think you stood me up. You weren't at work when I swung by, after my shift. You weren't at The Room, either." Jerome looked at Max's hand on my arm and came to a conclusion even more outrageous than me dating him. "This your boyfriend?"

"No!" I snapped, yanking my arm away from Max. "This is my brother."

Jerome's eyes lit up. "Really."

A voice came crackling over a Peacekeeper's comlink, and Jerome turned around to hear the orders. "Excuse me," Jerome muttered, turning away from me as he grabbed his own comlink with a flourish. From that little move, I surmised that they didn't contact him often. "Headquarters has orders for me."

I leaned toward them, wondering if the orders had anything to do with us, when Max grabbed my elbow again. While the Peacekeepers were distracted, we moved toward the fence that marked the perimeter of the market.

"Here," Max said, holding aside the chain link where it had previously been cut, probably by thieves. Or escaping Elementals, who knew? Anyway, we slipped through the fence and into the scrubby field beyond, seemingly undetected.

"I can't believe they didn't know who we are," I murmured.

"I don't believe it," Max said. "Your old boyfriend can't be that thick."

"He was never my boyfriend," I insisted, but Max wasn't listening. He was on his hands and knees, pawing through the dry, dusty soil. "Ah." He triumphantly lifted up…something.

"What's that?" It was a shiny, clear disc, somewhere between a shard of ice and a dull mirror.

"Portal." Max tossed it into the air, then he grabbed my arm and pulled me through the shimmering door along with him. A heartbeat later, we were behind the tavern in the Whispering Dell.

"It's an old trick of Dad's," Max continued, as if we hadn't just evaded the enemy and leapt across dimensions. "He would stash portals around the places he frequented, just in case he needed to make a fast getaway."

"Won't the Peacekeepers have detected it?"

"Nah. They break down after one use. Even if they know we hopped over, we're long gone." I let out a breath I didn't know I was holding and leaned against the tavern wall. "Drink?"

I nodded, too relieved to speak; I couldn't believe that I'd evaded Peacekeeper Jerome for a second time. And to think, Max spent his all his days like this, a hair's breadth in front of trouble. I wondered if he wasn't really of steel, rather than copper.

11

The next morning, I found myself once again left to my own devices. Micah, whose reaction to the news that his consort had been traipsing around the Mundane realm had been remarkably calm (would it have killed him to have been a *little* mad?), was off dealing with his magistrates, handling matters of taxation and laws and such. Mind you, I thought he deserved a day off, being that he'd just spent the prior afternoon explaining to Oriana the whys and wherefores of the damaged iron warriors. According to Micah, the queen had accepted his explanations without batting a single golden eyelash, which was further proof that I was right about Old Stoney being a troublemaker. However, these sorts of important matters, whatever these important matters may be, were among the few things that he handled directly in the village, which meant no day off for Micah, and no day for me to spend with Micah.

Someday, I am really going to have to learn what he does all day. I mean, I had no idea of how he managed to run the Whispering Dell. Did he pay craftsmen like Ash wages? Hmm, probably not, since I had watched as Micah gave Ash the payment for my sword. So, did that mean that Ash paid some sort of a duty to Micah? And what about the gatekeepers? Were they on Micah's payroll? Was gatekeeper a hereditary title, or was there an army somewhere around here, training gatekeepers and varied other law-enforcement types, that no one had told me about? And what about all the other people who made the village run smoothly, the street sweepers and the garbage collectors and—

Yeah. Clearly, I had no idea what was going on down there.

What made the whole mess even messier was that there weren't only Elementals living in the Whispering Dell. As one could well imagine, the Otherworld was home to all sorts of creatures, magical and otherwise. Micah Silverstrand, the reigning Lord of Silver, was also the lord of quite a few other sorts of beasties; there was Ash, for one. On the day we'd visited the filthy smith, we'd also encountered those lovely shapeshifters, not lycanthropes, as Micah had pointed out, which just made me wonder exactly what was howling at night. This wasn't even considering the countless other beings, like the blood-drinking tailor and the sentient tree, that were living out their lives in Micah's village.

No matter their country, or gene pool, of origin, all who resided in the Whispering Dell, Elemental and otherwise, deferred to Micah as their lord. When I took the time to consider the vast number of beings Micah wielded power over, it gave me a migraine.

I sighed, rubbing the back of my neck. As much as I didn't want to deal with all of those taxes and gatekeepers and other assorted beasties, if I wanted to be a part of Micah's life, I would need to learn something about all of this…stuff. I mean, I'd been telling Micah all along that I didn't want to be a kept woman whose only purpose in life was to be arm candy. I wanted to be his partner. Dammit, I wanted to be his equal.

Well, I can't really learn anything until he comes back. I sighed again, then I rolled over and beat a few pillows into submission. If I decided to be honest with myself (and I wasn't so sure if that was such a good idea), it really, *really* bothered me that Micah had been so calm about yesterday's adventure at the Promenade with Max, especially after all the concern he'd showed when Max and I had gone down to the village without a silverkin escort. It was like Micah thought that the puny humans weren't a threat, so I might as well come and go from the Mundane world as I pleased.

I'm one of those puny humans.

Resisting the urge to scream, barely, I reached toward the side table and scooped up the pendant I'd hurriedly purchased at the jeweler's booth. It was a base metal, likely rhodium or nickel (or maybe even wolfram, ha ha), and featured an abstract fairy with multicolored enamel wings. It was the sort of charm one gives to a little girl for winning the spelling bee; she'd smile and wear it every day, until the chain broke or it turned her neck green, whichever came first. In short, it was hideous. Maybe I would give it to Sadie. Her birthday was coming up.

I rolled over and stowed the fairy pendant in the jewelry case on my bedside table, then I dragged myself out of bed. As I made my way downstairs, I made a few mental notes about the things to ask Micah when he returned to the manor. I would ask about his day, of course, as any good consort should, but while I did that, I'd try and work in a few other questions. Namely, why interdimensional travel was okay, but a short walk to the village required a day pass and a guard. As I mentally ticked off my list of queries, I passed through the kitchens. After I grabbed a cup of coffee and a scone, I went for a walk in the orchards.

Mind you, the orchards brought up a whole new set of questions. For instance, what did Micah do with all of this fruit? I mean, I often saw the silverkin harvesting baskets full of apples and plums, but the five of us weren't eating all of them. I don't think we *could* eat all of it, not with all the sugar and piecrusts in all the worlds, Other and Mundane. And what had happened to all the fruit when Micah had lived here by himself? Did he sell it? Compost it? Make burnt offerings to the fruit gods?

"Going for a walk?" I turned around and found Mom leaning against an apple tree.

"Yeah. No." I sighed yet again, a sure sign of my brain developing a slow leak, and leaned against a tree of my own. "I'm just bored."

"Your most common complaint," Mom observed. "If you plan on making the manor your home, you'll need to develop some sort of a hobby." I heard what she'd left unsaid—I couldn't always wait around for Micah to amuse me.

"I ordered a sword from the blacksmith," I offered. I decided not to bring up the near-purchase of jewelry supplies at the Promenade. With my luck, Mom would scream at Max—or me—for not remembering to pick up her favorite brand of ice cream. "Once it's done, I'm going to learn to fight with it. Micah's going to show me how." My voice trailed off at the end, since there I was, once again waiting around for Micah.

"Oh, we don't need him for that," Mom said, pushing off from the trunk. "I can teach you swordplay quite well."

"You can?" I left my empty cup and half-eaten scone at the base of an apple tree and followed my mother toward the edge of the orchard. Mom had made a beeline toward one of the many heaps of pruned branches.

"Of course," she replied. "When I was queen, I led every charge and every raid myself. If I couldn't have handled a blade as well as my men, I would have been a liability. Any leader worth her salt knows not to distract her warriors with her squalling." Mom selected a branch that was about as long as her arm, handed it to me, and proceeded to dig about for another.

"Was this when you were the Seelie Queen?"

"Aye, and before, when I was Queen of Connacht."

Having figured out why Mom was digging through the branches, I ventured, "Micah said I should begin with hand-to-hand combat."

"Why? So you can get your head lopped off?" Once she found a second branch to her liking, she set about stripping away the smaller twigs and leaves. Not knowing what else to do, I followed suit with my own branch. Once both branches were as swordy as they were going to get, Mom began instructing me on how to hold a sword and on proper fighting stances. No more yoga poses for Sara.

"So," I ventured, after a few practice swings, "are you a fairy or a human?" Mom cocked an eyebrow, but answered me anyway.

"Truly, I do not know," she replied. "I was born human, that's true enough."

"But then you went under the hill," I prompted.

"Yes, I went into the *brugh* to escape a few... Well, to escape. And I reigned as the Seelie Queen for far longer than any queen of Connacht had ever reigned. Or king, for that matter." Mom motioned me toward a tree and pointed toward the trunk at the approximate height of a man. "Since you're on the smaller side, you need to aim your swing slightly upward, toward your opponent's head."

"Wouldn't it be easier to hit an opponent in the chest?" I asked. "Bigger target and all."

"Aye, but not all beasties carry their hearts where we do. Decapitation is the surest way to halt any foe."

A childhood memory of Mom hacking up an innocent chicken in the Raven Compound's kitchen appeared behind my eyes; her one home-cooked meal was fried chicken. She had always been so fast and efficient, her knife lightning-quick with an economy of movement; I used to wonder if she'd ever worked for a butcher. "You learned this when you were the Seelie Queen?"

"Aye, and before," she replied, with a blood-chilling smile. After I practiced my swing until my shoulders ached, I returned to the subject of mortality.

"So, is it true that fairy wine takes away your humanity, the more you drink it?" I asked, remembering one of the few tidbits of information she'd once shared about the *brugh*.

"It does, indeed," she replied, with a sideways glance. "What're you after, Sara?"

"I was wondering if I'm a fairy."

"Hmm." Mom dropped her eyes and became engrossed in her tree-branch sword, two signs that meant that sharing time was over. I understood her reticence to speak of her past, since she had apparently just wandered away from the *brugh* with Dad, leaving her throne and her people behind. Still, we were in the Otherworld now; shouldn't she be able to speak of those things without fear?

Or, I thought, considering a few of the more unusual things I'd witnessed of late, *maybe that fear is well-founded*.

"You know, a sword never was my favorite weapon," Mom murmured. "During raids, I always wielded an axe."

"Really?" I asked. "Was that because you couldn't touch iron?"

She gave me a knowing look. "Sara, I'm not fey-born. Iron does not harm me."

There's an advantage for the Seelie Queen. "Wasn't an axe heavy?"

"Aye, but a heavy weapon flies truer and is better at splitting through armor. You don't want to waste precious time on the battlefield trying to hack through your foe's helmet." She hefted the branch as if it were an axe and took a practice swing at an innocent tree. I refrained from mentioning that she looked like a baseball player. "Not to mention, an axe is much better at chopping through bone."

"Huh." I wondered if Ash could make Mom an axe. *Now there's an unusual Mother's Day gift*.

"If any of my fey blood yet remains, it has certainly gone on to you, Sara," Mom said; I almost asked her what she was talking about.

"You really think so?"

"I do." She tucked a stray piece of hair behind my ear and patted my cheek. "You've always taken after me, just as surely as Sadie and Max take after your father."

"But we're all of copper," I pointed out, rather unnecessarily.

"And Sadie's the Metal Inheritor, yes. You, however, you have a strength about you that's not just fey or Elemental, but a bit of both. You, Sara, are the one to be wary of."

Me? Regular old Sara, strong and wariness-inducing? I'd never done anything particularly strong or amazing. I mean, I did find Max, but that wasn't a very well thought-out plan. I had destroyed the Institute, too, but that was only because I was mad. It's not like I'd done those things on purpose. My inner struggle must have been obvious, since Mom continued, "You've tried to be ordinary for so long that you've never really learned how to blossom. All of this—you living in the Otherworld and being with Micah—this is your chance, my darling."

I blinked back tears, awed and shocked and so proud that my mother—a queen twice over—would say such things about me. Before I could blame the tears on the sun being in my eyes, Mom spoke again.

"Now that I've filled your head with ideas, let's work those muscles. No victory is worth having unless you've fought for it, and, without good, sweaty training, you won't be winning much of anything."

I dropped back into my modified yoga pose and raised my branch. "All right. Show me how to take a *brugh*." Mom laughed at that, and we spent the afternoon hacking away.

12

That particular gathering of magistrates and such must have been quite the meeting, since Micah didn't return to the manor until long after I was asleep. When I woke, I found my elf snuggled around me and the usual disarray of clothing that accompanied his return. *No matter if they're human or elf, boys do tend to be messy.*

I wondered how Micah would react if I told him he had some common traits with Max. He is cute when he frowns.

Since he'd obviously returned very late, I decided to let Micah sleep in. I took care to gently unwind his arms from around me and made my way to the kitchen, intent upon securing breakfast. I'd hardly touched my third cup of coffee when the elf himself joined me.

"Oriana would like to meet with us," Micah announced, his eyes bleary and his hair even wilder than usual. His left hand clutched a scrap of parchment, which I assumed was an invitation from the Golden Court. Leave it to the silverkin to hand-deliver the mail despite the fact that their master should be sleeping. "Today."

"The Gold Queen?" I considered my present self—unbathed, unbrushed, and with a liberal coating of toast crumbs. "Right now?"

"Not quite yet. We are to attend her midday meal." Well, that was a relief. "Our queen desires to meet with all of the remaining metal lords, in private, before making her first public appearance."

"All of the metal lords, all at once?" Now, please believe me when I say that ruling anyone—and I mean *anyone*—was far, far from my mind. However, I still hadn't met anyone of copper, save for members of my family, and I couldn't help but wonder who was ruling them. I mean, there had to be someone, right? Or, were they all on their own out there, scattered across the Otherworld like pennies in a wishing well? Then I considered the heap of gifts left languishing away in the atrium, and my morning toast became a ball of lead in my stomach.

"Not all at once," Micah replied. "Such a gathering would likely be too much for Oriana's delicate nerves." His voice carried no inflection as he said that last bit, but I couldn't help wondering exactly how loony this woman was. And she was supposed to be our leader?

I let the question go unasked, since I'd be witnessing her looniness in person soon enough. After a long bath (that's right, the silverkin had not only figured out how to manage espresso, but indoor plumbing as well; sadly, showers remained beyond their abilities, so I was doomed to whiling away my time in a deep, comfy tub) and an even longer time spent in my dressing room, I still wasn't ready.

Okay, the first thing that bugged me was that I *had* a dressing room. Back home I'd had a single closet that held every item of clothing I owned, along with a small cabinet for my unmentionables. And socks— lots and lots of socks; really, one can never have too many pairs. Now that I'm the reigning consort to the mighty Lord of Silver, my wardrobe situation has changed.

My dressing room—an *entire room*—was stuffed full of dresses and gowns and frocks and whatever else came with an attached skirt. It also contained all the assorted extras—shoes, hats, petticoats, corsets, and various other torture devices. And the worst part of all this frippery wasn't the itchy lace or stiff crinolines, but that Micah loved nothing more than the sight of me in a dress.

I sighed and gazed longingly at the neatly folded stack of jeans. I was resigned to my fate, at least for today, since a visit to the Gold Queen was certainly a dress-worthy event. It wasn't that I didn't like the silks and velvets and whatnot; in fact, my wardrobe was gorgeous. And I *liked* dressing up. I just wasn't accustomed to such finery, and the yards and yards of fabric made me feel like nothing more than a little girl playing in her mother's closet.

Well, if I'm gonna play dress up, at least I'll dress well. Eventually, I selected a bronze silk gown. The bodice and sleeves were edged with vines, skillfully embroidered in emerald green. It involved a corset, as all these costumes inevitably do, but only one petticoat, and delicate green shoes that matched the embroidery. The silverkin had coaxed my copper-colored hair into elegant sweeps and curls, but I disappointed them by refusing to wear any jewelry other than Micah's token.

When Micah had first given me his token, a silver oak leaf and amber acorn strung on a delicate silver chain, I hadn't known what a token really meant. I'd thought it was just a nice piece of jewelry, not something that bound me to him. What I also hadn't realized was that I'd already fallen, *hard*, for this handsome silver elf, but then again, that had become apparent when I'd rushed out to make Micah my own token, the copper cuff studded with malachite and amber that I was so pleased with. He wore it, proudly, each and every day.

I'd never seen my mother wear any jewelry save her wedding rings, and a set of earrings Dad had given her right before he disappeared, despite the fact that her jewelry case back at the Raven Compound was huge, packed with gold and platinum and gems in every color. *Jewelry should be given with love*, she'd say if we asked her why, *and no ever loved me as well as your father did*. So, since I can't really imagine loving anyone other than Micah, I guess I will only wear his token, until he decided to give me something else.

Once the silverkin had gotten me as good-looking as I was going to get, I exited my dressing room and found Micah waiting for me in our sitting room. Yes, our little corner of the manor, which comprised the requisite bedroom, along with a sitting room, bathing chamber (bathroom just sounded so utilitarian, whereas this space was nothing if not devoted to luxury), and a dressing room for each of us, was quite spacious, indeed.

Anyway, I found Micah reclined on the window seat, gazing toward the orchards. Since I was carrying my shoes, I almost managed to sneak up on him. I wondered if he'd yelp like a little girl.

"My Sara," Micah said, turning to greet me at the last moment. I vowed that, someday, somehow, I would catch him unaware. Maybe I would even tickle him. "As always, you are lovely."

I blushed as I murmured my thanks, then looked over Micah's attire. He wore a white shirt that laced up the front, topped with a dark-blue velvet coat, along with his usual leather leggings, though these were black instead of tan, and black boots. Yep, he looked pretty darn good. I let my hand stray to the hilt of the sword that hung at his side.

"Mom and I did some practicing yesterday," I said. "She's pretty good with a sword."

"Is she?" Micah noticed the shoes I was holding and motioned for me to sit. "Let me." Not one to refuse assistance of the Prince Charming variety, I plopped down in a nearby chair and offered him a foot. In case you were wondering, the silverkin had painted my toenails a shade of emerald green that coordinated nicely with my spiky-heeled, open-toed shoes. After murmuring his approval of the color, Micah knelt before me and proceeded to kiss my ankle before placing the shoe on my foot. After he repeated the process, kissing included, with my other foot, he smoothed down my skirts and smiled up at me.

"Is it time to go?" I asked in a rush. If he kept looking at me that way, we weren't going anywhere, and I didn't think the Gold Queen would take kindly to us standing her up.

"It is." Micah helped me to my feet and kept his hand on the small of my back while we walked through the manor. It was devious of him, since my mark, already aroused by that little shoe incident, flared at his touch.

"Stop that," I said, wiggling away. "You'll make us late."

"I will do nothing of the sort." He replaced his hand and rubbed. Oh, if you could die from pleasure. "I'm merely thinking of later."

"No thinking," I said, forcibly removing his hand from my back and lacing my fingers with his. "For now, just going."

He grumbled at that, but remained on his best behavior as we descended the stairs and stepped outside to the metal pathway. Thanks to Micah's excellent navigational techniques, in a few short moments, we stood before Oriana's estate.

The Golden Court was, well, gold. It looked like the standard-issue storybook castle, straight from the old-time illustrations, right down to the drawbridge and the turrets. The midday sun caught the light of dozens of stained glass windows, turning them into blazing jewels. Warriors, not like the metal monsters that had guarded Ferra's home, but actual men— perhaps they were even Elemental men—clad in gold-washed mail guarded the entry. Also unlike Ferra's iron warriors, not one of them made a lewd comment or even hazarded an inappropriate glance in my direction. And they say chivalry is dead.

Once we were inside the courtyard, I saw the court's occupants going about the varied routines of sustaining such a grand establishment. To my left, a maid carried a stack of linens, a porter scurrying behind her with cakes of soap. Someone from the kitchens, likely the cook's apprentice, inspected a cartload of vegetables, while another haggled with a wine merchant. I spied a few grooms off the side, who sang while they cleaned and oiled a set of tack. The horse looked on, politely munching his hay. Everything seemed to be in perfect order.

And yet, it wasn't, not by a long shot. Now, don't get me wrong, the Golden Court was nothing at all like the Iron Court, what with the latter's flagrant debauchery and rampant lack of boundaries. No one had smiled in the Iron Court, unless they were caught up in the moment of harming another; far more common had been cries of hopelessness and despair.

However, the Golden Court, for all its smiling inhabitants and cheery decorations, was far from welcoming. It was a sterile, falsified happiness, as if all the denizens were actors who had missed out on the roles of their lives and were doomed to go through the motions at a community playhouse. I really shouldn't have been surprised at all the forced cheer, since Oriana had spent five long years as Ferra's favorite pet.

I didn't know, not specifically, anyway, what sort of tortures Oriana had endured at the Iron Court. No one still living did, save Oriana herself. But I had some strong ideas. So did Micah, and I suspect that others did as well, since a generous allowance was being given toward Oriana's lunatic behaviors. Since she had been rescued, she'd alternately insisted upon sleeping out of doors in the rain, in a pool of mud, and once in a stable covered with hay. And there was the singing. Oriana had taken to singing, or, based on Micah's descriptions, wailing, instead of talking. Apparently, she was also tone deaf.

Her eating habits had also been affected by her captivity. Reportedly, Ferra had only fed her stale bread and dungeon mice. As a result, Oriana had subsequently banned all baked goods from the Golden Court, from bread to cookies. Rodents, however, were still allowed on the menu.

Are there any vegetarians in the Otherworld?

The possibility of rodent fricassee notwithstanding, I was on my best behavior as Micah and I approached Oriana's steward. After a few brief introductions, we were ushered into a grand dining hall by two smiling, perfectly-appointed servants, and I saw Oriana for the first time since she'd been hauled out of the oubliette. Her element had, indeed, been restored, and I noticed that her mark showed upon her hands, with her fingers being robed in solid gold. The metal then twisted and twirled around her hands and up her arms like so many shining ribbons. That, coupled with her wavy golden hair and sky-colored gaze, made the Gold Queen look like a true fairy princess.

"Micah," she exclaimed, rising to greet us. Thank the gods, she was speaking instead of singing. Oriana approached Micah and extended her arms as if to grasp his hands, only to withdraw at the last moment. I recalled the effect that Micah's touch had had on my own mark and wondered if Oriana's brought her more pain than pleasure.

Unperturbed, Micah bowed. "My lady," he intoned, then he drew me beside him. "I have brought my consort for you to meet. Allow me to present my beloved, Sara Elizabeth Corbeau."

"My lady," I said as I curtsied, rather elegantly if I must say so myself. Sadie and I had been practicing.

"Consort?" Oriana repeated, her head cocked to the side in an avian manner. "And a Raven fledgling, at that. Micah, when did this happen?" Huh. Were consorts supposed to be cleared with the queen? Oops.

"Shortly before your rescue," Micah said smoothly. "Sara and her family were instrumental in Ferra's demise." Oriana's gold brows peaked; I hoped Micah had just won me some points. "Are you ready to dine, or would you care to walk first?"

"Walk. Let's." With that, the Gold Queen turned on her heel, leaving Micah and me to follow. She led us on a meandering path throughout her estate, passing through the same rooms two and sometimes three times. The floor in her throne room was gold, as were the floors adjacent to it. After a few twists and turns, the floor took on a pinkish hue, then it deepened to crimson. Oriana seemed unperturbed by this, but when a black floor loomed ahead she cried out, then scurried in the opposite direction. She'd learned a thing or two from the rodents.

The queen visibly relaxed once we reached a blue floor and sighed with relief once the floor had lightened to green. Before I could ask Micah if this was a newly built castle, or if our queen had a terrible sense of direction, Oriana led us to a courtyard.

"That was the strangest half-hour of my life," I muttered. Micah squeezed my hand, and we stepped into the sunshine.

"Now, tell me," Oriana said, once we were out in the open air, "where did you find your consort?"

"The Mundane realm, my lady," Micah replied. "Sara has since consented to share my home in the Whispering Dell."

"How nice," Oriana muttered. "And why does she not wear her element?" It took me a moment to realize that the last question was directed at me, and I looked down at my dress.

"I thought others could tell that I am of copper by my hair," I said. "I didn't know I was supposed to wear it."

"It is not that you have to," Oriana clarified, "it is a matter of pride. Micah, I'm surprised you didn't inform your lady." I looked at Oriana's clothing, which was a white toga-like garment that draped from a heavy gold collar, leaving her arms and shoulders bare. The cloth was bound about her narrow hips with several lengths of fine gold chain, and gold sandals wrapped around her feet. Oriana must be very, very proud of her element.

"I...I forgot," Micah murmured, his silver brows furrowed. I looked closely at Micah's clothing; his white shirt was edged in silver, and silver buttons graced his coat. "My Sara, please forgive me."

"It's fine," I said. "After all, I'm only copper." Not an important metal or anything.

"Never see yourself as 'only' copper," Oriana said, rounding to face me. She stroked my hair, then her golden fingers travelled to my shoulder and danced down my arm, finally alighting on the small of my back. Even though my clothing separated our skin, I was acutely aware of her fingers as they pressed my mark. Being that Oriana was nuts, I decided to forgive her the personal trespass. "Copper is strong and beautiful, one of the most noble metals in existence."

"Is it?" I murmured. "But I'm not precious, not like gold or silver." Hell, where I come from, they make sewage pipes out of my metal.

"Does it matter if others see you as precious? Only you can truly assess your worth." Oriana smiled, her eyes shining like the sun reflecting across a lake in summer. "Always be proud of who you are, my non-precious friend, and show the world your best side. Others cannot judge you by your weaknesses if you only show them your strengths."

I opened my mouth, only to shut it with a *clack*. For the first time, I felt like I had an ally in the Otherworld. I mean, Micah was on my side, but that was different. Other than the pixie, Oriana was the first non-relation who had offered me any guidance in this strange land that was now my home. And having an ally in the Gold Queen must be a good sign.

"Thank you, my lady," I said. "I will do my best to follow your advice."

Oriana smiled at that, then she applied a bit more pressure to my mark. A sudden jolt, like lightning, shot to my core, while Oriana's eyelids fluttered and her cheeks flushed.

"See that you do," she murmured, caressing my cheek. "Come, let us enjoy our meal." With that, Oriana wandered off; luckily, Micah took my arm and helped me along.

"I think I just had sex with the Gold Queen," I murmured, more than a bit shaken.

"That was far from an act of love," Micah said. "Oriana simply favors you. She finds companionship with very few. You should feel honored."

"What I feel like is another bath," I mumbled. *And to never let my mark within touching distance of that one, ever again.* Before Micah could remind me to behave, we were again inside the dining hall. Oriana must have been hungry, since she had decided to take the direct route on our return. The most notable feature of this hall was the entire lack of a table and chairs; instead, there were several long couches gathered in a semicircle. Oriana lounged across one in true Greek-goddess fashion, and indicated that Micah and I should do the same.

"Shall we begin with wine?" Oriana asked, then she answered herself. That's not a sign of the crazy, no, not at all. "No, first a footbath."

Without waiting for our response, Oriana clapped and several servants stepped forth, all of them female. They were clad in identical heavy gold belts and diaphanous white skirts, the layers cut to resemble tulip petals. Armed with gold basins and neatly folded linen, they immediately set about removing our shoes and washing our feet. I must admit that, while I initially thought this procedure was more than a bit odd, having a servant girl clean and anoint my feet was an unprecedented luxury.

Once we were cleansed to the standards of the Golden Court, at least to the ankles, a new team of girls stepped forward. One carried a pitcher, presumably the wine in question, and the rest bore surprisingly plain glass goblets.

"Now," Oriana began, once she had sampled the wine, "I am aware that many things changed while I was…captive. Please, Micah, tell me of the all the good things that occurred. I am all too familiar with the rest."

13

Our meal with the Gold Queen stretched long into the afternoon, though I must admit that I ate precious little. Knowing that mice—and rats!—could be included in any and all of the dishes laid before us, I stuck to fruit presented in its original, tree-ripened state. I assumed that any rodent I found inside an apple or peach would be the fault of the rodent, and not Oriana's kitchens.

If the queen noticed my lack of appetite, she didn't comment on it, though she herself seemed far more interested in liquid refreshment; I don't think she'd recognize the bottom of a goblet if it snuck up and kicked her in the arse. Just when I was making a mental note to schedule an Otherworldly intervention, Oriana began recounting one of many ways Ferra had tortured her—after stripping all the gold from

Oriana's body, Ferra had kept her chained to the iron throne with golden shackles. It had been hideously painful, yet Oriana had refused to complain, terrified that Ferra would remove her only contact with her metal. That nightmare became a reality when Ferra grew bored with her docile prisoner, and threw Oriana into the oubliette.

Yeah. Oriana gets to drink all she wants.

Once Micah had told the drunken queen everything that had occurred with regard to the Metal Elements, and had shared what bits he knew about the other four Elements, three frickin' times, Oriana suddenly stood. She declared herself to be both exhausted and filthy, and let her tulip-skirted attendants lead her away, I assumed to bathe and sober up a bit. Or maybe she only wandered off to find more wine, who knew? Having gotten the impression that we'd been dismissed, Micah and I let ourselves out.

"All the floors are gold here," I murmured. I looked up and down the corridors; everything was gold, with no trace of the multicolored tiles we'd trekked over earlier. "Why is part of the Golden Court not gold?"

Micah pursed his lips, his signal that I was asking about something that nice people didn't talk about in public. "This site is very old," he said, at length. "There was magic here long before Oriana."

"Before Elementals?"

Micah squeezed my hand. "Yes."

Huh. I'd thought that Elementals had always existed. Before I could ask who was here before, and where they'd gone, we'd reached the bustling courtyard. Micah squeezed my fingers even harder, but I'd already gotten the hint. When I squeezed back, he smiled.

"I'm glad to see our queen so improved," Micah said, once we were outside the palace.

"That was improved?" A vision of Oriana having a conversation with her wineglass flitted behind my eyes.

"Oh, very much so. Not once did she fall to the ground wailing, nor did she rend her garments or her hair, and she set nothing on fire. I'm quite pleased with her progress."

If that was evidence of progress, gods help us if she regressed. I kept my thoughts to myself as we travelled the metal pathways back home, and once we were back on the manor's grounds, I was so excited to soon be out of those pinchy green shoes that I forgot all about our insane queen and spooky pre-Elemental magic. Before I could change, or even put on a pair of sneakers, I was met by a pleasant surprise—while Micah and I were off at the Golden Court, Ash had completed my sword.

The blacksmith had personally delivered it only a short while earlier, and Mom had accepted it on my behalf. From the way she kept absently wiping her hands, I assumed that Ash had arrived in his usual filthy state. Nice to know that he didn't bother cleaning up when he made deliveries to his lord's home.

Regardless of the dirty hands that forged it, the sword itself was a thing of beauty. It was perfectly balanced, and I held it as effortlessly as if it was an extension of my arm. Delicately engraved ravens and oak leaves swirled down the length of the wickedly sharp blade, and the steel hilt was accented with incised copper filigree.

"Ash knows that I'm of copper?" I murmured, tracing the delicate hilt that had somehow been wrought by that oafish man. Micah and I had retreated to our bedroom, since I felt that meeting one's first sword was a somewhat private matter. "And a Raven?"

"All know that the Lord of Silver has lost himself to a copper girl," Micah said. "And all know that the Raven clan was instrumental in Ferra's demise." He stood behind me, his arms wrapped around my waist while we admired the sword—*my* sword—together.

"Let me change, and then you can give me my first lesson," I said as I wiggled free of his arms.

"I advise against changing out of your lovely clothes," Micah said. "You should learn sword fighting while wearing one of your gowns, so you will understand how to compensate for their restrictions."

"Micah, that's ridiculous!" I suspected he was having some sort of damsel in distress fantasy that featured me waving a sword while my skirts whipped around my legs. "And I hardly ever wear dresses."

"You know I wish you'd wear them more often."

Good gods, if it wasn't babies, it was dresses. "Okay. I'll let you teach me sword fighting while I'm wearing a dress, on one condition."

"Name it, my Sara."

"You, Mr. Silverstrand, must wear a skirt."

His smile faded, and his eyes glazed over in mingled horror and disbelief. "Why would I do such a thing?"

"Well, you seem to think it's no big deal for me to wield an edged weapon while dressed to kill," I explained. "Prove it."

"Your argument is flawed."

"How so?"

"As a man, I would never don such a garment."

"In the Mundane realm there are entire countries where men wear skirts. All the time."

"You're making—"

"Are you insinuating that your consort is lying to you?" My hand flew to my breast in mock outrage. "How could you ever, *ever*, suggest such a thing?"

Micah stared at me, his mouth smushed into a crooked line. "When next I venture to the Mundane realm, I will verify this claim," he warned.

"Go ahead. The place is called Scotland." After a bit more glaring and grumbling, we fashioned a passable kilt from one of our bed sheets and Micah's sword belt. (He outright refused to wear one of my gowns. Spoilsport.) He wouldn't even put it on in front of me, but retreated to his dressing room, muttering curses that would make even Mom blush. And I think I heard him throw a few things.

When Micah finally emerged in his skirted glory, he proclaimed that our lessons should take place in the gardens, as much for the open space as the soft ground to land on. And, you know, the fact that it was somewhat removed from the manor so no one would see his bare knees. Being that I had no reason to dispute his logic, off we went.

The walk through the manor was entertaining, to say the least. We encountered no one but silverkin, yet Micah's eyes darted after every noise. Who would have thought the confident Lord of Silver could be so undermined by a simple garment? I felt like I'd won already.

The ideal sparring location turned out to be the far side of the maze, that had no stone benches to stumble over, or potential onlookers to witness Micah's humiliation. It really was a shame that we didn't have an audience; what with Micah's sword, black boots, and white lace-up shirt, he was totally rocking the sexy pirate look.

"You'd make a great pirate," I teased.

"Pie rat?" Micah repeated. "First, you trick me into donning this humiliating garment, and now you compare me to a rat that eats pies?"

"No, not a rat." I sighed; he was just tormenting me. I hoped. "A pirate. Buccaneer. Sailor of the high seas." Silver eyes stared blankly at me. "Have you ever been to an ocean?"

"Of course."

"A pirate drives a boat on the ocean."

"Sara, one does not drive a boat. One sails a ship."

So he did know what I was talking about. "Can you start teaching me now? I don't want your legs to get chilly," I added, smiling sweetly.

Micah's eyes narrowed, but he began my first real sword fighting lesson. First, he glided his hand along both of our blades, his palm flush to the edge. I shrieked when he did this with his own sword, but after he showed me he wasn't bleeding, he explained that he'd added an enchantment to our weapons, to make them safe for our little practice session.

"Did you blunt the edges?" I asked, watching intently as he repeated the procedure with my sword.

"They are as sharp as ever," he replied, to my relief. I wanted to have a sword for at least an entire day before it was wrecked. And I wanted to do the wrecking. "I merely asked the blades to harm neither me nor my consort."

Magic just seemed to get cooler by the day. "And they agreed?"

"They did."

"Huh." I flicked the pad of my thumb against the edge; it still looked sharp, but it felt smooth, almost like the edge of a porcelain plate. "How long does the spell last?"

"Not a spell, love," Micah clarified. "The metal has agreed to abide by our terms. Treat your sword well, and you will have an ally for life."

"I like allies," I murmured. I stroked my thumb against the not-sharp-to-me edge again, then I grinned at Micah. "Well? Let's get started."

After a few brief instructions about the proper way to hold a sword, and a few terrible (even for me) pirate jokes, I stood back and affected the stance Mom taught me. Based on Micah's expression, it was quite an improvement from the yoga pose.

"*En garde!*" I waved my new sword with a flourish. At that, Micah shook his head and smiled, and our lesson began.

Perhaps it was because the sword was made for me, or maybe I really had inherited some of my mother's warrior-queen blood, but swordplay seemed to come naturally. Before the wars, and our lives taking the express route to hell in a hand basket, I'd taken classical dance lessons. Swordplay turned out to be quite similar, with the feints and jabs like a graceful dance between opponents. Micah said as much, complimenting my fast learning after a successful parry that neither of us thought I'd make.

"It must be the skirt slowing you down," I teased. "What have you got on under there, anyway?" I used my sword's point to lift the edge of his makeshift kilt, but Micah knocked the blade away. "Oh, so you're modest now?"

"I am nothing of the sort," he snapped. "This is… unnatural." He gestured at his decidedly unmanly getup.

"That's what I've been trying to tell you! Really, Micah, this dress obsession of yours has got to go."

"A wager, then?"

The man in the skirt wants to make a bet. Intriguing. "What sort of wager?"

"One more bout. If you win, I will never speak ill of your man's clothing again."

"And if you win?"

"You'll wear that dress for each and every one of our lessons." He was grinning as he spoke, and, being that I was panting like I'd just run a marathon, I couldn't figure out why. Then I followed his gaze to my heaving, sweaty, pushed up by a corset bosom.

The poufy-haired bastard really *was* having a damsel in distress fantasy.

Oh, now I was mad.

I came at him in a flurry, swinging and striking like a madwoman. In fact, I was acting like such a madwoman that Micah had no trouble fending me off. He even laughed as he parried my ineffectual blows.

"If you could only see how lovely you look," he said, executing another parry that left our hilts locked together.

I'll show him what's lovely. I dug my heels into the soft ground and braced myself, shifting the brunt of his force onto my shoulder. Grinning wickedly, I slipped my free hand underneath his skirt, grabbed him, and squeezed. Micah's eyes went big as saucers, but he did not admit defeat. Instead, he ducked his head and bit my breast. Hard!

I yelped and hopped backwards, dropping my sword in the process. Being that I still had hold of Micah's most valued possessions, he moved with me, and we hit the ground as a tangled knot of limbs, thankfully with neither of us accidentally injuring the other. Once we stopped laughing, talk turned to who had won the bout.

"I made you fall," Micah said. "And you dropped your sword."

"I think the fight was done when I grabbed you," was my retort. "After all, you wouldn't want to get hurt here." Since I'd retained my handful of Micah, I gently traced all the places he'd rather not enjoy an injury.

"That would be terrible," he murmured, pressing a kiss to the pink impression his teeth had left in my breast.

"I can't believe you bit me."

"Does it hurt?" he asked, now intent on unfastening my bodice. It was always much easier for Micah to get me out of these confounding outfits than it was for me to get into them.

"It does," I murmured. "You should kiss it. Twice." He did, and again and again, while his deft fingers worked on my corset. Once he freed me from my bone and satin cell, I sat up and shook out my hair, having decided that he owed me somewhat more of an apology. I was still in my gown, from the waist down anyway, and Micah was technically fully dressed, but my, that skirt of his did make things easier.

Afterward, we snuggled on the sheet that was recently a skirt, my dress folded into a pillow beneath our heads. "About my next lesson," I began.

"Yes, love?"

"Can we get you a proper kilt for that one?" I asked, tracing small circles on his belly. "I'm beginning to see what you like about all these skirts."

He laughed, hugging me a bit tighter. "I thought you were against this…how did you put it?…'damsel in distress' nonsense."

"Maybe it's not all bad," I conceded. "After all, what if you were the one in distress, and I needed to rescue you?"

"What if, indeed."

14

The day after our swordplay/wardrobe lesson, Micah was off somewhere, doing something important yet again, and I was once more trolling the manor trying to find new and interesting ways to amuse myself. This particular important event of Micah's had something to do with the annual tithe from the village. Yep, he used the word "tithe," which I then learned was really just a fancy word for taxes. It also meant that I now knew one of the ways Micah managed the Whispering Dell, not to mention how he earned some of his money. Finally, I'd learned something about how Micah managed the village. It was just my luck that I learned the most boring part first.

It seemed that taxes really were unavoidable, even in the Otherworld. Being that I have no great love of tax payments or bureaucracy, I wasn't exactly pining to join Micah. I was just bored. Again.

Mom's advice echoed around in my skull, mostly because she was right. If I wanted to be happy here in the Otherworld, I needed more in my life than just Micah. I mean, even when (and if) I became his full-fledged wife, he won't always be around to entertain me, what with his many obligations as the Lord of Silver. Then I remembered that being his wife meant having babies, *lots* of babies, and realized that too much free time probably wouldn't be one of my problems. I hope this tithe was large enough for us to hire a few nannies. For the sake of the babies, of course.

I sighed and stepped outside the manor to walk in the gardens. I suppose I could have passed the time by helping Sadie set up her library, but with the exception of a few comic series and some trashy prewar paperbacks, I'd never been much of a reader. Of course, I'd never done much of anything in my spare time, except go to happy hour and watch television. So much of my life had been devoted to being unremarkable that I'd never bothered developing any hobbies, not even a lame one like stamp collecting. All of this unremarkableness had led directly to my current plague of boredom. Now, when I was finally free to do whatever I wanted, I couldn't think of a damn thing to do with myself.

Maybe I'll take up sculpturing. My feet had led me to the knot garden, and I was contemplating the statue of Micah's mother that was its centerpiece. I was a passable artist, at least where drawing was concerned, even though all I'd ever really done was copy my favorite comics. While I didn't think that qualified me as an *artiste*, I figured that my metal abilities should give me an edge in sculpting; I remembered Max telling me how he had made tiny metal flowers for a girl he liked. I decided not to dwell on the fact that those flowers were what made him the Institute for Elemental Research's favorite science experiment.

I can start with roses, I mused, fingering a velvety petal. *I can make the thorns sharp as needles, like barbed wire, and the petals will be so lush and—*

"Sara."

I turned to see my mother skulking behind the boxwood hedge, axe—or rather, one of the hatchets the silverkin used for chopping wood—in hand. Being that the boxwoods were only knee high, she looked utterly ridiculous, like an extra in a low-budget slasher film. Just like that, I wished for more boredom. "Yes?"

"Shh!" she hissed. "We've a boggart loose." She motioned for me to follow, and we headed toward the orchard.

"One of Max's?" I whispered.

"Aye," she replied. I wondered if Mom realized that, the longer she was in the Otherworld, the more her Irish accent returned. Before I could ask, she held up her hand. "Look, the wee beastie's eaten itself into a stupor."

I followed her gaze and saw that the boggart was propped up against a tree, belly swollen and peach pits scattered around its feet. With its mud-colored skin, elongated snout, and pointy ears, it looked like a cartoonist's acid trip.

"What is it?" I asked. When she quirked a brow, I added, "You know. Is it a boy or a girl?"

"Does it matter?"

"To other boggarts."

Mom glared at me, and then she started up with these obscure hand movements. Eventually, I figured out that all those slashing motions meant that she wanted me to find a weapon of my own. I trotted off to where the silverkin kept the firewood and found myself a sizeable branch. "Are we going to kill it?" I asked, once I returned.

"That would probably be best," Mom replied. "We can't have these sorts of things turning up here, making a mess of things."

"He didn't mean to make a mess. He was just hungry."

"Sara, you don't understand. Once a boggart is tied to a family, only misfortune will follow."

"Is that why Max was cursed with boggarts when he couldn't pay his debts?"

"Most likely." Wow. That bookie had a cruel sense of humor. "I broke the curse upon the others, but it looks to be well and truly stuck to this one. It was probably laid on this poor creature first, so it's strongest with him." Mom stood and hefted the hatchet. "Well, best get it over with."

"You mean now?" I stood and grabbed the back of her shirt. "You're just going to walk right over there and kill it while it's sleeping?"

"That is the plan, yes."

"But that's…that's not fair!" I shrieked.

"Sara, it's the boggart or Max's fortune." Mom's eyes softened. "I know that killing a creature in cold blood is a terrible thing to do, but I must. What kind of mother would I be if I left this beast alive to torment my son?"

A sane one. "Can't we re-curse him? Or bind his powers, or…or something?"

"Mmm." Mom let the hatchet's blade rest against her leg, one hand rubbing her chin. "How do you propose we bind him?"

Well. It looks like we do have options. "Salt!" I all but shouted. "A circle of salt!" *Salt binds everything, right? Hopefully?*

Mom stared at the boggart, her lips pursed. "If we also use a poppet, it may work," she said. I attributed her disappointed tone to the impending work of binding the boggart, not over missing out on hacking it to bits. "But if it doesn't—"

"Then we'll deal with it." Before she could change her mind and go all psycho-killer, I called for Shep. Moments later he appeared, and I asked him for a sack of salt, some old fabric, thread, and stuffing for the poppet. I figured I could manage the pins and needles as sculpting practice.

To my surprise, my nascent metal-sculpting skills wouldn't be needed, since Shep delivered not only a sack of salt and ball of twine, but also a lump of brown clay from which to fashion the poppet. How the little guy had known that I hated sewing, I had no idea, but at least I still got to work on my sculpting. While Mom poured the circle of salt around the boggart, I carefully molded the clay into a reasonable facsimile of the creature, pointy ears and all.

When I'd considered taking up sculpting, this was *not* what I'd had in mind.

"Now we bind the poppet," Mom murmured, once the salt circle was complete. Just as we'd completed winding the twine around the clay, Shep appeared with a shovel. Mom gave me a look (apparently, queens do *not* dig holes), and I started digging next to the tree it snoozed against. Throughout all of this, the boggart snored away, clearly the Otherworld's heaviest sleeper.

"What are the chances of this working?" I asked, as I patted down the loose earth.

"Fair to middling," Mom replied. "If nothing else, it should work until the poppet's disturbed or the salt washes away in the rain. Hopefully, by then it will have attached itself to another poor soul."

"And if it doesn't?"

"Then I shall take care of it." The hardness in Mom's eyes, the set of her jaw, made me wonder exactly what she'd done in the past in order to keep her children safe. She did seem to know an awful lot about boggarts.

"Have you done things like this before?" I asked. "You know, have you had to deal with *things*," I gestured toward the boggart, "like this?"

"Aye."

"Even at the Raven Compound?" I pressed.

Mom sighed, her lips pursed. It was the oldest I'd ever seen her look. "Being Beau's children has always made the three of you targets. It's one of the many reasons I couldn't go off and look for your father, and later for Max; who would have protected you and your sister? And, once you two were grown, there was the matter of the family artifacts…" She shook her head, then grinned. "Why, I remember one good fight, not long after Sadie went away to that university of hers."

"Fight?"

"Nearly a battle," Mom confirmed. "Why, it was a hand of goblins, led by a *glaistig*, of all things. They must have had old information and thought that your brother was still in residence."

I rubbed my temples; this was why I didn't ask Mom too many questions. She tended to answer them. "You fought off five goblins and a twig all by yourself?"

"*Glaistig*," Mom corrected. "A seductress with the legs of a goat. Really, Sara, you should learn more of your heritage." I nodded, pinching the bridge of my nose; yes, I think I finally understood why Sadie had started hanging out in the library so much.

"Come, now," Mom said and began walking toward the manor. "I've a mind to be gone when the beastie wakes. Think your Shep'll let bygones be bygones and brew me some tea?"

15

I went to bed early that night, bone tired after all the cursing of boggarts and burying of poppets. When I woke the next morning, I was in Micah's arms. To call me content would have been a severe understatement. I kissed his nose while he was sleeping and again once his eyes opened.

"Hi," I murmured, drowning in his silver gaze. I could just stay there forever, and, from the way Micah kissed me back, I suspected that he felt the same way.

"What are my Sara's plans for the day?" Micah asked, after we'd snuggled for a while.

I opened my mouth to say that I had no plans beyond breakfast and a walk in the orchards, when Mom's advice came rushing back to me. If I ever wanted to be more than an ornament on the fringe of

Micah's life, I was going to need to develop my own interests.

"You know, I think I'd like to go back to the Promenade Market," I said.

"In the Mundane realm?" Micah asked, his brows peaking.

"Yeah." For a moment, I thought Micah would forbid me to go. Wait—could he even do that? I was his consort, not his subject! I was his almost-equal, right?

Since he remained silent, and I really didn't want to learn the answer to those questions just yet, I continued, "When Max and I were there the other day, I wanted to get a few things from the jeweler's stand, but we didn't have time. The stand is the same one where I got the supplies for this." I traced the edge of Micah's copper cuff, the token that marked him as mine. "I thought I could make a few more things. You know, like a hobby."

"An excellent notion," Micah murmured.

"Really?"

"Of course," he replied. "The few items you've created have all been exquisite. If visiting this jeweler's stand is the first step in creating more beautiful things, then I encourage you to go." Relief cascaded over me; I'd been so worried that Micah wouldn't approve of me traipsing across dimensions with Max. Then he said, "May I accompany you?"

"Don't you have stuff to do?" I blurted out.

"Yes, but nothing so important it cannot wait. Nothing more important than being with you." He kissed my hair, and I had to admit, a day spent strolling around the Promenade Market with Micah seemed very inviting. "Besides, I do still need to verify your claims about this Land of Scott."

"All true," I said, kissing his nose once more before I leapt up to dress. "We can bring Max with us."

"Max?" Micah repeated. I ignored Micah's frosty tone, just as I ignored my brother's equally bad attitude when I told him about my plans over breakfast.

"You think he'll like it there?" Max asked, eyeing Micah over the rim of his coffee mug. The rest of us ingested our caffeine from the dainty silver teacups Shep was so proud of, like civilized folk, but Max's cup was as large as a beer stein. He was such a caffeine addict, he'd snort the stuff if he could figure out how to do it without drowning.

"I think so," I murmured. "He likes to travel."

Max snorted. "Yeah. Well. I don't know if I want to go to the Promenade today."

"Bullshit." Max and I, both startled, looked at Sadie, who had just lobbed a curse at us without even taking her nose out of her book. "You love the Promenade; you always have. You just feel stupid because Micah had to clean up your mess with the iron warriors. Just go and make nice with our brother-in-law, okay?"

When the Metal Inheritor tells you to do something, you do it, and in a short time, Max, Micah, and I were walking along the border of the Whispering Dell. We easily found the static portal secreted amongst the pines, and, a heartbeat later, we were in the Mundane realm. Micah had used some innate navigational talent, and instead of arriving in REES' parking lot, we were only a few blocks from the Promenade. The short distance let us walk right up to the gates, lest any drones spy the three of us appearing out of thin air. It also gave Max time to go on ahead and pretend that he didn't know us. Jerk.

Once we were inside the market, Max immediately took off for the newsstand. Instead of following him, I grasped Micah's arm and led him toward the flower sellers. Before we'd entered the portal, Micah had donned his human guise of Mike Silver, a tall man with brown hair and a genial smile. We walked practically unnoticed through the customers and stalls, almost like we were a regular couple. As if I had any idea what regular people did.

Micah had also magicked up some metal bits into an approximation of Mundane money, and what was his first purchase? He bought me a bouquet of daisies.

"For me?" I squeaked, far more pleased that a few limp flowers usually warranted.

"Of course," Micah murmured, closing my hands around the stems. "Did I not once promise to gather flowers for my consort?" My cheeks warmed, and I hid behind the petals. "Now, let us find some refreshment."

A few stalls later, Micah and I shared some tasteless lemonade; after these many weeks being fed from the manor's kitchens, I'd forgotten just how terrible Mundane food tended to be, and that the government liked it that way. Still, the liquid was a welcome coolness on a hot day, and Micah's arm around my shoulder made me forget all about the lack of citrus in my citrus-based drink. Then we turned a corner, and I came face to face with one of the last people I wanted to see—Peacekeeper Jerome.

Frickin' Peacekeeper Jerome.

"Sara!" Jerome's eyes lit up at the sight of me, thus ending all hope for a quick getaway. "I was hoping I'd run into you again soon."

"Were you?" I said shakily. Micah pulled me closer, an action that Jerome didn't miss.

"Is this another one of your brothers?" Jerome asked.

"No." I took a deep breath and introduced my elfin consort to a Peacekeeper. Luckily, Jerome wasn't one of the smarter Peacekeepers. "This is Mi—Mike Silver, my boyfriend. Mike, this is Jerome. He's a Peacekeeper."

Micah didn't miss a beat. "A pleasure," he acknowledged, with a nod. Jerome, however, proved to be less than mature.

"I didn't know you had a boyfriend," Jerome said with a pout, which was quite possibly the least becoming expression a grown man could wear.

"Sara is mine," Micah declared. "We are quite taken with one another."

Jerome's brow furrowed at Micah's wording, then his eyes settled on my left hand. "At least there's no ring," he commented with a grin. "I guess I'll see you around, Sara."

With that, Jerome sauntered off down the aisle, and I breathed a healthy sigh of relief. That relief was short-lived, since Micah was less than pleased about that little encounter.

"Explain to me what a boy friend is," he murmured in my ear.

"It's what a girl calls her special man," I replied. "When they're not married, but exclusive. Like us."

"And the ring he mentioned?"

"The rings are like tokens," I replied. "Humans exchange them when they get married." I finished off my lemonade and turned to toss the empty cup into a trash bin.

"Do you come here often to see that man?"

Micah's voice was soft and even, but it froze me where I stood. "Micah, I didn't want to come here to see him. Today was only the third time I've spoken to him."

"The third time I spoke to you, I gave you my token."

Those words might as well have been a knife in my heart. If there was anything I would never, ever do, it was cheat on Micah. I didn't know what to say or do, or how I could possibly convince Micah that nothing would ever happen, not with Jerome or any man—

Wait, why was he freaking out?

"Are you jealous?" I asked. Micah frowned and looked at the ground. "You are!"

"I am nothing of the sort!" he snapped.

"Of course not." I took his hands in mine and stepped close so I was looking up into his eyes. "Micah, you have nothing to be jealous of. I would never be unfaithful to you."

"My Sara, I do not doubt you," he murmured. "Still, I cannot help that it heats my blood when a man looks upon my consort with lust in his heart."

I couldn't help it; I laughed. "I don't think anyone's ever looked at me that way."

"Many do. Remember, I myself am quite well-versed in looking upon you in that way." I laughed again, but he silenced me with a quick kiss. "If that man comes looking for you again, I will glamour you."

That was fine with me. "Can you make me taller? And blonde?"

"Perhaps I'll make you appear as a copper frog," he countered.

"Ribbit." I hopped, but it was more like a bunny than a frog. Micah nipped my ear, and we resumed walking.

"It is not as if you have never felt jealousy," Micah said.

"When was this?" I asked. The only women I ever saw him with were Mom and Sadie. Well, and the Bright Lady, but that was different.

"When you first saw the shapeshifters in the village," he replied. "And when Oriana touched my mark."

At least the shapeshifters had kept their distance. "Anyone touches your mark again, I'm breaking their fingers, queen or not."

Micah wrapped his arm around my shoulders and kissed my temple. "I wouldn't have it any other way."

Me either. Remembering my failed attempt at buying supplies for my newly-chosen hobby the other day, I pulled Micah toward the jeweler's stall.

"The jewelry booth is right around this bend," I explained, when Micah asked where we were off to. I grabbed his hands and walked backward, telling him all about my favorite merchant. "She's so nice, and she has the best, shiniest stones, and—"

Micah stopped abruptly and pulled me against his chest. His mouth was a slash across his face, his eyes hard. I peeked over my shoulder and saw charred cardboard walls and a wooden counter that had been smashed to bits. I could see a few bits of metal glinting in the debris; this must have happened recently, being that the scavengers hadn't yet picked over the remains.

"Is that—"

"Yes." I said quickly. I didn't want him to say it out loud; somehow, saying it would make it too real. Far more real than the evidence scattered before me.

"Let's find your brother," Micah murmured. I nodded, numb, and we made my way across the market to the newsstand. We found Max engaged in a lively debate with an older lady about tomato sauce, of all things. As if Max had ever cooked anything in his life.

"I think rosemary's too harsh for a fresh sauce," Max was saying. "It's like chewing on a pine branch. Hey, sis." Max's brow furrowed at my rattled state, but I shook my head. "Me and Vincenza here are talking lasagna."

After we'd performed the requisite introductions, I learned that Vincenza sold ribbons, both new and gently used, and that her stall was not too far from the jeweler's. When I asked her how the fire had happened, I'd hoped she would say that it had been a freak accident with a soldering iron. Much to my dismay, Vincenza shook her head.

"She would have been lucky if that's all it had been. Rana was never one to think before she did anything."

Rana. Huh. So that was her name. "So, the fire was her fault?" I ventured.

"Oh, it was her fault, all right," Vincenza said. "She was caught fraternizing with enemies of the state." She leaned closer and whispered, "Elementals, you know."

My stomach dropped to the ground like a safe let go from the top floor of a skyscraper. Luckily, Vincenza assumed that our mingled looks of horror were due to Rana's questionable choice in friends. "Oh, a drone even recorded it," she continued. "Here, I'll show you what they did with her."

Like lambs to the slaughter, the three of us followed Vincenza. I, naïvely, assumed that the Peacekeepers had posted a writ detailing Rana's crimes, or that she herself was suspended in a cage for the lawful folks to throw rotten cabbages at. When we reached the center of the market, I cried out in shock, clutching at Micah's shirt for support.

Rana's head was impaled on a pike set atop a raised platform, her gummy eyes staring out over the stalls, both as a warning and a promise of the price of defiance. Beneath her head was a video screen, playing my interaction with Rana on an endless loop, followed by head shots of me, Max, Sadie, and even Mom.

Recognition sparked in Vincenza's eyes, and she slowly looked from the video screen to Max, then to me. Her face bloodless, she backed away in terror. "Elementals!" she shrieked, pointing at us. "Peacekeepers! Help me!"

Micah struck her hard enough to knock her out, then he clapped his hands on either side of my face. My world wavered, but I didn't realize what he'd done until he did the same to Max—he'd glamoured us, which was probably the only way we were getting out of the Promenade alive.

"This way," Micah said; then, his hand clasped in mine, we took off for the nearest exit, dodging other market patrons, and narrowly escaping a pair of bewildered Peacekeepers. When we reached the aisle that led to the main exit, my heart jumped into my throat.

Peacekeepers had formed a perimeter around the edge of the market and were slowly, methodically checking everyone's paperwork.

"I need room to cast a portal," Micah said. "If I do it in the open, we may bring back something extra."

"Extra is bad? Bad like 'so bad it's good,' or bad like raining terror?" I always make jokes when I'm nervous.

"The second," Micah replied.

As my mind raced with images of Peacekeepers shooting up the Whispering Dell, Max grabbed a handful of my shirt and dragged me inside a tent. I caught Micah's hand, and we found ourselves standing among about a million bolts of fabric. Not to mention people buying and selling fabric.

"We're Elementals," Max shouted. "Peacekeepers are coming. If you don't want to get shot at, get out now." They all stared back at Max, unsure if he was an Elemental or an asylum escapee, so he raised his hand and made the metal table twist into a pretzel.

"Out, now!" he bellowed.

As the Mundanes scrambled to safety, Micah reached inside his shirt and drew forth a portal, nearly identical to the one Max had used during our last escape. I heard Peacekeepers force their way into the tent, but I didn't turn to look. Micah cast the return portal, and the three of us leapt through. It wasn't until we'd rolled to a stop in the Otherworld, hitting every small stone and branch on the way, that I realized that Micah had glamoured Max to look like a girl.

"What?" Max demanded as I stifled a giggle. Then he looked down at his newly ample bosom, straining against his shirt.

"You frickin' bastard," he grumbled. "You just couldn't resist, could you?"

"Whatever do you mean?" Micah asked, brows arched and eyes wide. "I disguised you so you may live to fight another day."

"You gave me tits!" Max shrieked, his voice squeaking.

"And?" Micah's own glamour faded away, then he touched my forehead. The edges of my vision shimmered, and I knew I was myself again. "Is there a form you would have preferred?"

Micah fixed Max in his level gaze, and if I hadn't been laughing so hard I'd have warned him to stop before Max—*Maxine*—punched him. As it was, Max was winding up for the hit. I was about to tell them both to cool it—I mean, we'd just seen Rana's head on a pike—when we were interrupted by yet another shriek.

"It's Mom!" I cried. The three of us ran toward the sound. We found Mom, hatchet once again in hand, catching her breath as she leaned against a tree trunk.

"Boggart," Mom panted when she saw us. "The one you let live," she added, with a nod toward me.

"Just the one?" Micah asked. Mom glared, but it was a logical question. Boggarts were annoying, but killing one was as simple as sneaking up and whacking it. Since they sleep for most of the day, you could exterminate a whole herd of the buggers in a single outing.

"Whoever cursed it against Max was not pleased by our binding it," Mom replied. "The wee beastie's not so wee any longer."

"You attempted to bind a boggart?" Micah asked, but we didn't have time to respond. As if it had heard its cue, the boggart, now the size of a midsized office building, crashed through the trees. Its crusty brown hide bore several slashes from Mom's hatchet, but they hadn't done much to slow it down. Its skin had to be a foot thick by now.

"What about the poppet?" I asked.

"It's gone," Mom replied.

"Oh." We were so screwed.

The four of us dashed behind a hedge as the boggart crashed by, its huge, smelly feet narrowly avoiding squashing us into pancakes. At least its intelligence hadn't seemed to increase with its size.

"Have you tried magic?" Micah asked.

"I've tried clouding its vision, making the ground beneath it soft, turning its feet to stone," Mom listed, "but all for naught. It's been rendered immune to my magic."

"Hmm." With that innocent sound, Micah stepped out from the hedge and started waving his arms and shouting. Once he had the boggart's attention, he grabbed my arm.

"Lead it toward the Clear Pool, but not in a straight line. Circle the orchard twice, perhaps thrice," he instructed. When I hesitated, he added, "Quickly, love!"

Then the monster was barreling down upon us, and I needed no more prompting. I took off toward the pool, running first to the left, then the right, in a wild loop around the orchards. The thing was so stupid that I had to stop occasionally and wait for it to catch up, and once I had to throw clods of dirt in its direction to remind it to chase me. Whatever Micah had planned had better not involve any higher thought processes on the part of our quarry.

Finally, I reached the shore of the Clear Pool. I saw Max and Mom standing on the opposite side, and, not knowing what else to do, I ran straight into the water toward them. As soon as I cleared the shore Micah appeared, waving his arms as a huge lump of silver grew out of the sandy bank. The boggart, possessing either too much velocity or stupidity to stop, tripped and splashed into the pool.

"They cannot swim," Micah explained as he helped me from the water. I nodded, still staring after the slowly sinking behemoth. It was still bellowing, or rather gurgling, as it settled on the bottom of the Pool. Boggarts, too dumb to die.

"And how will this beast be removed?" squeaked a voice behind me. I peeked over my shoulder, and saw the Bright Lady standing there, bare as ever, arms crossed and foot tapping. "I'm to host a company of Satyrs this evening. I cannot have my waters so befouled!"

"I'll have the carcass removed directly," Micah soothed. "Many thanks for your assistance."

That placated her a bit. She produced a comb and started arranging my mother's hair, much to Mom's annoyance. "An admirable job cursing, Maeve," the Bright Lady murmured. "However, next time, maybe consult with me first?"

"Perhaps," Mom grumbled, swatting the Bright Lady's hand. "Who's the lass?"

Confused, I followed Mom's gaze. Even Max looked over his shoulder, before realizing that Micah still hadn't unglamoured him. Max's ears turned red, in rage or embarrassment I couldn't tell, but before he could start screaming, Micah touched his forehead. Just like that, my scrawny brother was returned to us.

"Pity," Bright Lady purred. "He was a lovely female."

Jennifer Allis Provost

Max's jaw dropped, and he watched as the Bright Lady turned and sashayed back to the edge of her watery home. Micah, Mom, and I headed back toward the manor, leaving the two of them to have some alone time at the Clear Pool.

Hours later, I found Max sitting alone on the manor's front stairs. I plopped down beside him, the silence between us heavy for a time. I suspected that we both had the same worries, but I was so hoping I was wrong. Then Max spoke, and I learned that I wasn't.

"They have us on vid chips," he muttered.

"Why didn't Jerome say anything?" I wondered. "He must have seen the display."

"Oh, he knew," Max said. "Ever hear about lambs going to the slaughter? That's what we were." He dropped his head to his hands, grumbling, "We can't even get a lousy newspaper without being hauled off."

"I know. I never..." I cleared my throat, willing my voice to hold steady. "I shouldn't have gone with you."

"Not your fault."

"I got Rana killed."

"Not your fault!" Max grabbed my shoulder, turning me to face him. "The Peacekeepers are a brutal, insane bunch of thugs. They alone are responsible for their actions, no one else."

"Uncle Mike's actions." I still found it hard to reconcile the image of Juliana's creepy uncle with

184

the mad-scientist-cum-renegade-politician of Mike Armstrong. But it was the truth, and it was far more true than any of the lies the Peacekeepers had shoved down our throats. All that remained was determining what we were going to do about it.

"Micah once said we should overthrow the Mundane government," I ventured.

"Yeah?" Max perked up at that. "He mean it?"

"Yeah."

Max grunted. "Let me think on it for a while, get a plan together. We'll show those bastards."

I smiled tightly, dropping my eyes. I had everything here in the Otherworld, from a man who loved me, to the silk that made up my bed and my clothes, to every food or drink I could ever desire. But none of it mattered if I couldn't go home again.

16

Who knew that there were holidays in the Otherworld?

Well, I sure hadn't known about any holidays, mainly because I had grown up in a place where one day was as banal as all the others. This was largely due to the fact that, once we Elementals had lost the Magic Wars, the new government had banned Every. Single. Holiday. Even the bank holidays! Although we did have one mandatory day off, each and every month—Tax Day. What did we do, you ask? Well, we hauled on down to our local government kiosk and paid our taxes.

I know. Hogmanay, it was not.

Since I was still pretty young when the wars ended, I hardly remembered those special days devoted to large meals and recreational activities;

the government was constantly reminding us that a good work ethic would do more for our health and happiness than any sort of observances, religious or otherwise, and that a hard day's labor was better than any day spent lolling about. So we worked and worked and worked until minor events like Happy Hour at The Room seemed like Christmas morning.

Therefore, Micah could hardly understand my elation when he informed me that he and I would be hosting the Whispering Dell's Beltane celebration, right here at the manor. What's more, we were going to play the parts of the May King and Queen.

"A *real* holiday?" I'd asked for the hundredth—maybe thousandth—time. "With cakes, and presents, and things?"

"There will be cakes, yes," Micah answered, again. So far, my incessant questions hadn't worn the bemused smile off his lips. "And those attending will bring offerings. As for these other *things* you desire…"

Instead of continuing, Micah grabbed me about the waist and pulled me against him. We were hiding out in the kitchens, seated on the bench beside the vast oven where the silverkin baked their breads and pies. If I could have spent every day surrounded by the aroma of baking desserts and wrapped in Micah's arms, it would have been my version of heaven.

"Micah." I swatted his shoulder, not that I wanted him to stop. Not that he had any intention of stopping, anyway. "By *things* I didn't mean this."

"Oh?" he murmured, while his lips caressed my neck. "I wonder if you truly understand the meaning of Beltane."

After a bit more, um, *education*, we managed to get the manor outfitted for a Beltane celebration. Long tables had been erected in the field that stretched between the Clear Pool and the Great Wood, and a massive pile of wood, which would be the first of many bonfires, was neatly stacked in the center. Garlands of flowers decorated the tables and surrounding trees, along with swags of ribbon and streamers. Platters of oatcakes and jugs of sweet May wine filled every available flat surface. Besides all the decorations and a truly enormous amount of food, there would be dancing and games and, perhaps most importantly, Micah and me dressed up as the May King and Queen.

I'd had a hard time explaining to Micah why dressing up in a costume was way more fun than wearing dresses on a regular basis. It wasn't his fault; since he was a boy, he saw a dress as a dress, no matter what day it was worn. Except for the time he'd worn a skirt, but he still didn't want to talk about that.

In the end, he just shook his head and pulled on his own costume. It consisted of buff-colored trousers topped by a white linen tunic, which was heavily edged with embroidered silver flowers. Over the tunic was a forest-green vest decorated with leaves just a shade or two lighter, cinched with a brown belt.

My costume wasn't as heavily decorated as Micah's, but it was still beautiful. It was a sleeveless white dress made up of many gauzy layers that floated and shimmered whenever I moved. The back was low, so low that a good portion of my mark was exposed, a first for me. Since I'd wanted to incorporate my metal in some way, now that I knew that that was what Metal Elementals did, swirling copper bands decorated my upper arms and ankles. Based on Micah's expression, my first attempt had been a success.

The celebration began around noon, but Micah and I waited to make our grand entrance until shortly after the food had been laid out. As we stepped onto the field, a hush rolled across the gathering, as the people of the Whispering Dell took in the sight of us, the May King and Queen.

Wow. That's a lot of people. I looked down and distracted myself by wiggling my toes in the cool grass. I grabbed Micah's hand and murmured how glad I was that we had both chosen to go barefoot.

"Micah. Sara."

I looked up and saw my mother standing before us, bearing a silver tray with two flower crowns upon it, along with two wineglasses. "For the May King and his Queen," she intoned, her voice rolling across the field. As Micah and I solemnly crowned each other, a dull roar replaced the respectful hush, with those around us claiming that the Seelie Queen offering the May King and Queen their wine was most auspicious, indeed.

Well, we knew she'd be recognized eventually. I glanced at Micah, but he only shrugged and reached for a wineglass; if he had any qualms about the fact that the Seelie Queen was now known to be bunking in his guestroom, he was content to let them be until tomorrow. Then the crowd parted, and I realized that my queenly mother was far from the most interesting thing in the field that day.

In the center of the field was a maypole.

I vaguely remembered dancing around a maypole when I was very young, during the Beltane celebrations held at the Raven Compound. Back then, Mom and Dad had dressed up as the May Queen and King, overseeing the bonfires and collecting dew, ensuring that all were happy and content. I remember lying under the fairy tree, exhausted, and wondering how my parents could keep up with the endless revelry.

Now that Micah and I were filling the roles of the May King and Queen, I understood. The flower crown upon my head filled me with an elated energy, so much so that I wanted to dance and leap around the field. Micah had laughed, and we danced for a time, but he stayed me when I tried to grab one of the long ribbons dangling from the maypole.

"That dance is for those seeking to find a mate," Micah murmured, his breath warm against my ear. "You, love, are well and truly attached."

I looked longingly at the pole. "We don't get to dance?"

"Ours will be later," he promised.

I smiled at that and leaned against Micah, his arms sliding around my waist as we oversaw the revelers. My eyes could hardly track all the multicolored ribbons as they were plaited together by the unattached, skipping in circles but somehow never knotting the ribbons. Sadie clutched a blue ribbon and as the dance ended found herself blushing, face-to-face with an equally embarrassed faun. I watched as the two of them wandered off for refreshments. After they'd disappeared, I saw Max skulking around the edge of the festivities.

"Why didn't he dance at the maypole?" I wondered. It was like he hadn't even noticed that the area around the maypole was teeming with available females, most of whom were looking for mates, if only for the evening.

"Perhaps his heart lives elsewhere," Micah offered. "I know that, when you are nearby, I see no other woman."

Before I had time to blush at the compliment, Micah and I were called to take our places at the head table. We were seated in two enormous wooden chairs, reminiscent of thrones, bedecked with so many swags of flowers that you could hardly see the high backs. No sooner were we settled than the other revelers lined up before us, each of them bearing packages.

"What are they holding?" I whispered to Micah.

"They bring offerings for the May King and his Queen," Micah replied.

"I like presents," I murmured. "Will there be more copper gifts?"

Micah shrugged. "We shall soon learn."

I watched, somewhat amused, as the revelers went about organizing themselves into an orderly mess; the fact that Micah's wine had flowed freely for the better part of the day made this look like an Otherworldly slapstick routine. In the midst of the semi-drunken chaos, a woman stepped forward.

She was tall, with flowering vines twisted throughout her long hair, their softness in stark contrast to her clothing of bark bound with straw. Her limbs were long and spindly, like dried-up twigs, as was her nose. She looked to be very old, yet her face and hands bore no wrinkles, and her hair was a vibrant blonde underneath the lush vines. Micah leaned toward me, probably to make an introduction, but I already knew who she was.

She was the Lady of the Great Wood.

"For the May King," she said, her voice as clear as a bell. She reached forward, graceful despite her gawky limbs, and placed a single perfect lily before Micah. It was a deep orange, tipped with red, the perfect complement to his silvery hair. Micah affixed the lily to his shirt with a bit of silver, and murmured his thanks.

"And for his Queen," the Lady continued, now placing a spray of yellow orchids before me.

Following Micah's lead, I pinned the spray to my bodice, though my pins were copper.

"Your gifts are as lovely as your Wood," I said, "Thank you for joining us today."

With that, the Lady of the Wood gracefully bowed her head and melted away into the crowd. "I thought you two didn't get along," I whispered to Micah.

"It seems that things have changed for the better," Micah replied. He squeezed my fingers, and we looked toward the next person in line, who happened to be one of Micah's magistrates from the village. He carried a crystal decanter filled with golden wine, a sprig of fresh woodruff poking out of it. It was a lovely gift, and Micah and I both said as much.

The next gift involved a basket containing a few bundles of herbs, namely ginseng, sarsaparilla, and something I didn't recognize.

"What's this?" I asked the giver, a youthful man who would pass as human if not for his glowing yellow eyes.

"Horny goat weed," he replied, his knowing glance explaining exactly what the herbs were used for. Hot blood spilled up my neck as I murmured my thanks, and turned my attention to those behind him.

Thankfully, no one else was carrying a basket of weeds, horny goat or otherwise. The next few offerings were mostly benign, ranging from loaves of still-warm bread to a lovely tapestry that rivaled anything on the manor's walls. Then there was a carved bone decanter of powdered rhino horn, then a basket of melons, which was followed by a platter of chocolate and the reddest strawberries I'd ever seen. When a bucket of raw oysters was presented to us, I finally asked Micah what the heck was going on.

"Like, half of these offerings are aphrodisiacs," I explained, when he'd responded by peaking those silver brows of his. As if he was in any way innocent. "You can't tell me you didn't notice."

"Of course I did," he replied, reaching so his long fingers could graze my belly. "The purpose of Beltane is fertility."

Babies. Do we really need to talk about babies during a holiday? I mean, come on. "That's all?"

"Well," Micah added, scooping me from my chair and settling me on his knee, "there is also the bit that comes before."

Micah's blatant affection for me was a hit with the crowd of onlookers, and a great whoop issued forth. I laughed, since a crowd of partiers cheering while Micah nibbled my neck was about as hilarious as you can get, and tried to wriggle free from his grasp. My May King was undeterred. Instead, he drew me tightly against him, his nibbling giving way to unabashed nuzzling.

"Silverstrand," boomed a voice. I tore my eyes away from Micah, and found that Old Stoney was at the head of the offering line. Just when I thought baby talk was the true buzzkill, the rocky king of buzzkills stepped up.

"Greymalkin," Micah returned, with a polite nod. "Have you come to join our celebration?"

"And further disturb the queen? Not I," he said with a sneer.

"Pray tell, Farthing, how is this gathering disturbing Oriana?"

"Look." Old Stoney spread his palms, gesturing to encompass the whole of the field. "You've set up a silver court, bright enough to cast hers in shadow."

I followed Old Stoney's gaze across the field. Was this a court? I suppose it was, what with the food and drink, and that gifts were being offered to the king and queen. But Micah and I were only ruling for this one day, and only in this one field. Besides that, didn't the Lord of Silver deserve a court of his own?

"Farthing." Micah nudged me off his lap as he stood, but he kept his arm around my waist. "If you have come here only to make trouble for me and mine, I will remove you without a second thought." Old Stoney opened his mouth, but Micah didn't miss a beat. "You know as well as I that I harbor no desire for the throne," Micah continued, stepping around to the front of the table. I followed him, taking my place at his side. "But don't take my word for it. Stay, mingle amongst my people, and when you return to Oriana's side, you can tell her beyond a shadow of a doubt that Lord Silverstrand remains true to his queen." With an ease that belied the tension crackling around him, Micah selected a loaf of bread from among the offerings. He tore off a generous portion and held it out to Stoney. "What will it be, friend?"

The field had gone deathly quiet, and every set of eyes and ears were trained on Micah and the rock. Old Stoney was so incensed that it looked like lava would leak out his ears, but Micah had well and truly trapped him. The Otherworld didn't have many enforceable rules, but hospitality was one of them. Once an invitation was given it must be accepted, or at the very least acknowledged. In short, as Micah stood there, smiling at Old Stoney, exuding nothing but good faith as he offered him a hunk of fresh bread, he had the rock over a barrel.

Gods, how I loved him.

Old Stoney grumbled as he accepted the bread, then he turned and stalked away. It seemed that he didn't enjoy our company any more than we enjoyed his. Good.

Things settled down after that, and the offerings resumed; things settled down even further when a few attendees produced instruments. Nearly everyone was softly swaying to the music, but even though I'd been so eager to dance earlier, I made no move to join them. I'd resumed my place on Micah's knee and was perfectly content to watch the rest spin and twirl about the still-unlit bonfire. Micah was murmuring about how he couldn't wait to see the flames against the night sky, when suddenly the crone from the apothecary was standing in front of us. I was so shocked I nearly fell off Micah's lap, but he was as composed as ever.

"Good woman, why have you come before us?" Micah asked. His tone was respectful, but I saw a muscle twitch in his jaw.

"To present my offering, of course," she replied, spreading her hands wide. "Is an old woman like me not welcome at your feast?"

"All of my people are welcome," Micah said, in such a way that had me wondering if he counted her as his. "An offering, you say?"

"I regret, my lord, that I have only a gift for the May Queen." With that, the crone reached into her colorless robes and set before me the reddest, shiniest apple I'd ever seen. It was beautiful, as tempting as the first fruit itself, and I coughed to hide my annoyance. What, did she think I was stupid? Like I would fall for that? My mother was the Seelie frickin' Queen, and she'd warned me off of spelled fruit before she had taught me to read.

"Thank you," I said, my voice hardly more than a whisper. "Your offering does much to ensure the land's fecundity for the coming year," I added, a bit more forcefully. Well, I was louder, anyway.

The crone said nothing, but bowed respectfully, her gray eyes never leaving mine. After she'd shuffled away, Micah grabbed my hands.

"You mustn't touch it," Micah warned.

"Don't worry. I won't." After staring at the apple for another heartbeat, I looked at his hands, his long fingers that were tightly wrapped around my wrists. "Is she dangerous?"

"She is powerful," Micah replied, "and arrogant. She swears allegiance to no one. While she is not what I'd call evil, she certainly isn't trustworthy."

I shuddered, remembering the tiny blue vial that sat on my dressing table, and the dubious bargain I'd struck with her. Misinterpreting my quivering shoulders, Micah called for a silverkin to take the apple and toss it into the center of the firewood.

"Worry not, love," he said, rubbing my arms as if he could rub away the crone's visit.

"I'm—I know you wouldn't let anything hurt me," I amended, mid-speak. I would never outright lie to Micah, not even to tell him I wasn't worried. My omissions about the birth control didn't count; yeah, I was still trying to convince myself of that one.

Micah smiled at that and leaned forward to kiss my hair. "The sun goes to rest," he said, gently turning my chin toward the west. "Come, let us light the bonfire."

We watched the sun paint the sky in oranges and purples for another moment, then we rose and wound our way around the tables and revelers toward the massive pyramid of wood. As we stood before the intimidatingly large heap, I suddenly found myself wishing for a pair of flip-flops. A splinter in the May Queen's toe would certainly not bode well for the coming harvest. Micah had somehow obtained a candle, and we both held it as we guided its tiny flame toward the kindling.

"This won't work," I whispered. "The flame's too small."

"Is it?" Micah had no sooner said the words than the firewood caught, and the entire mound was ablaze. We stepped back as others stepped forward, lighting their own sticks so they could create their own fire.

While there had been no shortage of libations earlier in the evening, once the bonfire raged, Micah's wine flowed like a river after the spring thaw. Revelers wandered off among the orchards, either to dance or sing, or maybe begin more private celebrations. Throughout it all, Micah and I walked among his people, ensuring that all had eaten and drunk their fill. Eventually, we happened upon our least-liked guest.

"Farthing," Micah said, with a polite nod. As Old Stoney turned to reply, the pixie he'd been talking to took the opportunity to flee. I was beginning to think that pixies were the smartest creatures in the Otherworld. "Enjoying yourself, I trust?"

"Always, Silverstrand." He turned back to the pixie, found that she was gone, and settled his gaze on me instead. "I could ask the same of you. I'd have given the lady a green dress by now."

I looked down at my dress, wondering what was wrong with white. Was I supposed to change after the bonfire was lit? Then, I heard a breathy moan from beyond the trees, and my toes twitched in the grass.

"Watch yourself, Farthing," Micah said, pausing to take a sip from his wine. "And watch your mouth around my consort. You may be my guest, but I've no qualms about tipping you into the Clear Pool and leaving you there to be taken over by so much pond scum." Old Stoney's eyes flamed and his neck bulged, but Micah ignored him as he took my arm and led me away from him.

"I hate him," I grumbled. "Why does he have to be here, today of all days? He's going to ruin—"

Micah silenced me the best way he knew how, by grabbing my shoulders and kissing me hard. When he came up for air, he said, "Only if you let him."

I opened my mouth to protest the many ways Old Stoney's presence had me less than pleased, when I caught sight of a line of dancers. In the Mundane world they would have been called a conga line, but here they were just happy. Carefree. Enjoying themselves.

Micah was right. Who cared if that stupid rock wanted to be a jerk? I kissed Micah's chin and asked, "Are we done being the May King and Queen?"

"Almost," he murmured, drawing me into the darkness beyond the firelight. "There is but one more matter to see to." And see to it we did.

17

Something was bothering me about that last boggart, the one Mom and I had needed to bind. And not just because the binding had turned out to be a total waste of time.

Okay, the fact that the critter was bothering me was a given, since the sole purpose for boggarts to exist is so they can annoy people. But something about that particular boggart was off...way more off than the usual boggarty shenanigans.

It wasn't that the original clutch had been Max's penalty for being a world-class failure at gambling; around here, Max screwing up happened often enough, and it was really only a matter of time before *someone* cursed him. But Mom had managed to break the curse on the rest of the clutch, so why did just the one boggart wander on back to the manor, first to eat nearly half the orchards, then as a supersized menace? What was more, the binding spells worked by me and Mom should have been more than enough to hold it. Of course, we hadn't expected anyone to dig up the poppet we'd buried, either.

So, who had unbound the boggart? And where had the poppet gone?

Those two questions had the same answer— someone had dug up the poppet and destroyed it. Most likely, that someone was the same someone who had then made Max's boggart the Largest Boggart Ever. But who could have done it? Who would have even known there was a bound boggart in the first place?

Even without knowing said digger/enlarger's name, I could puzzle out a fair bit of their identity. It would have to have been someone of considerable power, and someone who knew that the Lord of Silver had recently begun hosting a few out-of-town relatives up at the manor. Granted, it was no secret that the Corbeaus were now staying in the Otherworld, especially with Max's epic losing streak, and all the associated brawls, being the talk of the village; now that Mom had made her appearance at our Beltane festival, I could only imagine what further surprises we were in for. Hopefully these future incidents would just be standard attacks, with swords and spears and the like, and not another plague of stinky, messy critters.

When I'd asked Micah who he thought had been responsible, he'd placed all blame on Max, since he'd been cursed with them in the first place. I admitted that Micah had a point, but when the boggart had made his third appearance at the manor, it had had nothing to do with Max. What's more, for someone to attempt removing a poppet buried on Micah's land, they must have had access to a ready supply of spellcrafting implements, as well as a heaping helping of egotism.

So yeah, I had a few ideas about who this individual could be. And I wanted to pay her a visit.

I found Max lying on a bench in the courtyard, halfway between the manor and the Clear Pool. He was flat on his back, staring at the clouds. "What's going on?" I asked.

"Absolutely nothing." He drew up his feet, giving me space to sit beside him, so I did.

"Are you going to visit her?" I asked, nodding toward the Clear Pool. My brother seemed to have hit it off with our resident nymph.

"Nah. She's nice, but…" His voice trailed off, and I didn't press him. I was actually kind of glad that Max wasn't too into the Bright Lady, since I needed his full attention.

"I have a theory about your boggarts."

"What kind of theory?" He hadn't moved, but I heard the edge in his voice.

"Not about the whole group, just about the giant one. I think I might know who cursed it." At that he sat up, eyes narrowed and mouth pressed into a thin line. "Want to head down to the village with me?"

Max is always game for causing a ruckus, and soon we'd passed the village gates and were walking down the darker path toward the apothecary. Just as Sadie and I had, we found the crone inside. This time there weren't any heaps of freshly skinned pelts, thank the gods for small favors. Instead, we found the crone sorting powders behind the roughly-hewn counter.

"How did the tincture perform?" she croaked, by way of greeting.

"I'd rather talk about this," I replied. With that, Max heaved a burlap sack onto the counter and dumped out one of the giant boggart's toenails. I'd been disgusted when Max had suggested that we should dig up the boggart's corpse and just rip off a trophy, more so when he explained that a toenail, which was curved and cracked (not to mention smelly) and the length of Max's forearm, would be the easiest, and least messy, body part to carry with us. Really, who could argue with that? And he assured me that he could match the residual magic on the toenail to whoever had cast it.

Based on how the crone's eye twitched at the sight of it, she also thought we could trace any leftover bits of magic. Or perhaps it was just an involuntary reaction to the stench of putrid boggart flesh. "Are you looking to sell this?" she asked.

"Would someone buy it?" I asked.

The crone cackled. "Fools will buy anything!"

She had a point. She also wasn't going to distract me from the purpose of my visit. "Well, someone cursed this boggart to make it a giant pain in my ass. Any idea who would do that?"

"Who are your enemies?" she countered.

"I don't have any," I said, while Max murmured, "Lots." Confused, I turned toward my brother. "Think about it, Sara. Micah's got lots of enemies—basically, any Elemental who doesn't want metal to rule, not to mention the rest of metal who think they should be ruling. If they take out Oriana, Micah's next in line. And you know what metal comes after silver."

I so did not need to be reminded about that. "Why a boggart?"

"Why not? It can annoy us, distract us long enough that we don't see what's really going on." Max was thoughtful for a moment, as he studied the yellowish, dirt-caked toenail. Then he raised his eyes, his hard gaze wiping the smirk right off of the crone's face. "And you're the one who did it."

"I did nothing—"

"Don't lie," Max commanded. "This powder is identical to the stuff in that jar." Max indicated a reddish, crumbly substance caked on the underside of the nail and jerked his head toward the shelves of jars. "Besides, I can feel your magic on it. It's as unique as a retina scan."

The crone's eyes burned, and I mean *burned*; flames actually leapt across her pupils. "Just because my powder was used on the beast does not mean that I cast the spell."

"But you know who did," I said. "We won't hold it against you. We know that you're only trying to make a living here, selling your wares." I leaned across the counter and asked, "Come, dearie, I thought you wanted a few friends in Lord Silverstrand's house?"

She glared at me for a long moment, so long that I worried she was about to blast us with her fiery eyeballs. As it usually does, self-preservation won out in the end. "Farthing Greymalkin."

Old Stoney. Figures. "Why?"

"I've no idea, other than it was easy enough to accomplish. You might want to take up something other than gambling," she added, with a pointed look at Max.

"Why did you give me an apple?" I blurted out. It was so not the point of our visit, but I had to know.

"It was a test," she hedged.

"A test of what?"

"Your intelligence." She cackled again and produced a basket of the shiny red fruit. "Had you been foolish enough to eat it, I would have been summoned to save you, and Lord Silverstrand would have been indebted to me. Since you chose to burn my gift, I know you aren't as stupid as other mortals. Be glad you passed the test, *Lady* Silverstrand."

"If I'd eaten it and gotten sick, Micah would have killed you," I said. "Or my mother, if she got to you first."

The crone shrugged. "Maeve would have been furious if her own child had fallen for such a common trick. Furious with *you*," she added.

That was true, but Mom would have worked out her disappointment in her daughter's bad judgment on the crone's hide. Being that I couldn't stand to be in the apothecary for another moment, I slipped a few silver coins onto the counter; in the Whispering Dell, they were worth far more than gold. "If Greymalkin asks you for anything else, come to me. I'll pay for the information. Well." With that, we turned to leave, leaving the rotting toenail on the counter. That's what the crone got for doing business with people like Old Stoney.

"I'll give you a bit of information at no charge, my lady," she called after us. "To prove my loyalty to the Silverstrand house, of course." We turned and waited. "Have you noticed that none of copper yet attend you in person?"

She was right; other than the steadily increasing heap of gifts, I hadn't seen a single copper Elemental in the Otherworld, save for Sadie and Max. "Are they in trouble?"

"They're quite well," she replied. "They've all been instructed that avoiding the Raven clan is the only way they will remain well."

Huh. Someone must really think we're a lot more powerful than we are. "Was it Greymalkin?"

"No, this is bigger than that foolish rock's influence."

I nodded, murmuring my thanks as Max and I exited the apothecary. We were silent as we left the village, and as we travelled the metal pathway. Once the manor loomed in the distance, Max broke the silence.

"There's no one vying for leading copper," Max said. "All the metals follow Oriana."

"I know."

"Not many have more influence than Greymalkin."

"I know." There was Micah, but he wouldn't try to keep those of copper from us, and Ferra, but she'd long since rusted away. That left one person with the power to keep those of our own metal away from us. Oriana.

Crap.

18

"Oriana would never do such a thing," Micah insisted. Again.

"Then who would? Who even could?" I pressed. "Who besides Oriana and you has more power than Old Stoney?"

"Firstly, you overestimate my influence," Micah said. "Secondly, that crone deals in deceit as much as tinctures. Take care, love, before you take her word as true."

I blew out an exasperated breath; yeah, I knew she wasn't trustworthy. But who around here was? "She practically admitted to cursing the boggart."

"That, I do believe." Micah took my hands, grazing his thumbs across my knuckles. "Why did you go to her alone?"

"I told you, I was with Max." Micah harrumphed, which I ignored. "Besides, you said she was of questionable loyalties. Anyone who would send a giant boggart to the manor must be of questionable loyalties, right?"

"You have a point," Micah murmured. Then he rose and buckled on his sword belt. "Very well. I will travel to the Golden Court and discuss this matter with Oriana directly."

"You will?" I blinked, surprised that he put such credence in my fears. "Right now?"

"If someone has denied my consort access to others of her Element, I demand to know who is responsible, and why they would do such a thing," he replied.

"What if it *was* Oriana?" I asked, my voice wavering only a bit. Micah squeezed my hand.

"Then we will deal with it," he assured.

I walked Micah to the manor's front door; before I let him leave, I clung to him for a small eternity. Once it became apparent that I was holding on to him for dear life, Micah gently reminded me that neither he nor I had any reason to fear the Golden Court and promised that he would return home as soon as possible. Reluctantly, I released him and leaned against the doorframe as I watched him approach the metal pathway. Then Micah was gone, on his way to the Golden Court and an afternoon spent questioning our insane ruler. I did not envy him.

Gods, I hoped he was back soon.

I retreated to the inner atrium, deliberately not looking at the ever-growing heap of gifts stacked in the corner. It made sense, now, why those of copper kept sending these offerings; they were sending us (I refused to believe that they saw just me as a ruler; that was just ridiculous) a signal, a clue as to why they couldn't present themselves in person. Why none of them bothered to send clues about who had ordered their silence, I couldn't answer. Maybe those of copper overestimated the Raven clan's influence, and our intelligence.

Or maybe not. In addition to the casks of ale and tiny sweet cakes we'd been getting all along, we were now receiving a few books and scrolls each day. Apparently, word had gotten out that the new Inheritor of Metal was into libraries, and those of copper wanted to help her out in any way they could. Or maybe they'd sent us the Otherworld's version of a treasure map.

I shuffled through the scrolls we'd received most recently; there was one that told the history of a family with an unpronounceable surname that looked like archaic French, an astronomical chart, and a third that was all about espaliering fruit trees. Frustrated, I dropped them back on the heap of other bric-a-brac. Either we weren't being sent any clues, or I was just too dumb to see them.

My stomach rumbled, so I left the atrium and made my way to the kitchens. As I helped myself to some still-warm bread, I saw one of the newspapers

Max had picked up in the Mundane realm. I leafed through it, only intending to read the funnies. Instead of the comics, my eyes fell on an event notice, given pride of place above the fold.

Mike Armstrong – Pre-Election Rally To Be Held Saturday, 12:00 PM

Hm. It just happened to be Saturday morning, and here I was with nothing to do.

I found Max in his immaculately clean bedroom, scanning the tabletops for stray particles of dust. It both irritated and confounded me that the same person who tracked mud and other detritus across Shep's gleaming floors would also have a conniption if someone wore shoes inside his room.

Max looked up and cocked an eyebrow, his way of inquiring why I'd dared to enter his space. By way of explaining what I was up to, I tossed the newspaper onto the table in front of him. "Want to go?"

"Micah won't like it," he said, after a quick glance at the headline. So yeah, he was in.

"I can call him back from the Golden Court and ask him to glamour us," I said, but Max shook his head.

"We don't need him to disguise ourselves." I stared at Max, wondering if he'd forgotten that our images were playing on vid chips all over the Promenade, and who knew where else. If we went to the Mundane realm unglamoured, we might as well ask Sadie to get started baking a cake with a file in it. Of course, that was assuming that the Peacekeepers would let us have visitors. And baked goods. Then Max smirked his "I'm the brilliant older brother" smirk, and produced a few knitted caps.

"Where did you get these?" I asked. The hats, black and burgundy respectively, were a bit lumpy, and the seams were puckered in places.

"Sadie made them." That explained the lumpiness. She'd gone through a knitting phase while in high school, which meant that Mom and I had been temporarily sentenced to wearing asymmetrical sweaters in varying shades of brown and puke.

"You think a couple of hats will be enough to conceal our identities?" I asked. I mean, my plan to go to the rally was crazy enough, but this was beyond the pale. Even for Max, this was reckless.

"Nah. I've got sunglasses, too."

I stared at my insane brother, then at the hat in my hands, mentally listing everything that could go wrong. Danger, capture, torture, death…the reasons for just staying put in the Otherworld were all sound. Still, I had to see for myself if this Dr. Armstrong was also the Uncle Mike I remembered, the fat guy who tried to be jolly but never quite got it, who had grilled hot dogs while wearing a "Kiss the Cook" apron. I know, I'd seen all those magazines with his image on the cover, but those were just pictures. I needed to see this with my own two eyes.

"How could I have never noticed that he was such an evil man?"

"Because he didn't know you were an Elemental," Max said softly. I hadn't realized I'd spoken aloud. "And, once he found out, he used you, just like he uses everyone else."

"Do you think he used Juliana?" I asked.

"I know it." Max jerked his head to the side, and I followed him out of his room, down the stairs and away from the manor. We made our way to the edge of the Whispering Dell, and one portal hop later, we were skulking around the streets of Capitol City, wearing our impenetrable disguises of knitted caps and dark glasses. It was a sunny autumn day on the Mundane side, in stark contrast to the spring currently being experienced in the Otherworld. I would have remarked on the opposite seasons, but it was hot as frickin' hell, thus making these stupid hats even stupider, and making us in our winter wear stick out like sore thumbs among the sandal- and tank-top-clad masses. We should have just portaled right into a jail cell and saved everyone the bother. At least our dark glasses were somewhat appropriate. Then we turned a corner onto the main thoroughfare, and the sight before me shocked the snark right off my lips.

There had to be hundreds—no, make that *thousands*—of people gathered on the lawn before the steps of Government Headquarters. There were so many that even the Peacekeepers who manned the barriers looked a little on edge, despite the fact that they stood shoulder-to-shoulder, each one of them clad in riot gear and armed to the teeth. I noticed that they carried the same plastic guns I'd been shot with at the Institute, though these had blinking red lights rather than green. Dozens of drones buzzed away overhead, and I wondered how they avoided having midair collisions.

Near the edge of the crowd was a candidate running under the Mirland party. Mirlanders espoused the belief that Mundanes could, and should, live in harmony with Elementals. They preached a dogma that was full of symbiotic relationships, illustrating how the two races complemented, even needed, one another. You would think that, since they hadn't won an election in years, they would have altered their platform somewhat, but Mirlanders are stubborn folk.

While we watched, someone threw a cabbage at the speaker's head.

I felt bad for the guy, since he obviously wasn't going to win, vegetal projectiles or no. Maybe twenty years ago he would have had a chance, but not in the Pacifica of today. In the Pacifica of today, no one was safe.

Max and I threaded our way through the crowd; earlier, we'd decided that we wanted to be as close to the stage as safety allowed. Okay, maybe a few feet beyond safety; I wanted a good view. We pushed past Uncle Mike's many supporters, at one point nearly becoming engulfed by a drum circle. After we navigated around a group holding aloft a pro-Mike banner the length of a tennis court, we found that we were only two or three bodies back from the stage. Finally, I dared to look up at the man of the hour.

There he was, Dr. Michael Armstrong, and yeah, he really was the Uncle Mike of my memories. He was the same as ever—a heavy, balding man, clad in perfectly pressed khakis and a collared shirt. He looked like a regular middle-aged man, not how I imagined a crazed politician who hated Elementals would look. He was standing to the side of the podium, conferring with his assistant, who I recognized from the magazine covers as Langston Phillips. In person, Langston was even creepier, all pale and bug-eyed, like a hermit crab that had slithered outside its shell. Then, I looked behind the two men.

Juliana was there.

She was seated between her mother and her younger brother, Corey. Mrs. Armstrong was the picture of the ideal housewife, from her perfect bun to her single strand of pearls to her white gloved hands, neatly folded in her lap. Corey, who must have been about seventeen, maybe eighteen by now, wore a slightly more rumpled version of Uncle Mike's outfit, along with neon-green sneakers. He was absently stretching his fingers, which led me to believe that he still played piano. They both looked at Uncle Mike attentively, fake smiles plastered across their faces.

And Juliana…well, she looked like hell. Her thick, dark hair, which I'd always been envious of, was slicked back into a severe bun, which was somehow made her look far more matronly than her mother. She was wearing a plain gray shift dress, which was a dull contrast to her mother's pink cardigan and blue skirt. There were dark circles under her eyes, and she looked like she'd lost about twenty pounds. She didn't wear the fake smile that her mother and brother did; in fact, she looked like she could hardly hold up her head.

I couldn't imagine what could have caused her to look so...so used. It couldn't have been the metal dome that I'd wrapped around the Institute for Elemental Research, where Max had spent time as the resident lab rat. No, whatever had happened to her had happened afterward. Don't ask me how I knew this, but her symptoms seemed to speak more of a mental exhaustion than physical problems. I wondered if the Peacekeepers had blamed her for Max's escape. I wondered if they were punishing her.

I quickly tamped down the tightness in my chest; Juliana had betrayed not only me, but my entire family. She wasn't worthy of my guilt, or my sympathy.

"I guess she survived," I murmured, and Max nodded.

"Armstrongs are tough cookies," he said. "Always have been." He stared at Juliana so intently I worried that she'd feel his gaze, and look over at us. "I bet the bastard's torturing her."

"Why would he do that?" I asked. "Aren't they bad guys together?"

"We got away. Someone needs to pay for that." Something dark skated across Max's face, and I wondered how often he had been on the receiving end of Uncle Mike's punishment. And Max had never told me exactly how he had ended up in the plastic tube, only that he'd made a few metal flowers for a girl. He'd even said that the Institute hadn't been such a bad place for a while. What could Max have really done to end up like that?

"She deserves it," I said. "After what she did to you, she deserves all the punishment she can get."

Max shook his head. "Sara, no one deserves *him*." He would have said more, but just then Langston approached the podium and thanked us all for coming. After a moment of ear-splitting feedback, he handed Mike the microphone.

"It...it humbles me to see such a large turnout today," Mike began. "I can hardly believe that you all are here to support me in my quest to bring all of us a better world. Thank you."

And thus he began relaying to the crowd his visions of a better future, so long as you were a Mundane. He sounded like the same old Uncle Mike, his low voice rich with emotion, as if he might be overtaken at any moment and left sobbing on the stage. His eloquent words, flowing around me as he spoke of improving our world not only for us, but the next generation, nearly swayed me to his cause. Me, a fugitive Elemental.

Then, everything changed. "Tell me, what is keeping us from living the good life? What keeps us poor, underfed, overworked?"

The stupid government. I however, was alone in my opinion.

"Elementals!"

"Magic freaks!"

"Bearded baby snatchers!"

Cold sweat broke out across my chest, and I moved closer to Max. He grabbed my arm, just above the elbow, probably to keep me from running or doing something else stupid. I'd never been so glad for anything as the knitted hats that covered Max's and my copper-colored hair.

"I ask you, good people, how can we break the hold the Elementals have over us?" Uncle Mike demanded.

"What hold?" I hissed in Max's ear. He shook his head, his eyes never leaving the stage. Then I heard what the crowd was shouting around me.

"Imprison them!"

"Make them work for us!"

"Keep them away from my children!"

That last cry was little more than a sob, but Mike, and the rest of the crowd, had heard it clear as day. She was probably a plant.

"I know your pain," he said, now staring right at the woman in the crowd. Yep, definitely a plant. Mike stretched his arm out behind him, beckoning. Seeing her cue, Juliana staggered to her feet.

"This is my niece, Juliana." Juliana stumbled, but Langston steadied her with a hand on her back and guided her to the front of the stage. A murmur rode over the crowd; evidently, this wasn't the first time she'd joined in on Mike's theatrics. "As you can see, she isn't doing very well." Mike made a show of whispering into Juliana's ear, as if he was asking her approval to tell her story. She nodded slightly, as if she'd had any other choice.

"Elementals ruined her," he said, with a pointed glare directed at the women in the crowd, just in case we didn't know what he meant by ruined. "Luckily, there was no permanent damage, not that the bastard didn't try."

Realization dawned on the more thick-headed in the crowd, and we were surrounded by shouts and gasps. Mike gave them all a moment to settle down before he continued. "You see, that's what they want. Elemental men set out to impregnate normal, healthy girls. That's how they plan to spread their foul race across our country."

"Was he executed?" someone called out.

"No," Mike admitted. "He escaped and remains at large." The crowd went deathly silent, eyes darting at their neighbors, as if the Elemental in question would leap out and abscond with their daughters at any moment. "But if you elect me, and grant me the resources to combat this evil, I will make sure that what happened to my dear Juliana will never happen to your children."

"What will he do with—" I stopped short when Max coughed, and I chose a different word. "All the Elementals. Will he imprison them, deport them, what?"

"Who cares?" grumbled a man at my left.

Another said, "He means to use them."

That had our attention. Max and I turned to look at the speaker; it was the Mirlander candidate, none the worse for wear after the cabbage incident. "Use them for what?" Max asked.

"He wants to dissect them, determine the origin of their abilities, and replicate them," the speaker replied.

"That's stupid," Max said. "Why would a man that hates Elementals want to make more Elementals?"

"Does he hate or is he jealous?" the man countered. "Read up on your history, kids."

With that, the speaker melted into the crowd. I was shaking, not trembling but actually shaking, as if I was outdoors in a blizzard. While I accepted that most Mirlanders were nuts (why else would you join the losing party?), what he'd said hit too close to home. No matter what Max had said about the Institute not always being so bad, based on the state I'd found him in, he'd only been a day or two away from dissection.

"What will happen to her?" someone called out, and I was glad, not only for the distraction from the Mirlander's conspiracy theories. I wanted to know the answer to that, myself.

"Langston here has been kind enough to care for her," Mike answered, giving his assistant a hearty clap on the shoulder. "Juliana is a lucky girl." Juliana nodded weakly, and Langston drew her to the side of the stage. Our side of the stage.

"Aww," murmured a woman beside me, "they're such a cute couple. Aren't they?"

I realized she wanted my agreement, so I nodded. "Yeah, they look like they belong together," I murmured. If you overlooked how Juliana shrank away from Langston's hands, and how Langston stared at her like she was a juicy pork chop, they looked like the King and Queen of Hearts.

"I read that they'll marry in the spring," the woman continued. "Isn't that sweet?"

"Mmm." I would have said more, but Langston and Juliana had stopped directly over us, so close I could touch their feet. Langston whispered something in Juliana's ear, to which she glared and looked away. And right at me.

We both went stock still, our gazes locked together. I couldn't risk running, not while she was staring at me; my only hope was that Juliana would keep her mouth shut. Then, her gaze moved to slightly above my left shoulder, and she gasped.

"Max," she breathed. Too late, she clamped a hand over her mouth. Langston had heard her, clear as a bell.

"Why did you—" he began, then his gaze shot out over the crowd. "He's here, isn't he?" When Juliana didn't answer, he grabbed her arms and forced her to face him. "Isn't he?"

Max's hold on my arm had become like a vise grip, and for a moment I thought he was going to leap onto the stage and deck Langston. I grabbed the back of Max's shirt, whispering for him to calm down, but just then Mike said something that made the crowd cheer. At the same time, Juliana's refusals had gotten to Langston, and he started shaking her.

"Where is he? Is he with the rest?" Langston demanded. "Tell me now!"

Juliana looked over her shoulder and scanned the crowd, then she indicated an area about thirty feet behind us, more toward the center of the stage. "There," she said. "Behind the people holding the banner."

Langston released Juliana as he barked orders to the guards, so abruptly that she fell to her hands and knees. Max reached forward, as if he was going to help her up, but Juliana shook her head. "*Go now*," she mouthed, then rolled out of the way as Peacekeepers leapt off the stage and into the crowd.

Langston had taken over the microphone and was ordering everyone to remain calm, despite the fact that Peacekeepers were detaining everyone within a twenty-foot radius of that banner. Taking what might be our only chance, Max and I slipped out of the audience amidst the ensuing uproar, and once we found an alley, we portaled back to the Whispering Dell, this time to the edge of the manor's gardens. As soon as we were safe in the Otherworld, my mouth started running.

"I can't believe she saw us," I muttered. "So much for your fancy disguises." Max snorted. "And she just *had* to say your name."

"She also distracted them," Max pointed out. "She gave us time to get out of there." Now I snorted. Since I didn't want to discuss any possibly noble acts committed by Juliana, I changed the subject.

"Is that really what they think Elementals do?" I demanded. "Run around kidnapping Mundane women, making little Elemental babies?"

"It's one of Mike's scare tactics," Max answered. "Sometimes, he accuses us of stealing all the good jobs, all the good food... You know, whatever people are upset about, he blames on Elementals."

"Like we have nothing better to do than be his lousy scapegoats." Max grunted in agreement, and we walked in silence for a time, which was just as well. I still couldn't get the image of gaunt, sickly-looking Juliana out of my mind. Or what Mike had insinuated.

"Hey, do you think Juliana really was sleeping with an Elemental?" I asked suddenly.

"Didn't you hear Mike? He said she was."

"Better an Elemental than shacking up with a Peacekeeper," I continued. "And that Langston, what a creep. What could she possibly see in him?" I recalled the guys Juliana had dated in the past; all of them had been athletic jock types. She never would have fallen for some nerdy creep like Langston. Then again, I was pretty sure that she hadn't been dating Elementals while we both worked at REES. Although, the way Langston had yelled at her, treating her like she was his property rather than his partner, made me think he wasn't exactly in love, either. And Max seemed to think that she was being punished…

"I wonder who knocked her up," I mumbled.

Max stopped short. "What?"

"You heard Mike," I explained. "He said that Juliana was ruined. When a girl gets pregnant and doesn't get married, they say she's ruined."

Max was staring at me, eyes wide and brows nearly touching. "I…I have never heard that expression."

I shrugged. "I guess it's not that outdated." Max nodded, and we resumed walking.

"Hey," I asked suddenly. "Was Juliana getting it on with one of the Elementals at the Institute?"

"Leave it, Sara," he warned. I noticed his clenched jaw, his hands balled into fists. Both signs meant that Max knew much more than he was telling.

"She was!" I squealed. "Did you know him? Was it an air man? Or water?"

Max stopped just ahead of me and spoke over his shoulder. "Honestly, I know nothing about Juliana being with any air or water Elementals."

He walked off toward the orchards, which is where he retreated to when he wanted some alone time. It was typical Max; he willingly thrust himself into all these volatile situations, but he couldn't admit how shaken up he got. I mean, it was nothing to be ashamed of; anyone would feel a little off after being surrounded by thousands of people calling for your head on a platter.

Since I wanted to give Max time to decompress, I went inside. To my surprise and relief, Micah was back from the Golden Court, safe and sound.

"I missed you," he murmured as he folded me into his arms. "I take for granted that you will always be here, waiting for me when I return."

"You didn't miss me nearly as much as I missed you," I mumbled into his shoulder. "Did you talk to Oriana?"

"I did." Micah held me for a moment before he continued, one hand stroking my hair. "I asked her, bluntly, if she knew of anyone who might want the Ravens separated from others of copper. She countered by asking me what evidence I had. I then made the mistake of mentioning the boggart."

"Mistake?"

"It seems that our queen is not fond of boggarts. She immediately ordered her guards to search the court, to ensure none of the creatures were skulking about." I felt Micah's shoulders quiver and tipped my head back. He was desperately trying not to laugh.

"The Gold Queen is frightened of boggarts?" You'd waste less energy being scared of wallpaper, most of the time. I raised my eyebrows, and that was more than enough to set Micah's laughter free.

"She went so far as to stand on her throne, as if one would bite her toes," he said. I laughed with him then, at the image of the crazy queen squealing at shadows.

"Suffice it to say," he continued, wiping his eyes, "I did not learn much this afternoon. However, what I observed leads me to believe that Oriana is not at the center of a plot against you."

Yeah, she was the wrong sort of crazy to be an evil mastermind. After a few more comments at our gracious queen's expense, Micah asked me where I'd been earlier.

"I went to the Mundane realm, with Max." I hadn't meant to just blurt it out, but my words came out in a rush, faster than I could check them. In a short time I'd told Micah everything, from the press of the crowd, to how they had shouted for all Elementals to be imprisoned or banished, to Uncle Mike's speech about Elemental babies. I even mentioned how Juliana had been on stage beside him, a haggard shadow of her former self. I left out how Max and I were spotted, and how Juliana might have helped us escape.

"It's bad, Micah. Really bad." We'd made it as far as the kitchens, and the silverkin served us tea and quiche, along with a side of grapes. How I loved these little guys. "I mean, there's always been anti-Elemental factions, but not like this. This hasn't happened since the wars ended."

"Do you think this is related to what you did at the Institute?" Micah asked.

"It must be," I replied. "How, I don't know, but it must be." I left out that Juliana's punishment, whatever it was, also seemed to be my fault. Now, I'm not saying she didn't deserve it, but we were friends once (well, *I* was *her* friend), and for a long time, at that. Sometimes, you just can't help the guilt.

"You and your family must be much more important to your government than you realize," Micah said softly. I began to protest, but he continued, "Your sister is the Inheritor; you and Max are powerful in your own right. Maeve—"

"They don't know about Mom," I interjected. "No one did, except for Dad. He didn't even tell Meme Corbeau." Hell, Mom's own kids hadn't even known about her royal status until recently.

"Then it is you, Baudoin's children," Micah said. "Your government wants the three of you found, and, from what you have told me, they will exhaust their resources to do so."

For a long time, I was silent. First I examined a fingernail; then I picked at the table's edge, and ended up staring into the bottom of my teacup. All the while, my mind was churning with the life I once knew in the Mundane realm, coupled with what Uncle Mike wanted the world to be.

A world with no place for Elementals.

A world with no place for me.

"We can't let him get elected," I said at last. "He'll ruin everything. For all of us."

Micah grabbed my cold fingers and squeezed. "We won't."

19

As it turned out, our plans for overthrowing the Peacekeepers would have to wait, since the next few days at the Silverstrand house were spent in preparation for Oriana's debut. While "debut" wasn't exactly the proper Otherworldly term, I thought it fit the situation quite well. I suppose I could have called it a coming-out party, but Oriana didn't strike me as a Southern belle. Although I once had a coworker who had told stories about his wacky Southern aunt, who used to sit on the front porch, rain or shine, drinking beer and yelling at the songbirds for making a ruckus. That, I could see Oriana doing.

One of Micah's and my biggest worries was abated when Sadie readily agreed to attend. Even better, Max was fine with staying home. We probably could have kept Max out of trouble for the evening, or at least pretended that we didn't know him, but I don't think even Micah was suave enough to explain away the lack of the Metal Inheritor's presence. Being that Sadie was finally starting to make an effort here in the Otherworld, I guessed I'd have to pick up something nicer than the fairy necklace for her birthday.

As most girls do, I've always very much enjoyed the occasional fancy dress party. For this event, I had the silverkin fashion me an emerald silk gown, not of the flimsy stuff but of the sort of heavy fabric one would use for draperies. These gatherings tended to occur in ancient stone halls, full of drafts and devoid of centralized heating, and I didn't want to spend the entire party shivering away.

In addition to staving off chills, my outfit was also pretty damn fine. It looked like the silverkin really had paid attention to the fashion magazines I'd brought over from the Mundane realm. My gown had a long, draped skirt *sans* petticoats and was topped with tight sleeves and a fitted bodice. And, since I now knew that it was customary to incorporate one's element into one's attire for these sort of events, I'd gone all out. I'd coaxed a length of copper to outline my torso and decidedly scandalous décolletage. More copper twined through my upswept hair, and my shoes were delicate copper platforms attached to ribbons that wound up my calves, vine-like, to my knees.

Once I—and Shep—was satisfied with my appearance, I stepped out of my chambers and found my little sister waiting for me in the hallway.

Sadie, who loved dressing up almost as much as she loved books, had chosen a sunflower-hued silk gown edged in stiff white lace and, of course, copper. Delicate copper filigrees cascaded over her arms and shoulders, covering her back and rising to a high, wide collar. A delicate copper tiara set with citrine wound through her hair; truly, she looked the part of the Metal Inheritor. She was so beautiful, I bet she would even outshine Oriana.

"If only I can act like the Inheritor as well," she said when I complimented her metalwork. "Should you be wearing a metal other than copper?" she asked, indicating Micah's token nestled in my cleavage.

"I think it'll be okay," I mumbled. Removing the delicate silver chain hadn't occurred to me, but Sadie had a point. "I guess I'll find out when we get there." After all, I could always take it off.

We descended to the front hall, and I nearly lost my footing at the sight of Micah. My Micah. He was wearing a coat of woven silver cloth over a black silk tunic and pants, and black leather boots, his wickedly sharp blade at his side. As always, his mass of silver hair had resisted all attempts at taming and floated around his pointy ears like an earthbound cloud.

"My Sara," he greeted, taking my hands. "By far, you are the loveliest vision that has ever graced my eyes." He twirled me around, and as his arm stretched, I saw the copper cuff on his wrist.

"You're wearing it," I murmured, touching the token that proclaimed Micah as mine. "I worried I shouldn't have another metal on me." Micah's brow quirked, then he moved my token aside and pressed a kiss to my cleavage. My breath caught, and I flushed from the roots of my hair to my toes, only to flush further at the sound of a throat clearing.

"Real classy," Max smirked. I'd been so intent on Micah, I hadn't even noticed that Max and Mom were also in the room.

"Leave them be," Mom said, stepping forward to arrange the tendrils that always seemed to escape my hair, no matter how many clips and pins I used. "Can't you see that he loves her?"

At that, Micah's cheeks darkened, but he didn't miss a beat. "It's true, Max," he murmured, reclaiming me from Mom's hairdressing attempts. "I've lost my heart to your enchanting sister. I only hope she'll give me hers in return."

He was grave at the end, and I wondered what he really meant. Wasn't it obvious that I loved him? I mean, I was here in the Otherworld with him, living in his house, traipsing to all these ridiculous events with him. Then his hand brushed my belly, and I understood his meaning all too well. Before I could think of anything not too horrible to say, Sadie piped up.

"That's great that you two are all sloppy over each other, but can we go now?" she asked. "I'd like to get this over with."

If Micah was offended by my lack of response, he made no mention of it. After saying our goodbyes to

Mom and Max and extracting a solemn oath from my brother to not leave the manor until we returned, along with another oath from Mom to keep the silverkin in one piece, we were on our way.

Earlier, Sadie had agreed to travel to the Golden Court along the metal pathways as Micah and I normally did, which was a relief. While I'd done all I could to make my copper shoes comfortable, high-heeled metal footwear was not meant for extensive walking. Besides, shouldn't the Inheritor of Metal make use of one of her basic abilities? In my opinion, that was a firm yes.

The metal pathway carried the three of us along, swift as a river bursting from the spring thaw, and in a short time we arrived at the Golden Court amidst other Elemental dignitaries. The entrance to the court was packed with Elementals, metal and otherwise. The first person I recognized was Ayla, the Inheritor of Fire. She was tall and slender, her lithe form swathed in rich crimson and orange silks that paled in comparison to her red, red hair. Close behind her was Old Stoney, who had granite plates affixed to his clothing like some kind of Paleolithic armor. He didn't notice our arrival, being that he was leering at Ayla with barely-concealed lust.

"Why are the metals all pure elements, but earth isn't?" I asked Micah. Something—let's be honest, *many* things—bothered me about Old Stoney, and I thought I'd just figured one of them out. "I mean, granite is made up of feldspar and quartz, but I don't hear about any brass or pewter elementals."

"At times, I think you look for strife where none exists," Micah murmured. Normally I would have been offended by the obvious brush-off, but the combination of Micah's amused smile and his hand firmly pressed against the small of my back placated me. That, and I couldn't risk an argument with one of the only two allies I knew I had in the Golden Court. Gods willing, a few others would step forward, and soon.

We gained entry, and once again I marveled at the beauty of the Golden Court. If anything, it glowed even more brightly than it had during my previous visit, the golden walls and floor so shiny it seemed like we were standing inside the sun. I looked upward and saw that the roof had been retracted, filling the hall with even more golden light. I squinted at the clouds and hoped it wouldn't rain.

"The queen can't afford a roof?" Sadie quipped. "Can't she just hock a couple gold lampshades or forks to get a few bundles of shingles?"

I laughed despite Micah's quelling glare, and the three of us entered the main hall. It was enormous, far larger than the room Oriana had received Micah and me in for our lunch date. The walls and floor were gold, as I'd expected, but that was where the queen's metal ended. Chandeliers of cut crystal hung from the arched ceiling, with matching sconces on the walls. Between the sconces hung solid crimson panels of fabric edged in swags of pearls and sparkling gems, and a matching carpet led up a set of steps to what I assumed would be Oriana's throne. I, who had become accustomed to the opulence of the Silverstrand manor, gasped at the wealth before me.

Before I could truly appreciate my surroundings, the other lords and ladies of silver arrived and nearly swarmed Micah in their adoration of him. I hadn't realized how many others of silver there really were, having only seen a few in the Whispering Dell. But here they were, at least fifty of them, each and every one of them nobility in their own right, and Micah's loyal subjects.

They clustered around him, and I automatically stepped aside. Micah wasn't about to let me hide, not this time anyway, and grabbed my hand.

"For those of you who were not yet aware that I have taken a consort," Micah said, drawing me beside him, "I present to you my beloved, Sara Corbeau."

Those of silver turned as one, and dozens of silver eyes gave me the same quizzical, sweeping gaze that I got from all the rest. They took in my copper hair, and that my belly was flat. A few females sniffed indignantly, murmuring to each other that they'd have birthed an heir or two by now; others commented upon the Lord of Silver taking up with a Raven. However, since I was just a consort, most of the crowd resumed fawning over the Lord of Silver, ignoring me in the process.

I didn't mind, really. At these sorts of events I preferred to remain in the background and observe, and the perfect time to do so was while Micah interacted with his subjects. Those of silver seemed truly devoted to him, so much so that they were constantly looking out for his interests.

But where were others of copper? The ones who had sent me gifts, the ones who saw Max and Sadie and me as leaders? Micah had assured me that Oriana hadn't ordered those of copper to keep their distance from us, but that didn't explain the lack of a copper presence here at the Golden Court; Micah had said that all of metal were to pledge themselves to Oriana. So, why would all those of copper ignore a directive from their queen? If I was a betting woman (and I wasn't, thanks to all the times Max had gotten beaten up), I would bet that they *had* been ordered not to appear.

If I was completely honest with myself, I'd been hoping to see at least a few copper Elementals here, thus proving my suspicions against the queen wrong. That, and right now I could really use a few friends. Their absence made me feel both wrong about the queen, and wrong about having any allies.

Somehow, someday, I am going to get something right.

"Who is that?" I heard someone ask, indicating Sadie. "Our lord has two consorts?"

"No," was the reply amidst knowing laughter, "she is the consort's sister, the Inheritor of Metal."

"Why doesn't Lord Silverstrand take the Inheritor as his consort, then?" asked the first. "It would be a wise move, what with Greymalkin again making his presence known."

"Yes, that certainly would be shrewd," the second stated. "Shrewd, indeed."

There was a small chorus of agreement, and it was all I could do not to run screaming from the hall. Remembering Oriana's advice, I mustered what little grace I had, turned on my heel, and walked toward the nearest door, which led me to a small, enclosed courtyard, the high walls creating a gloom that matched my mood. I sank down onto one of the benches, fully intending to hide for the rest of the evening.

I'd just gotten settled when I heard the door open and softly close, then Micah's arms were around me. I leaned my head on his shoulder, waiting for him to ask why I was out here all alone, but he didn't. After a time I sighed and told him anyway.

"They don't like me," I whispered.

"Who doesn't?"

"Your people. Those of silver." I fingered the edge of his silver coat. "They think you're wasting your time with me."

"I don't care what they think," Micah said.

"They think you'd be better off with Sadie, since she's the Inheritor and I'm a nobody."

"I don't care what they think," Micah repeated. He moved to look into my eyes, holding my chin so I couldn't evade him. "Do you hear me? *I do not care*. I love you, my Sara, and that is all that matters."

"But, your people—"

"I love them too, but I have only ever bestowed a token on one person," he murmured, tracing the silver chain about my throat. "Only you."

"You never had a consort before me?" I asked, a bit bewildered.

"It is not a situation that one enters into lightly," he replied.

"I thought that was what royalty did, take consorts and…such."

Micah's brow furrowed. "You thought this was a temporary arrangement?"

"Um, yes."

Micah sighed, then buried his face in his hands. His shoulders trembled, I thought with anger at his useless, stupid consort. Then he raised his head, laughter creasing his features, and reached inside his fancy silk shirt. He withdrew a few items, small and dull, like little pebbles. "Do you remember these?"

I squinted in the dark, my breath catching as I recognized the three pennies I'd given him that day before the Lovers' Pine. "You kept them?"

"Of course. They were the first things you'd ever given me, freely and without expectation." He dropped them into my palm, then tightly closed my hand around them. "At the time, I hoped they were given with love."

"They were," I murmured. Though I hadn't realized it at the time, I'd fallen fast and hard for my silver elf. "I thought they weren't good enough for you. That's why I made you the cuff."

"They were—they *are*—perfect. But the cuff is nice too." We laughed at that, then Micah reclaimed the pennies and slipped them once more against his heart. "You see, my love, I have never considered us to be anything but permanent. As soon as you are with child, you will be my wife. My only wife," he added, pressing a kiss to my temple.

I so did not want to have the baby talk here, so I opted for a drastic subject change. "Your people, they were also talking about Old Stoney hanging around again. What's that all about?"

Micah's face clouded. "He was Ferra's lover."

Those two? Oh, ick. "Does that mean he helped the iron bitch capture Oriana?"

"Yes. He is now embroiled in the arduous task of begging for her forgiveness." Micah smoothed back my hair. "Do you understand?"

"About Stoney?"

"About us."

I sighed; that was all the subject change I was going to get out of him. I took his hand onto my lap, pushing up his sleeve and tracing the copper cuff he wore. It was my first real experiment with the metalwork that was my birthright, not to mention my first real defiance of the Peacekeepers. Oh, sure, I'd done little things, like rig up my Picture Vision to watch prewar movies and cut the government tracker out of my arm, but those were different. They had been nothing but petty acts of defiance, a child thumbing her nose at her elders. The magic I'd used to make the cuff was real defiance, defiance that could have gotten me killed, or worse. And I'd done it all for him. What's more, I'd do it all again, that and more.

"I understand that I love you, and I will rip to pieces anyone who stands between us," I said softly. "More than anything, Micah, I am yours."

He kissed me then, with far more passion than I imagined was normally seen in the Gold Queen's courtyard. After a few more moments of calm happiness, I said the other terrible thing that was on my mind.

"Micah, there's no one of copper here."

His arms tensed around me. "I know."

We didn't discuss it further, being that if Oriana, or someone close to her, really was ordering others of copper to stay clear of the Corbeaus, her courtyard during a gala event wasn't really the ideal place to examine her motivations. Micah kissed me once more, then we returned to the hall stuffed full of non-copper Elementals. Instantly my eyes landed on Old Stoney, who was hitting on my sister.

"Sadie!" I exclaimed, having crossed the floor in record time. Maybe copper shoes are made for speed. "I've been looking for you!" I plastered a giant grin across my face, alternately staring at her and Stoney.

"Have you?" Sadie countered, her irritation at being abandoned plain. "Grey here has been nice enough to keep me company while you two were wandering off."

"Grey? Oh, yes. He knew Ferra, you know." Old Stoney's face went stone cold, pardon the pun. I found that I liked irritating him, so I babbled on, "Yes, they were great friends. Allies, even. Do you know our father, Grey? A copper man by the name of Baudoin Corbeau?"

Old Stoney responded by trying to eviscerate me with his eyes. When that failed, he offered Sadie a shallow bow. "Good evening," he muttered, then he stalked off to other rocky sorts.

"Do you think he knows what happened to Dad?" Sadie whispered.

"Very little about him would surprise me," Micah replied, joining the two of us. "He is a devious man, loyal to no one. Ah," he said, nodding toward the dais, "our queen has arrived."

I followed Micah's gaze, and indeed Oriana was ascending the dais to her throne, looking like nothing so much as a fairy-tale queen. I remembered that cold morning three months past when she was hauled out of the oubliette; she'd been shrouded in darkness for so long she had been practically blind and had snapped and clawed at her rescuers like a feral beast. Since the gold had been stripped from her body after her capture, restoring her element was crucial to her recovery, physically as well as mentally. To my horror, the newly-free Oriana had been immediately bound immobile with golden chains and a cairn of gold built above her.

At first, I'd thought such actions foolish. How could a heap of metal cure one's crazed state, and wouldn't she suffocate? Well, cure her it had, as was well evidenced by the graceful being before me. Oriana's golden hair was loose, cascading down her back in heavy waves, her blue eyes reflecting the same sun-colored hue. Her arms and shoulders were bare, showcasing her mark from her golden fingers to the spiraling tendrils that glinted on her shoulders. Of course, Oriana wore her element in her clothing, her choice being a golden breastplate over a deep crimson skirt.

"She's so beautiful," Sadie murmured. "I used to think Mom was of gold, what with her hair."

"Me too." I squeezed Sadie's hand, and Micah escorted the two of us as we navigated amongst the other Elementals. It was quite the daunting task, since everyone wanted to make the Metal Inheritor's acquaintance, toast her good health, and offer her their assistance in whatever tasks she might need. Imagine their surprise when all she asked for was donations to her nascent library.

Those who weren't immediately enamored with Sadie desired a few moments of Micah's time, inquiring about matters of silver politics that I hadn't even been aware of. Apparently, the Whispering Dell was one of the richest communities in the Otherworld, due in no small part to Micah's management of the land and its resources. I'd known that Micah was wealthy, but I'd never appreciated just how wealthy, or that Micah was what we in the Mundane world would call a shrewd businessman. While Micah talked shop, and Sadie talked books, I stood there with a smile on my face and tried to stay out of the way.

After an endless barrage of politics and well-wishers, and my cheeks aching from holding on to my false smile, an excited murmur rolled across the hall. Naturally, all eyes turned toward the queen. Upon the dais, Oriana rose from her throne, her golden breastplate melting away. With a flick of her wrists, her golden nails elongated and became ten wickedly sharp blades. Another flick, and she slashed herself above her heart. Sadie gasped and grabbed my hand while I tried to retain enough composure for both of us.

"What's going on?" I asked Micah.

"It is time to pledge ourselves to our queen," he replied, loosening his shirt to expose his chest. I watched those closest to Oriana and discerned what sort of a pledge this was. Each supplicant approached the queen, also with a bared breast, and those golden nails slashed above the supplicant's heart. Oriana touched her own breast, then her subject's, thereby creating a blood bond with her people. As far as Otherworldly ceremonies went, this was a piece of cake.

"I can't do it," Sadie said.

"It'll only be a minute," I soothed. "No one's going to see you."

"It's not that," she said, taking a step backward. "The blood…all that blood."

"Sadie." She looked at me, her brown eyes full of irrational fear. "You must. You're the Inheritor."

"I won't," she whispered, though it was still loud enough for all those nearby to hear.

"What's the matter?" growled Old Stoney. He had fully opened his robe, showing off his gigantic stone member as it knocked against his thigh. "Afraid we won't keep our hands to ourselves?"

"Speak to my consort, or her sister, in such a way again," Micah said, putting himself between the moronic boulder and us, "and I *shall* take issue." While Old Stoney was still too incensed to reply, Micah turned to Sadie and me.

"Sadie, stand between Sara and me," he instructed. "We shall pledge our queen as one."

Sadie insisted that she couldn't do it, but Micah was unrelenting and practically dragged her through the throng of Elementals. The crowd parted for the three of us, murmuring of the implications of the Silver Lord and Metal Inheritor approaching the queen together. We were doing well, walking with our heads held high and not noticeably dragging Sadie, until we stood at the foot of the dais. At the sight of Oriana's naked blood-smeared breasts, Sadie squeezed her eyes shut and pressed her face against

Micah's shoulder. Only his arm about her waist kept her from running. Micah and I shared a look, then we locked hands behind Sadie's back and hauled her up the steps.

"This...this child, she is the Inheritor of Metal?" Oriana inquired, taking in the sight of the three of us as we knelt before her. Sadie was curled against Micah's side, protecting her breast as if Oriana sought her heart, not a few drops of blood.

"Forgive her, my queen," Micah murmured. "She is young yet, new to our world and not accustomed to our ways. My consort and I will pledge ourselves now, of course."

At that, I lowered my bodice and allowed Oriana to cut me between my breasts, much as Oriana had done to herself. She performed the movements of creating the blood bond like an automaton, first to me, and then to Micah, devoid of all emotion or comprehension. Where was the vibrant if unstable woman I'd lunched with? Where was the inappropriate touching, the insane commentary? I ventured a glance directly at her eyes and saw that they were clouded, lacking their typical warm glow.

Had someone drugged her? Before I could alert Micah to my suspicions, Oriana cast a wary glance at the throngs waiting to bleed for her and visibly swallowed. She wasn't drugged, far from it. She was terrified.

My righteous indignation flowed away, replaced by no small amount of pity. "Perhaps, if it so pleases you, my sister may pledge herself to you once she is recovered?" I ventured. Stiffly, Oriana turned to regard me, her head cocked to the side in one of her odd, birdlike mannerisms.

"Yes. That would please me." Oriana reached toward my trembling sister, first resting her golden fingers on Sadie's chin, then trailing them down her neck and breast, leaving a violent red ribbon in their wake. "I only hope it won't be too late."

I nodded, both appreciating that Oriana had given us a warning and terrified that she'd felt the need to do so. One thing was certain—I needed to convince Sadie to play nice with the rest of the Elementals, and the sooner the better.

20

After the near-debacle of Sadie's outright refusal to swear fealty to the queen, we left the Golden Court as soon as we could shove our way out the door. Due to Sadie's position sandwiched between Micah and me, it seemed that no one, save the three of us and the Gold Queen herself, had realized that the Inheritor of Metal hadn't completed her oath to serve Oriana, probably because the queen's bloodied fingers had left a noticeable red stain on Sadie's neck and breast. At least, no one had made mention of any lack of pledging on Sadie's part within our hearing.

Instead of levying accusations of indifference or worse, treason, as the three of us descended from the dais we were pelted with comments and well-wishes, along with invitations to dinners and dances and all sorts of glorious rendezvous. Well, Micah and Sadie were pelted; I might as well have been carrying the bags.

"It was like no one even saw me," I grumbled. Once we'd returned to the manor, Sadie had gone off to boil herself in a bath, while Micah and I removed our formal attire and washed up in a much calmer fashion. Since we'd left directly after the pledging ceremony, it wasn't even time for dinner, and Micah had promised me another lesson in swordplay before nightfall. "And where were the others of copper?"

"We left quite early; perhaps they arrived afterward," Micah murmured. He paused to dab a bit of ointment on the cut above my heart. "And, love, when an invitation is extended to me, it is naturally assumed that my consort shall accompany me."

"Assumed." You know what happens when…I shook my head, unwilling to explain why that was such a bad idea. I pulled on a T-shirt and sat on the bed in order to tie my shoes. "So, I'm expected to just follow you everywhere? Because that's what consorts do?"

"If you do not wish to attend a particular event, you may remain in the Dell," Micah replied. "No one is forcing you to attend any functions, Sara."

I don't know what was more irritating—Micah's blasé attitude or the fact that I really did want to go to at least some of the parties. I just wanted to be more than arm candy. "If I was your wife I bet I'd get my own invitations," I pouted.

"Most likely," Micah agreed, "but that has not happened yet." Oh, yeah? I'll make it happen. I stood and grabbed the coverlet, shoving half of it into my shirt.

"See?" I turned to the side, showcasing my falsely burgeoning belly. "Wife here. Now people will pay attention to me, too."

"This," Micah murmured, stepping forward, "is unnecessary." He withdrew the wadded-up coverlet, then smoothed down my shirt. "Soon enough, your belly will swell."

"Micah." I grabbed his hand, but I couldn't manage to say anything further. When he spied a certain blue glass bottle on my dressing table, it turned out that I didn't have to.

"Is this something new?" he asked, picking up the unfamiliar bauble, his eyes widening as he read the label. "Sara, where did this come from?"

"I bought it. In the village." I dropped my eyes; even though I hadn't done anything wrong—hell, I hadn't even uncorked it yet—it felt like the bottle's very presence was a betrayal.

"Have you taken any?" he asked quickly.

"No." He blew out a relieved breath, and I tried not to wince.

"Sara, my Sara," Micah murmured, gathering me into his arms. "Please, love, you must be more careful. Whoever sold this to you did not explain its true purpose."

Micah—trusting, genuine Micah—assumed that I'd bought the extract because it smelled nice, or because the bottle's color was pretty. "I know what it's for."

"Sara—"

"I don't want a baby," I said in a rush. At that his entire body drooped, and I regretted my words. No, no I didn't; the truth is better. More painful, but better. At least, that's what they say.

Who are *they*, anyway?

"Not ever?" Micah asked softly, his hand cupping the nape of my neck. I felt the disappointment in his voice; truly, Micah's strongest, most heartfelt desire was for an heir.

"I…Micah, I'm so young. And we really haven't really known each other for very long. And—" He turned up my chin, and I met those silver eyes. "Not never, but not now. Not for a long time, probably." Micah sighed and leaned his forehead against mine. "I'll go. We'll all get out of your hair—"

"My hair?"

Right. "My family. We won't trouble you anymore."

"Sara, you do not trouble me," he murmured. "Max is troubling, yes, and your mother may yet be the death of me. But you," he threaded his fingers through my hair, his eyes searching mine, "the only trouble you give me is when we're apart, and I can't see to the tasks before me."

"Why can't you?"

"Because I can't stop thinking about you."

"Oh." When we were apart I thought about him constantly, too—what he could be doing, if he would laugh at this or that, when he would be home. When he would hold me again. Max and Sadie both thought that our closeness was unusual, unhealthy even, but I didn't. To me, nothing had ever felt so right as being with Micah. "But if you can't have an heir…"

I couldn't finish, not while he was staring at me like that. I'd had this conversation in my head a hundred—no, a thousand—times, and I knew exactly how it ended—me leaving the manor, off to fend for myself in the Mundane world. Oh, wait, I couldn't go back there, so I guessed I would just be homeless here in the Otherworld.

But when I had mentally rehearsed these conversations, Micah hadn't looked at me as if his heart was breaking.

"Micah," I began, knotting my fist in his shirt. Before I could continue, a silverkin appeared out of frickin' nowhere, chattering away like mad. After a few moments, I learned that Max, who had gone out the moment we'd returned, was back, and he was a bit the worse for wear. Micah nodded toward the silverkin, muttering under his breath about my inconsiderate fool of a brother. I moved to follow the little guy, but I was captured in Micah's arms.

"You are not trouble," Micah said, grasping the token I wore. "You are mine, and you will remain so. Mine," he repeated, this time kissing me hard for added emphasis. He abruptly released me, and we went downstairs to see what sort of trouble Max had gotten into this time.

21

We found Max seated at the head of the dining room table, bruised and bloodied with his feet propped up, muddy boots and all, slurping coffee. The long table had been polished to a glasslike shine... emphasis on the "had been." Good gods, we'd been gone all of two hours, which meant that Max had been away from the manor for *less* than two hours, yet he couldn't manage to stay out of trouble for that extremely short amount of time. I had a strong suspicion that, if Micah wasn't already done with Max's nonsense, he would be now.

If I hadn't been trailing a step or two behind Micah, I wouldn't have noticed the muscles in his shoulders tighten when he saw Max's deplorable state, or the abrupt way he halted when he saw my brother's filthy, disrespectful pose. Somehow, despite his anger, Micah kept his voice calm when he spoke.

"Remove your feet from my table," Micah said. "Now."

Max opened his mouth, probably to finally utter the words that would cause Micah to throw him out once and for all, but he never got the chance to speak. Two of the silverkin yanked Max's chair backward, his feet hitting the floor with such force that coffee splattered all over him. Shep, who was even less of a fan of boots on the table than Micah, began wiping up the muddy mess while ignoring Max.

"Hey," Max said, trying to get Shep's attention, "can I get a refill? Or a towel?" It was only when Shep bustled off to the kitchen that Micah continued his interrogation.

"Whose property have you destroyed this time, Max?" Okay, Micah was a bit condescending, but Max had earned it. The last brawl Max had gotten himself into had cost Micah a prized orchard in recompense, and the damage from the most recent incident with iron warriors had been considerable. "Or was the fight here, and only my home has been damaged?"

"There's nothing for you to worry about," Max grumbled. "I was down at the tavern. We were throwing dice, and it got out of hand. It's fine now."

"We?" Micah asked.

"We." Max and Micah stared at each other, each of them refusing to give ground. Just when I'd had enough of this macho pissing contest, Mom and Sadie entered, the former carrying a bowl of water, the latter clean cloths.

"Whoever this 'we' is," Mom said, wetting a cloth and dabbing at a gash over Max's eyebrow, "you'd do best to avoid them. As strong as you are in the Mundane world, there are forces here you would not like to tangle with. Believe me, I know." Max snorted but wisely held his tongue. "If you insist upon gambling, you should employ a guard to accompany you."

"Ma, I'm not a kid," Max said. "I've been going to the market alone since I was twelve!" At that, Mom dropped the cloth. Too late, Max realized his error.

"Market?" Sadie asked innocently.

"Yes, Max, what market?" Mom prompted. Max visibly swallowed the lump in his throat; my brother might be reckless and irresponsible, but he knew better than to let a direct question from Mom go unanswered.

"The Goblin Market," he mumbled. Sadie gasped, Mom squeezed her eyes shut, and I moved toward the safety of Micah.

"Please, explain to us why you found the need to patronize the Goblin Market at the tender age of twelve?" Mom demanded as she opened her eyes, holding Max in that gaze we all knew far too well. While that look remained, lying was *not* an option. Max opened and closed his mouth like a fish, unsure what, if anything, would salvage him after such an outburst. Little did he know that Micah would be the one revealing his secrets.

"Likely, that was where he met with Baudoin," Micah said. Slowly, Mom rose to her feet, her head swiveling around so that the murderous gaze was now fixed on Micah. My elf was no longer the safest person in the room.

"What do you know of Beau?" Mom ground out. Behind her, Sadie sat heavily, gripping the table's edge for support.

"Max has told us that he was in regular contact with Baudoin after the wars," Micah replied, apparently unfazed by the fury boiling in Mom's eyes. He was either remarkably courageous or had taken a blow to the head. "As you are no doubt aware, Maeve, the Goblin Market is an excellent place to meet while concealing one's identity."

Mom bristled but let it go. "Is this true?" she demanded, turning back to Max.

"Yes."

I watched the emotions skate across Mom's face anger and outrage and, lastly, hope. I couldn't remember the last time hope shone in Mom's eyes. Then she stood, yanking Max to his feet by his collar.

"Ma," he began.

"I've heard enough from you," Mom cut off, before turning to the rest of us. "Don't just stand there gaping. Off to market we go."

We walked in silence, Mom's fury effectively muffling the sounds of our feet on the gravel path and, to an extent, the surrounding landscape. And since Mom had outright refused to travel by the metal pathways, it was taking forever to reach the Goblin Market on foot. Not that any of us were foolish enough to make that observation.

Max, the uncontested king of fools in both the Mundane and Otherworld, slunk along behind Mom, head hanging and shoulders hunched. Somehow, I resisted the urge to smack him. Barely. He could have told Mom about his meetings with Dad at any time since his rescue from the Institute, but no, he had been too busy with his harebrained plan to find Dad by gambling, boozing, and getting into public brawls. What was more, if Dad ever found out where and how Max had been spending his days, he'd probably box his ears.

And now, thanks to my idiot brother, we were trudging across the countryside, under the brightest, hottest sun imaginable, toward the Goblin Market. Everyone, Mundane or otherwise, knew about the market, where you could buy and sell anything, and I do mean *anything*. From roses bearing poisoned thorns to a past lover's still-beating heart, all could be had, so long as you had the coins to trade.

I shivered, realizing how much that description sounded like the Promenade Market I'd frequented in the Mundane world. I hoped that no one's head ended up on a pike today, especially mine.

Decapitation was far from my most pressing concern. Not only were we all about to sashay directly into this lair of evil, I didn't have the slightest idea what was going through Micah's head. Now he knew, in no uncertain terms, how I felt about babies, and he said that he still wanted me around, but... Don't get me wrong, Micah was no liar. If anything, he was painfully honest. However, I was also painfully aware of the importance the greater houses placed on heirs, and how Micah's lack of one was commonly discussed or, rather, ridiculed. Mind you, the Gold Queen didn't have any living heirs, but everyone overlooked that piece of trivia. Being a recently freed and somewhat insane ruler did have that advantage.

Come to think of it, I don't think Ferra had any heirs, either. What a turn of good fortune *that* was.

Micah, who I would swear was telepathic, chose that moment to wrap his arm about my waist. He didn't say anything, and neither did I; we just walked along, one form with four legs. I pressed myself against his side, loving the feel of him, hoping he wouldn't soon be lost to me because of my lack of maternal instincts.

Maybe I should have a baby, just one, just so I could stay with Micah. I mean, he was so good to me, and really, who else was ever going to put up with me? One baby wouldn't be so bad.

But what if he wanted more? What if I was a horrible mother, and he found someone else to care for his children? What if—?

"Sara," Micah murmured in my ear. "The dark magics of the market are affecting you. Do not allow them to take hold."

"Wha—?" I blinked and shrugged off the psychic weight I hadn't noticed a moment before. "How did you know?"

"I felt you tremble." He wiped away the tears that had streamed down my cheeks, and I burrowed further into his arms, now grateful for his warm solidity for a whole new reason. Before I could ask how much further until we reached this wretched place, and when could we leave it forever, Sadie spoke.

"Is—is that it?" she asked, pointing a shaky hand. We'd just crested one of the hills that formed the border of the Whispering Dell, and nestled in the valley below was a dark, obviously well-populated area. Even at that distance, I could sense the wrongness of it; it was filthy on more than just its surfaces, the taint ground in so deep that sunlight hardly penetrated between the walls. Strains of discordant music, along with shouts and wails and an oily black smoke, wafted toward us.

"Yes, that is the Goblin Market," Micah answered. I resisted the urge to hide behind him, but only just.

"I didn't think it would be so close," Sadie murmured. "I mean, we walked pretty far, but I didn't think the manor was within walking distance of such a place."

"Such places are always close by," Micah said softly. "You're just not the sort to look for them." Max shot Micah a glare, which Micah ignored.

"I've never gone looking for them, either," Max grumbled. "I was just meeting Dad."

"Why here?" Sadie pressed. "Why didn't he just come to the Raven Compound?"

"Yes, Max," Mom said, rounding on the rest of us, "please explain why this was the most convenient meeting place for the two of you." Max looked away, but Mom wasn't in a mood to let things drop. "And please enlighten me as to why my young son was the best emissary for such a task?"

"Well, who else was there?" Max retorted. Mom pursed her lips and turned away. Sadie's eyes widened.

"You mean you never told Mom that you saw Dad after the wars?" Sadie demanded.

"No," I murmured, "Max *and Dad* never told Mom."

Sadie gasped, her hand over her mouth. "Oh, Max," she murmured, "you really screwed up this time."

Max opened his mouth, only to clamp it shut again. Looking much like the kid he had been when he used to frequent the market, he approached Mom. After a bit of coaxing, she turned toward him, shaking her head and staring at her feet.

"I just don't understand," she said, over and over. "Why didn't he just contact me?"

"Because you would have moved heaven and earth to get him back," Max replied. "And that wouldn't have been safe for us, or for him."

"We could have kept him safe," Mom insisted. "I could have hidden him in the old basement or the *brugh*—"

"If he could have come home, he would have," Max replied. "Ma, Dad didn't have a lot of options, and none of them were good. It…" Max raked his hand through his hair, then he hugged her. "I'm sorry. I bet he's sorry, too."

"He will be, once I get hold of him," Mom muttered. Max smiled tightly; hopefully, we still had a father left for Mom to yell at.

"Okay, here's what you need to know," Max began when he turned to the three of us, leaving Mom to collect herself. She hung back for a minute, her blue eyes narrowed, staring at the dark mass of the market. As she stood there with her wind-tossed hair, she looked like an invading queen assessing the opposing army's weaknesses. In a way, I suppose that's exactly what she was doing. "When I came here before, I would just hang out in the square until someone approached me."

"I thought you were meeting Dad!" Sadie squeaked. "It was random people?"

"It was never the same person twice. They'd give me a sign, and I would follow them toward one of the shops—usually it was the carpet weaver, but a couple times we went to a sweet shop—and we would talk, but never for more than a few minutes."

"What about Dad?" I asked. "Did you ever see him?"

"Not all the time," Max replied. "During those last few months, I didn't see him at all. I just got messages, which I read and burned."

"How did you know it was your father who wrote those messages?" Micah asked. "Baudoin's enemies could have easily manipulated you."

"I know. That's why I stopped coming."

And why you let the Institute take you. I didn't say it out loud, but it was plain as day on Max's face.

"Then why are we coming here now?" Sadie asked, eyes darting toward a particularly chilling screech. "If you stopped hearing from Dad way back then, what makes you think he'll be here today?"

"This is the last place he was known to be," Mom said quietly. She rubbed her nose, then she tossed her golden hair over her shoulder. "We know he was here, or close by, after the war ended, for at least a few years. We'll start looking here. If we find no trace of him, we'll look someplace else. I will find my husband, of that you can be certain."

Based on the fire in her eyes, I believed her. So it was my mother who led us to the gates of the Goblin Market, which were little more than pale wooden planks crudely lashed together with blackened, fraying ropes; the haphazard construction was due to the market's need to uproot and flee at a moment's notice. Not that they were doing anything wrong, of course.

A set of ragged guards flanked the gates; no, "guard" wasn't really the right term. They were more like bouncers, the scary kind you only find outside the not quite legal hangouts. What's more, they didn't care if we were criminals or thugs, they just wanted to ensure we weren't there to shut them down. Being that they'd set up shop so close to the Whispering Dell, Micah could have ordered them to pull up stakes or had them apprehended and sent to Oriana for judgment. Since that wasn't what we wanted, at least not for now, Micah swept a hand over his hair, glamouring the distinctive silver to a rich brown, and the Lord of Silver passed unnoticed into the Goblin Market.

And what a market it was. To the left was a group of stalls that sold odd food items, and by odd I mean that some of the food was still moving, wriggling odd tentacles and limbs. To the right was a random collection of tents, stained with smoke and blood and who knows what else. The largest tent belched a thick reddish smoke whenever the flap was raised, along with a chorus of laughter and screams. While those entering the tent appeared healthy, those leaving were gray-skinned and frail, their eyes sunk deep in their skulls. What was worse, the not-yet-dead food and questionable goings-on in the tents and stalls were far from the creepiest aspects about this place.

Even though it was a bright, clear day, darkness hung like a chill blanket over the aisles and stalls. I couldn't put my finger in it, but there was a wrongness that seeped from every hawker. The evil permeating the Goblin Market was much stronger than anything I'd felt in the dark quarter of the Whispering Dell's village, and it made the crone at the apothecary seem like a fairy godmother.

We are so out of our league here.

"Why did you come here in the flesh?" Sadie whispered to Max. "Why didn't you just dreamwalk?"

"This is no place for dreamwalking," Max answered, nodding toward a nearby stall. Among the dried herbs and incense was a display of tightly capped containers, some made of fine crystal, others constructed out of badly thrown clay.

"Those are pretty," Sadie murmured. She tried to get a closer look, but Max grabbed her.

"Don't get any closer," he hissed. Sadie stared from the jars to Max, uncomprehending, but I instinctively knew what those jars were for. Souls.

"Later," Max grumbled when Sadie questioned what good a jarred soul would be. "The more you act like a dumb kid, the worse it'll be for you."

"I *am* a dumb kid," Sadie reminded him. "Remember, you and Mom kept all of this from me."

"With good reason," Mom said, indicating the Goblin Market with her gaze. "Would you have rather spent your youth hiding here, or in that library you so loved?" Sadie dropped her eyes; yeah, no one likes having the truth held from them, but sometimes it's done with good reason. "Max, where would you wait for Beau?"

"Here." We'd reached a fountain, so shiny and black it could have been carved from obsidian. The water, which had long since ceased flowing, was choked with slime and stank like a week-old corpse.

"All right, Maximilien Laurent." Mom surveyed the square; the fountain was the centerpiece of a common area, surrounded by somewhat permanent-looking shops. If the placards hadn't all been made from bleached bones and bloody skins, it would have been a nice spot for a picnic. "Sadie and I will watch from that shop," she declared, indicating a storefront across the way, "and Sara and Micah will take a post behind you. Once your contact approaches, go with them. We will follow."

With that, Mom turned on her heel and dragged Sadie toward the weaving shop, which I deduced from the shopkeeper's resemblance to a black widow. Once they were inside, I understood why Mom had chosen that shop: it had a large front window, affording them an excellent view of nearly all entrances to the square.

I murmured for Max to take care, and then followed Micah across the square. Instead of entering one of the shops, we took up a shadowy spot at the mouth of an alley, which was fine with me. I did not like this market, being that I was still engaged in a mental battle to keep the black magic from again reducing me to a quivering heap of self-doubt, and I wanted to be away from here as soon as possible. Once we'd found a good position, Micah's arm snaked around my waist, while his other hand grasped the token I wore.

"I worry that you still do not understand the meaning of this token," he whispered, holding the leaf and acorn before my eyes.

"It means that the oaks are your friends," I replied, trying to focus on Max. This was not the time or place for relationship discussions. Micah, however, had other ideas.

"By wearing my token, you proclaim to all that you are mine. My consort. My lover." He pressed a kiss behind my ear. "My equal."

"But I'm not your equal. I won't be, not until I'm your wife." He turned me around, tilting my chin up so he could look me in the eye.

"You will be, once—"

"An heir, I know." I couldn't look at him and keep my voice steady, so I stared at a point above his shoulder. "Not until then."

"Sara, I cannot alter the way of things. This has been our tradition for many, many generations." I nodded since I already knew these things. Really, I understood his predicament. It didn't mean that I had to like it. "You want to be my wife so badly?"

At that, I met his eyes. "Yeah. I do." Micah's eyes widened, and I feared I'd said something wrong. Like there was even a right thing to say. "I mean, it's just not what I'm used to. Humans get married before they have heirs. Children." Well, it didn't always work that way, but I decided to forgo a discussion on the ramifications of unplanned pregnancy. "I mean, if I got pregnant today, by the time I have the baby, we still wouldn't have known each other for a year."

"Thirteen months," Micah corrected.

"Still. That's not very long." Something behind me caught Micah's attention; I peeked over my shoulder and learned that it was just Max, throwing pebbles in the fountain. "And, it's not like I know anything about babies. I was only two when Sadie was born. I don't know how to feed one or bathe one." It was easier saying these things when Micah wasn't looking at me. "I wouldn't know what to do."

Micah tightened his arms about me, pressing his face against my hair. "Sara, my Sara, you will be a fine mother," he murmured. "Forgive me for not considering your customs."

"Forgiven." As if I could stay mad at him, anyway. After a quick kiss, I turned sideways in his arms so we could both keep an eye on Max.

"Humans marry before children?" he murmured, and I nodded. "Tell me how."

"Well, the easiest way is to go to your local Hall of Records and get a certificate. There's usually a Peacekeeper on duty who can perform the ceremony."

"These ceremonies, they are complex rituals?"

"No. You exchange rings and a few words and it's done." I went on, describing the basic ceremony, all the guests and food at the reception, and the huge, gaudy rings celebrities tended toward. Throughout my explanations Micah remained thoughtful, his eyes resting on Max while one hand stroked my neck, his other hand firm on my mark.

"Very well," Micah said when I was done. "We shall go to the Mundane realm, and I will exchange words with you."

"What?" I gasped.

"I will make you a ring, too," Micah continued, turning his eyes to mine. "A ring so large all will know that you are mine."

"I don't need a huge ring," I mumbled.

"Then a plain band."

"Micah, we can't go back to the Mundane realm," I argued weakly. "We're fugitives. We'll be captured."

"I'll glamour you."

"But—"

"Are you going to keep arguing with me, or are you going to say yes?"

I blinked, my last protest dying on my lips. I'd been so sure that Micah would cast me aside once he learned that I didn't want a baby just yet; all this time, I'd thought that an heir was his fondest desire. That desire, it seemed, was for me.

"I'll make you a ring, too," I whispered, pressing myself against his chest. "A heavy copper one, with oak leaves etched all around." I twined my arms around his neck. "Or is it not proper for Micah Silverstrand to wear a copper wedding ring?"

Before he could answer, movement caught his eye. Silently, Micah turned me around, and I saw Max conversing with another creature, their heads bent toward each other. The creature was short and stout, with waxy yellow skin that reminded me of a half-burned candle.

"Goblin?" I whispered, and I felt Micah nod.

"One of the enforcers," he breathed. "Has your brother always dealt with such unsavories?"

"Max thinks he *is* one of the unsavories," I replied, shaking my head at the sight of my scrawny brother trying to act tough. Well, since no one had bothered to kill him when he was a kid, he probably wouldn't get killed today.

"You father's reach must be far and strong," Micah observed. "Like as not, the enforcers have been ordered to leave Max be."

"I wonder if Max realizes that," I mused.

"Doubtful." Micah pressed his hand over my mouth to muffle my laughter. "Look, he's being led away."

Across the market, Mom and Sadie stepped out of the shop, brushing away a few stray webs in the process. The four of us exchanged a look, then we were off after my brother.

22

The four of us followed Max as he wended his way through the market. After a few minutes, the first goblin had melted into the crowd, and another took its place. This little replace the bad guy routine repeated itself until a grayish creature beckoned Max into a narrow stretch between stalls. He went, all but disappearing into the shadows.

"Max," Mom called, the rest of us close behind her. "Maximilien, do not—"

Then the world tilted, and everything went dark.

I was vibrating, slow and steady. Earthquake? Slowly, stickily, my eyes opened, and I learned that the vibration was caused by Micah. His hands were on my shoulders, and he was gently shaking me awake.

"Hey," I mumbled. I noticed the faint shimmer in Micah's eyes, a telltale sign of his dreamself. And, he was naked, an unexpected but not unpleasant development. "When did we go to bed?"

"We did not. We were captured."

"Captured?" For a moment, I thought he was joking. Not that he was being funny.

"Um, when did this happen?" I ventured. I felt like hardly any time had passed, but then I had been unconscious. "And who exactly captured us?"

"We were captured by whomever Max made contact with at the fountain. That was yesterday afternoon, and it is now two hours before dawn." Fountain, fountain... Dimly, I remembered a shiny black monstrosity, filled with stagnant, stinking water, and my brother standing before it. It felt like all of that nonsense had happened a thousand years ago. As I struggled to a sitting position, Micah put his hands on the sides of my head, his features creased with concern. "Are you well?"

"Yeah. I guess." I pressed my hand to my forehead; I wasn't in any pain, but I felt like I had the hangover of the century. "My brain's fuzzy."

"You are being drugged." Micah indicated an incense burner belching sweet smoke into the room, which explained my lack of both memory and consciousness. I mumbled something about putting it out, but Micah shook his head. "No. As long as the three of you remain here, you are safe."

Three of us? I turned around, and saw that myself, Sadie and Max were heaped upon a ridiculously ornate bed. It seemed that Micah wasn't the only one dreamwalking here. Then I took in the rest of the room; it was full of brightly colored cushions and drapes, bedecked with all sorts of tassels and fringe. And wouldn't you know it, not a speck of metal in sight. "Is this a harem?"

"More like a brothel."

Cold dread filled my stomach. "Micah, tell me why you're naked."

"I was stripped before being escorted to a cell," he replied, as nonchalantly as if describing checking his coat at the opera. "Nothing untoward has happened to my body."

Nothing untoward? "You're in a cell?" He nodded. "Take me there. *Now*."

In the blink of an eye, our dreamselves went from the lush harem to a dank, dark cell. Crumpled against the far wall was a corpse. It twitched and I jumped; so, not quite a corpse, not yet, anyway. Whoever it was had been badly beaten, his skin covered in bruises and sticky clots of blood. Then the body twitched again, into the light, and I noticed a thatch of hair like a dandelion gone to seed; Micah had once warned me that a glamour would dissolve if its wearer fell asleep. Or was beaten to a bloody pulp.

"Micah," I cried, falling to my knees before his body. "What did they do to you?" I tried to caress his bruised cheek, but my hand, insubstantial, passed through him. Then his dreamself's arms were around me, and I buried my face in his chest.

"I'm so sorry," I sobbed. "You're so hurt, all because of me and my stupid brother. You'd be better off without us."

"It looks worse than it is," he soothed. "I will be fine."

"Fine? You're unconscious!"

"I needed to sleep in order to dreamwalk and find you." He pried me away from his chest, and turned my face toward his body. "Have a look at my back." Hesitantly I crept around his prone form, and gasped when I saw his expanse of caramel skin, marred by bruises and blood, but devoid of his mark.

"They took it!" I shrieked. "Your silver!"

"No, love," he murmured, once again taking me into his arms. "I drew my silver deep into my body. Even now, it is healing me." I eyed his body dubiously; he certainly didn't look like he was healing. "Those who captured us were intent on the rest of you, Baudoin's children and mate. They did not realize who I am, or that I am of metal."

"Still, we need to get you out of here," I began, when Micah hushed me again.

"Love, truly my predicament is not as dire as yours. Look." He crouched at his body's feet and indicated heavy shackles that chained him to the floor.

"I'm chained with metal. And the door is fitted with metal hinges. When the time comes, I will merely walk out."

"When the time comes," I repeated. "Where's Mom?"

Micah's face darkened. "When I last looked in on her, she was being interrogated. Come, I'll take you there."

We slipped through the heavy wooden door and navigated a bustling corridor; while our dreamselves could instantly reach our physical forms, once we were actively dreaming, we were limited to far more basic means of transportation. Though no awake persons could see us while we were dreamwalking, I was decidedly embarrassed to be walking alongside a naked elf.

"You may keep looking," Micah commented, catching me before my eyes could dart away.

"Why did they strip you?" I mumbled. Until now, I'd had no idea that my dreamself could blush.

"Looting, most likely," he replied. "Ah. Here it is."

We slipped through another door and found ourselves in a larger, cleaner version of Micah's cell. Mom was tied to a chair, thankfully with her clothes on, and surrounded by several small creatures, squat and gray-skinned and so ugly I couldn't stop looking at them. Micah, after laughing at my description, agreed that they were orcs, though these few were smaller than those in the Whispering Dell. Then again, those orcs had been mostly beer belly.

"Again, where do we send the message?" the smallest orc, standing on a table in order to be at Mom's eye level, shouted in her face.

"Again, I do not know!" Mom spat. Her blue eyes blazed, and I almost felt sorry for the orcs. They had no idea what they'd gotten themselves into. While her children were being held, Mom would pretend to play their games, but once she knew we were safe, they would feel the full wrath of the Queen of the Seelie Court.

"What message?" I whispered to Micah, though only he could hear me.

"They wish to send a ransom note to your father," Micah replied. "They believe Maeve knows of his location."

Stupid orcs. They knew nothing of the Corbeau family dynamic. "Will they hurt her?"

"Perhaps, but not seriously. If they kill her, not only will they risk Baudoin's wrath, but they won't receive their coin." I nodded, and we withdrew to the corridor, mostly because I could hardly hear over Mom shrieking curses in Gaelic.

"So, what's our plan?" By the time I'd finished speaking, we were back in the harem room with Max and Sadie. Oh, and my body, too.

"You will wait here, and I will come for you," Micah replied.

"Micah." I placed my hand on his arm, which was foolish. I couldn't stay his dreamself like I could his physical form. "Are you… Will you be able to make it here?"

"Of course." He brushed his thumb over my cheek, catching a tear. "I am nearly healed. Once my dreamself returns, I will wake, and then I will come for you."

Infuriating man! So calm and confident, while I was terrified for his life. Since our captors hadn't gleaned his identity, Micah was the least safe among us, the expendable one. I could deal with being captured, my mother being interrogated; hell, I could even deal with a crazy queen and Old Stoney's hatred. What I could not deal with was Micah being expendable.

"If you die, I will kill myself and follow you to the underworld," I declared. "If you dare leave me, I will torment your soul until the end of time."

The bastard smiled. "Good." Then he kissed me, lightly at first, but when he would have moved away, I threw my arms around him and held him fast. Since he wasn't wearing anything, I was very aware of how much he enjoyed that.

"Sara," he began, but my kisses silenced him. Right then, I needed him more than I'd ever needed anything, more than breath or water or sunlight. Micah drew me to the far side of the room, down onto a heap of the oversized floor cushions. We'd only made love once before while dreamwalking, and it had been amazing, so amazing that I hadn't wanted to repeat it, in case that one time had been a fluke.

It wasn't.

Afterward, Micah stroked my back while I lay on my stomach, watching my slumbering body. "My body's wearing clothes, but my dreamself isn't," I mused.

"Did you think your clothes would just disappear?" he asked, and I laughed. We cuddled a few heartbeats longer, then Micah went from teasing to grave.

"I must go now. We've dallied long enough." He rose then and murmured a few words that extinguished the drug-laced incense. Someday, far from here, he was going to have to teach me a few of these tricks. I was starting to think he was leaving all the good stuff out of Sadie's Magic 101 lessons. "By the time your body wakes, I will be here."

"If you're not, I will come for you," I promised. "We will leave this place together."

"I am counting on it." Micah squeezed my hand, and then he was gone.

23

Vibrating again…

I opened my eyes—my physical eyes this time—and saw Micah's hands gently shaking my shoulders; once again, he was the source of my seismic event. I opened my mouth to speak, realized that that wouldn't be happening, then rolled onto my hands and knees and retched violently. Aw, I ruined the pretty silk pillows.

"The incense," Micah murmured as he rubbed my back. The nausea passed soon enough, and Micah went on to wake Sadie and Max. They had similar, disgusting, reactions to the smoke.

"What was in that stuff?" I rasped. Sadie had gotten over it fairly quickly, but Max's skin had taken on a grayish cast. He was coated in a thin sheen of sweat, and he couldn't stop puking. "Will he be okay?" I asked, jerking my chin toward Max.

"He will," Micah assured as he helped me to my feet. I saw that he wasn't naked any longer, but had covered himself in dark iron armor. He'd even fashioned himself a short sword, complete with a belt.

"The manacles and hinges?" I asked, to which he nodded. "Did any guards see you?"

"They won't be following," he said flatly. As a rule, Micah avoided violence, mostly because I couldn't stomach it, but since these people—goblins, orcs, whatever they were—had captured us, I was fine with Micah doling out whatever punishment he saw fit. And after the beating they had given Micah, I wouldn't mind seeing this place razed to the ground.

Once the smoke had dispersed and Max's stomach was somewhat calm, Micah informed my siblings of our recent capture and Mom's interrogation over Dad's whereabouts.

"I don't remember being captured," Max protested, rather weakly, since our current situation proved otherwise.

"I remember you walking into a deep shadow, then the shadow moved," Sadie whispered. "Mom yelled for you to stop, but you were too far ahead to hear her. Then, we woke up here."

Micah nodded. "They took Max first, as an enticement for Maeve," he said. "They could not risk her flight."

Max pushed himself upright, wobbling only a bit. "All right. Let's get Mom and get out of this hellhole."

Our progress toward Mom was ridiculously slow, being that Max needed to vomit every few minutes, the retching punctuated by some Olympic-caliber belches. I wondered if, as the first one captured, he'd been exposed to some other drug along with the smoke. Whatever it was seemed to be working its way out of his system, albeit in the most revolting way possible.

"Maybe you should sit," Sadie suggested after he yakked on her feet.

"Nah," he said, shaking his head. "I'll be fine."

"Then puke on a bad guy next time!" she huffed.

Eventually, we made it to the last bend in the corridor before Mom's cell. We'd only encountered two guards along the corridors, both of whom Micah had quickly and quietly dispatched.

"Wait here," Micah murmured, then he crept forward and peered around the corner.

"Hey, sis," Max rasped, his rampant puking having wrecked his throat. Not to mention his breath.

"Yeah?"

"Next time you want to get it on with your boyfriend, get your own room."

My mouth fell open, while my face went flaming hot. "I-I don't know what you're talking about."

"I'm a Dreamwalker too, remember?"

I banged my forehead against the slimy stone wall; no, at the time I'd forgotten all about Max's supernatural abilities. Sadie started pestering Max for information, wanting in on the torment of me, when thankfully Max puked again. *Wow. I'm glad that Max puked. That smoke must have made me as nutty as Oriana.*

Before Max could recover himself, Micah returned, wearing an interesting look on his face. When I asked why, he replied, "That guard happens to be the fellow who stole my belongings. I'd rather like them back."

I peeked around the corner and looked at the goblin, who was standing guard about half the corridor's length away, monitoring the final turn before Mom's cell. Like the one who'd approached Max at the fountain, he was short and stout, with the same generous paunch and waxy yellow skin. He had crammed his bowed legs into Micah's pants, the leather bunched up around his ankles, and Micah's sword, the point of the scabbard scraping the floor, dangled from his belt. I saw a crumpled shirt and pair of boots behind the creature, as if he'd tried to wear them but had long since given up. Clearly, goblins and elves did not frequent the same tailors. I opened my mouth to question if, since Micah's things were already ruined, this distraction was worth it, when I saw the token I'd made for Micah hooked onto the creature's belt.

"Kill it," I said. Micah grinned and pressed a kiss to my forehead before returning to the corridor.

"My friend," Micah announced as he stepped into view. "Do you remember me?"

The goblin's jaw went slack, his curved, cracked toenails scraping the floor as he backed away, trapping himself between Micah and the wall. Micah grabbed him by his loose, wrinkly throat and slammed him into the stone wall once, twice, thrice. As the goblin's body slid downward into a pool of blood and filth, Micah retrieved his sword, his shirt, and, most importantly, his copper token.

"I did like those boots," Micah said wistfully, toeing the heap of ruined leather.

"I'll get you new boots," I promised.

He smiled at that, then he turned and beckoned us to follow. We rounded that last turn, then we were outside Mom's cell. Presumably, the guard who was supposed to be stationed by the door had heard the commotion down the hall and abandoned his post, probably to round up reinforcements, so we needed to make this rescue quick.

Things inside the cell were much the same as when Micah and I had dreamwalked in; Mom was still tied to her chair, and the orc in charge was still on the table, but now he was jumping up and down as he bellowed threats in Mom's face, threatening her family's lives as spittle sprayed everywhere. Not wise behavior on Mr. Orc's part, not wise at all.

At our entry, the orc spun around, his spindly arms flailing as he called for his goblin guard to apprehend us. Little did he know his guards had either taken off or been more permanently relieved of their positions. And the rest of the orcs in the cell seemed content to let him handle us newcomers.

Mom leaned to the side, saw that the four of us were relatively unharmed, and stood as her rope bindings fell away. The head orc fell silent for a moment, but only one; then, he resumed screaming and hopping. Mom, who'd long since had enough of this nonsense, leaned forward and clapped a hand on the orc's bald little head.

"Silence!" Mom commanded, and the orc's mouth was instantly replaced by a smooth patch of skin. This only got the little critter even more worked up, so Mom yelled, "Cease, or I'll do away with something far more dear!"

At that, the orc stilled himself. "I don't know if this feeble, ill-advised plan was your doing, or if someone else has directed you," Mom continued, "but risk coming after a Corbeau at your peril. We are *not* to be trifled with." She glared in turn at each of the orcs, most of whom were now cowering against the back wall of the cell; I noticed that some were missing ears or noses. Mom's curse had affected more than just the orc in charge, then. Good.

"You're going to let them live?" Max asked, looking over at the furious, grunting creature. Despite his lack of an orifice, he still had a lot to say.

"It sends a message," Mom replied. "Attack my family, be horribly maimed. Attack my family again, and you will perish."

"Won't he starve?" Sadie asked, glancing over her shoulder at the mouthless orc.

"The curse only lasts forty-eight hours. Though he still has his teeth and may well gnaw his way through before then."

Sadie, now a lovely shade of green that coordinated nicely with Max's sickly pallor, placed a hand over her mouth as she nodded. Mom patted her youngest's shoulder, then turned on her heel and marched us out of the cell. Disheveled and filthy, she nevertheless walked down the murky corridors like the queen she was, with her head held high. We encountered no guards, goblin or otherwise, though if they had any sense at all, they'd long since fled.

When we reached the public areas of this fine establishment, I saw that Micah's assessment was correct—we were in a brothel. Not one of the nicer brothels, either, if nicer versions of that sort of place existed. Based on the jaded faces of the workers, and the empty eyes of the patrons, this was nothing more than a study in hopelessness.

Heads swiveled toward us; wouldn't you know it, all the workers, and more than a few patrons, recognized the Lord of Silver, despite the fact that Micah was clad in iron. I was definitely going to have to ask him about this notoriety. Thinking that they were about to be shut down, apprehended, or worse, all the patrons and workers fled at once, out of doors and windows or any other conveniently placed opening. Once the place had emptied, we made our way outside into the welcome sunshine.

It was just after dawn, which meant that we'd spent half of yesterday and the entire night as the orcs' captives. We quickly navigated our way back to the square and soon reached the obsidian fountain where this little adventure had begun. Now that the adrenaline high of our escape was wearing off, we took a moment to rest. Sadie moved to dip her hands in the water, attempting to wash up, but Micah stayed her. By way of explanation, he dropped a pebble into the water, which hissed and smoked as it dissolved.

"Oh," Sadie croaked. "I guess I'll stay filthy." The dissolving stone reeked something awful, and Max retched. Again.

"Now what do we do?" I asked. "Clearly, that wasn't the way to Dad."

"Dad never dealt with orcs," Max said, wiping his mouth on the hem of his shirt. "No matter how deep in hiding he was, he never compromised his morals. Dad just wouldn't do that."

"This was some fool's notion of a way to earn coin," Micah said. "They saw Baudoin's son, and assumed—rightly so—that the son sought his father. The orcs attempted to intercede, but their sloppy kidnapping failed. Like as not, Baudoin has not set foot in this market for a long, long time." Micah looked at Mom while he spoke. Mom didn't acknowledge him, instead she stared at the fountain, scrutinizing the trail of noxious bubbles. All that remained of the once-solid stone.

"So, where could he be?" Sadie asked. She went on to ask Max what else he remembered, when Mom shook her head.

"Perhaps he isn't anywhere," Mom said. "Perhaps...perhaps when he stopped meeting Max, it was because he was...gone." I slipped my hand into Mom's and squeezed. She'd been holding onto Dad's memory for so long, I wondered if it had ever occurred to her that he had died, maybe quite some time ago. Rationally, we all knew that his death was a possibility, but out loud, we had always denied it. Out loud, we claimed that Dad was in hiding, and that he would come back.

Gods. Why were we always wrong about these things?

"What I do not understand," Mom said, blinking from something other than the rising sun, "is how they managed all of this so swiftly. It is not like we frequent the Goblin Market. Well, *most* of us don't," she added, with a withering look at Max.

"Maybe they were waiting for Max," I offered, but Max shook his head.

"I never come to the fountain anymore," he said. "I stick to the bars and the gambling dens. This square is too exposed."

"Makes no sense," Mom muttered.

"Come," Micah said, wrapping his arm around my shoulders. The iron armor he'd fashioned from his manacles was certainly not his finest work, and it had rough edges that bit into my flesh, but I didn't mind. At least he was with me. "Let us leave this vile place."

24

We trudged back up the hill and away from the Goblin Market, silent save for Max's occasional bouts of nausea. It had been proven, far, far beyond a shadow of a doubt, that Dad was not anywhere near us, not in body, or spirit, or…Well, let's just stop there. As much as the evidence pointed toward the obvious, I was not ready to consider my father as passed on. Not now, and maybe not ever.

I squeezed Micah's hand, grateful for his calming, solid presence. When I called him my knight in dirty armor, he didn't get it, but he smiled anyway. His battered leather shirt was tossed over his shoulder, and he was once again wearing the token I'd given him. Since he'd regained his own sword, he'd given me the iron one he'd made on the fly. It was a lot heavier than the one Ash had made me, and nowhere near as beautiful, but the edge was razor sharp; it seemed that Micah had been wrong in sending me to the blacksmith, since he managed to create quite fine weapons all on his own. I only hoped I wouldn't need it.

I also hoped that Mom would be okay. Since we'd left the Goblin Market, she'd done nothing but mutter away to herself. I wondered if Dad's lack of presence at his last known haunt, coupled with the years of mistreatment by Peacekeepers, had finally done her in.

"Do you think she'll be all right?" I asked Micah, my eyes on Mom. He didn't answer, so I tugged at his hand. When he still didn't answer, I followed his gaze down the road and gasped.

Iron warriors blocked our path.

"Stand aside," Micah boomed, for all the good it did him. The iron warriors, true to their nature, remained immobile. I counted seven standing shoulder-to-shoulder across the road, and a group of at least ten behind them, clustered together as if they were shielding someone important. That someone was probably the person in charge of this little event.

Micah, frustrated that the warriors refused to move or even acknowledge him, the Lord of Silver, raised his arm to fling them aside. They wobbled a bit, and one toppled over, but they remained on the road.

"You think you're so strong," came a gravelly voice from behind the cluster of warriors. "All you of

metal, thinking you're so much better than the rest."
In another moment, Old Stoney stepped around to the
front, a pair of orcs flanking him. The very same orcs
that had been in the Whispering Dell's tavern the day
Max and I were attacked by that iron warrior.

I glanced at my brother, and he nodded. Great.
We'd been captured, drugged, interrogated, beaten,
and then I find out that we'd also been followed by
orcs and iron warriors, for who knows how long, and
they had been on Old Stoney's payroll. Could my day
get any better?

"Interesting words, Farthing Greymalkin, coming
from one of stone who surrounds himself with iron
warriors," Micah observed.

"We of earth and stone have always been
stronger!" Old Stoney shouted, indicating the
warriors before him. Their feet were held fast by
fingers of living stone, thus keeping them in place
when Micah would have flung them away. "We
ruled the Elemental court for centuries! Nearly a
millennium, until you of metal betrayed us!"

"Fool, there was no betrayal," Micah countered.
"Those of stone had been challenged countless times
for the right to rule us all. You merely despair now,
because, the last time, you lost."

"And you now ally yourself with his children!"
the granite madman continued.

"Wait!" I shouted. Surprisingly, Old Stoney paid
attention to me this time. "What about *his children*?
What about my father?"

His face split like a fissure carved out by a river long since dry. "He was our greatest rival, for all that he fell before us."

"Our?" I demanded, but Max got it right away.

"Ferra," he ground out. "You and Ferra killed my father?"

"We did him one better," Stoney said. "You recall when iron warriors attacked your prison, boy?" Max, too shocked to be offended, nodded. "That was your father's feeble attempt to rescue you. We captured him ourselves and turned him over to the human magistrates."

And, just like that, we were all struck dumb. Now we *knew* that Dad hadn't died when he'd stopped meeting with Max, and that he'd tried to rescue Max from the Institute, which meant that he had been alive just a few years ago. Thanks to Old Stoney, this was the first new information we'd had about my father in more than a decade.

Thanks to Old Stoney, we now knew that he and Ferra had betrayed my father and turned him over to an enemy even worse than the two of them combined. Who knows what the Peacekeepers had done to him since then.

"Disappointed that you allied yourself with a loser?" Mom said, her voice dead calm. "It must pain you, Greymalkin, to have betrayed your kind, only to watch Ferra falter and die." Mom crossed her arms and raised her chin, her eyes glazed as if she was about to take on Old Stoney hand-to-hand. "Pity you weren't there to watch her rust. It was a fitting end for one like her."

"Mom," I warned.

"*Mom*?" Stoney sneered. "Baudoin's whore, here in the flesh?" He laughed, but Mom didn't so much as flinch.

"Don't you dare talk about my mother that way!" I shouted. As Stoney opened his mouth for one of those "who do you think you are" retorts, the warriors before him melted. And when I say melted I mean *melted*, as if they were butter left out on a hot day. The pain behind my eyes told me that I was the one responsible, and that I was about to faint.

"Sara," Micah began, catching me about the waist. I shook my head in reply; I wanted his focus to remain on Old Stoney, not shift to me.

"You've no one left to hide behind," Mom observed. "So, Greymalkin, why don't you tell me everything you know about my Beau, and I'll consider letting you live."

Instead of speaking, Old Stoney grinned. Later, I understood that melted metal is similar to magma, the even hotter, liquid rock that flows beneath the earth's surface, the stuff that's called lava once it erupts from volcanoes. I would also understand that my reducing the iron warriors to their liquid states had given Stoney an idea, and that he was a diabolical man, more than a bit crazy, and that he had gone into this meeting knowing that he wasn't coming out alive.

Old Stoney raised his arms, and stone caps grew over the pools of cooling metal, far out of our reach. Stoney cackled, chilling my blood despite the great geysers of lava bursting from his feet. Max shouted something about not being able to reach the metal below the bedrock, and I felt Micah's influence tug at the sword in my hand, saw his armor rattle against his limbs. Then Micah grabbed my shoulders and threw me behind him amidst a gale of oppressive heat and impossible loudness. I passed out before I hit the ground.

25

Black ash rained around me, like a dusting of dry, dirty snow. I brushed it away from my face, coughed a bit, then took a few deep breaths. I explored the ground with my fingertips, feeling for my sword; when I found it, the hilt didn't seem right. Sluggishly, I realized that it was the sword Micah had fashioned from the iron manacles, not the beautiful weapon Ash had made especially for me.

Micah. My last memory was of him shoving me away, and then...

I struggled to a sitting position, shaking off more cinders in the process, and took in the scene around me. There was Sadie, lying on her side, but alive and breathing. Behind her, Max was helping Mom to her feet. Before us lay cooling puddles of iron and lava, belching great billowing clouds of steam, and beyond that was Old Stoney's body, his chest cleaved in two by a mass of white metal. By a mass of silver.

Where is Micah?

"Micah?" No answer. "Micah? Micah Micah Micah Micah MICAH!"

I remembered him standing on my left side, shoving me behind him and shouting. Now, all I could see was ash, blanketing the ground, no shapes that resembled bodies. I crawled forward, feeling with my hands, my feet, searching for any sign of him. At last, after far too long, I came upon a small heap of stones mixed in with the ash. I pushed the topmost layer aside, and found a hand.

Gods, it could have been a corpse for how cold it was; the skin had already gone bluish. Still, I knew it was Micah, *my* Micah, and as I dug him out, my skin and nails tearing against the stones and cinders, I knew he wasn't dead. He could not be dead. He was not allowed to be dead. When I unearthed his face, eyes closed and mouth slack, my heart almost stopped.

"Silverkin!" I shrieked. If anyone knew how to help him, it would be the silverkin. Shep always knew what to do.

"Sara." I looked at the hand on my shoulder, unsure why it was there, and followed the attached arm up to Max's face. His eyes were sad, resigned. "He's gone. Let him rest."

"Not gone," I said, holding Micah's cold cheek against my neck. "He promised me he would be okay. He promised me we would leave together."

"Sara—"

"Silverkin!" And then they were there, crowding around Micah and me like a diminutive cavalry. "Shep!" I called, finding their leader amongst the masses. "Shep, I don't know how he's hurt. Can you tell me?"

"He's sacrificed himself for you," answered a gravelly voice. I turned and saw the crone hobble toward us through the clouds of steam. "He had nothing left, no weapons he could use against so great a foe, so he used his silver in your defense."

Her gray head nodded toward Micah's chest; I looked and saw that his armor had melted away, leaving behind a bare expanse of skin. Then I looked to Old Stoney's corpse, and the mass of silver that had killed him. I was awed by Micah's sacrifice.

"How do I help him?" I demanded, my tears mixing with the ash and stinging my eyes.

"Oh, but if I told you, you'd surely owe me," the crone sneered.

"I'll owe you!" I shrieked. "I'll owe you anything! Just tell me how to save him!" Perhaps it was only the ash in my eyes, but I thought I caught a satisfied smile on the crone's lips.

"If he cannot manage to replenish his silver, and quickly," she continued, "our Lord Silverstrand will not be able to heal himself, and he will surely die."

"Then how do we replenish him?" Before the crone could reply, the silverkin began molding themselves into a flat surface, the base for a silver cairn. I remembered when Oriana had been rescued from the Iron Court, and how she had been bound in golden chains, and gold had been piled upon her to replace the element she'd lost.

If it worked with Oriana, it would work with Micah.

It had to.

He was not allowed to die.

Methodically, I removed what was left of the iron armor from Micah's body, then I helped the silverkin move him onto the silver platform. Without a moment's hesitation, I lay down beside him as the silverkin fitted themselves together above us, like a tiny metal igloo. Dimly, I heard Sadie bawling, Max and Mom yelling for me to stay away, that I'd suffocate beneath all the silver. Honestly, I didn't care. Micah needed me, so I was staying.

I don't know how long we were under the silver cairn, hours or days or maybe even years, before Micah twitched. I'd fallen asleep against his chest, my cheek against his throat, one hand laced into his while my other arm pillowed his head. Images floated behind my eyes, like a greatest hits episode of our short time together. The first time Micah had kissed me, both in a dream and in the flesh. The time I had been sick, and he'd brought me tea and toast in bed. The first time I'd felt his tongue against my mark.

But then, the twitch.

I held myself still, not quite believing that he'd moved, not breathing for fear I'd miss the next sign of life. Then, he twitched again.

Carefully, I pulled myself up to look at his face, cast in a muted silver glow. His eyes flickered behind his lids; I hoped he was having a good dream, like I'd been, and not reliving his last few waking moments.

"Micah," I murmured, the silver cairn creating an odd echo. "Micah, please be all right. Please." A tear splashed onto his cheek; as I wiped it away, he turned toward my hand.

"Micah!" I kissed him, then held him close, then kissed him again.

"Sara?" he croaked, his silver eyes slowly opening. "What…" He got a look at our silver ceiling, and began again. "Where are we?"

"You used all of your silver to kill Stoney. The silverkin had to heal you." He looked again to the cairn, recognition lighting in his eyes.

"And you stayed with me?"

"I did." Micah brought my face directly before his, so close our noses touched.

"Sara, you might not have survived this," he whispered, his hand trembling as he stroked my hair. "Love, never put yourself in danger for me."

"Why not? You do it for me all the time."

Micah couldn't really argue with that fact. "My copper girl," he murmured, caressing my cheek. "My copper girl, who means more to me than my life."

After a few more moments of cuddling, Micah placed his hand flat against the roof of the cairn, which was evidently the signal for the silverkin to disperse. We blinked as we sat up, joints creaking, bathed in the bright sunlight. As we stretched the kinks from our bones, something on Micah's arm caught my eye.

"What's this?" I asked, grabbing his wrist. There was a band of copper around his left wrist, spiraling up his arm like a ribbon.

"And here," Micah murmured, indicating my right wrist, which now bore a similar ribbon of silver. Somehow, during the healing process, we'd gotten marks of each other's metal. "We are truly joined, my Sara."

I couldn't help it, I laughed. Maybe I was a bit hysterical, being that Micah had nearly died, and his healing had involved both of us being buried alive under a mountain of metal, and we'd received permanent jewelry as a parting gift. Yeah, only a bit hysterical.

"Better than rings, huh?" I teased.

"But you will still give her one." I turned and saw Mom, smiling, along with a worried Sadie and a pissed Max; the crone was nowhere in sight, thank the gods. Of course my family had waited here for us, though I wished they hadn't. If this venture hadn't worked out, I'd have hated for them to be burdened with two bodies.

"I will, Maeve," Micah murmured, gathering me against him. "On that, you have my word."

26

Our return to the Whispering Dell was, thankfully, uneventful. I was concerned about leaving Old Stoney's body out in the open, but Micah and Max both assured me that scavengers would be by to collect the metals and stone; Micah hadn't even wanted the silver that had come from his own mark, claiming it was tainted. At least, if he was rebuilt into a shop, or maybe into an outhouse, Old Stoney would finally be doing something useful.

Micah's recovery was slower that I would have liked, but some things, like healing, can't be rushed. Why they can't be rushed no one could adequately explain to me, but as long as he got stronger every day, I held off my complaints. Since Micah still needed close contact with his metal in order to complete his healing, our bed had been transformed from the heavenly feather and down confection I so loved into a solid silver couch. It was the most uncomfortable thing I'd ever experienced, more like a torture device disguised as modern art that any sort of bed, far worse than even a corset could be.

And every night I gladly laid myself down on that metal monstrosity, because it meant I was lying next to Micah.

As much as I complained about the slow healing process, it only took six days of sleeping on metal before Micah proclaimed that his silver was fully restored. We then started taking daily walks, ranging a bit further each day until Micah could walk to the orchards and back without tiring. Then he started getting frisky again, chasing me around the orchards, leaping out from behind trees to capture me, weaving flower crowns as apologies for knocking me to the ground. It was as sure a sign as any that my Micah was going to be okay.

One morning, after a late-night swim in the Clear Pool, I awoke alone. We'd gone back to sleeping in the real bed, which was so deep and luxurious that I slept late more often than not. On this morning, not only had Micah risen first, the silverkin were waiting for me.

"What's up?" I asked Shep. He chirruped and waved his hands, then quickly ushered me downstairs. I found my family lounging around the atrium, wearing their Sunday best along with a few smug grins. When I asked what was going on, they refused to answer and practically ordered me to have breakfast with Micah. Being that I was sore, sleepy, and starving, I took their advice.

My pajama-clad self shuffled into the dining hall, where a lavish meal was set out on the long table. At the head of the table stood Micah, resplendently attired in the silver coat and black breeches he'd worn for our audience with the Gold Queen. He'd taken to wearing his sword again, and the sight of him made my mouth water almost as much as the food did.

"What's all this for?" I asked.

Instead of answering, Micah pushed three copper pennies, each now brightly polished, toward me. "Make me a ring." I stared at the pennies for a few moments, wondering why he had such a dire need for jewelry before we'd even had breakfast, when I all but lost my breath. "Today?"

"Unless you've changed your mind," he replied. I took that last step toward him and wrapped my arms around his neck.

"No. Today is perfect."

And it was. We went to the chapel where Mom and Dad had been married, which, like so many other religious institutions, had been converted to a Hall of Records. Micah had thought to glamour the lot of us (unfortunately, he did not make Max into Maxine again), so the drones just passed obliviously overhead.

After we'd spoken to the Peacekeeper on duty, a stiff little man called Corporal Rawson, and filled out the required forms, the ceremony got underway. My official paperwork said that I, Sara Evans, was marrying Mike Silver, but I didn't care what a few scraps of paper said. All I cared about was the man waiting for me at the end of the aisle.

"You ready?" Max asked. In Dad's absence, he'd agreed to walk me down the aisle, though Sadie had balked when I'd asked her to be my flower girl.

"Yeah," I replied, tucking my fingers into his elbow.

"Nervous?"

"Nah. I can handle this." With that, Max squeezed my fingers and led me to Micah.

The Peacekeeper droned on for a bit, mostly about our duty to our government, but I hardly heard him. I don't think Micah was paying much attention either, since when it came time for the vows, he had to be prompted.

"Have you written your own vows?" the Peacekeeper repeated. Micah blinked, then he nodded.

"I have." Micah took my hands. "My Sara, my love. You are my reason for waking, for breathing, for being. From the first moment I saw you, you have intrigued me, infuriated me, enthralled me. You are mine, my Sara, for now and always." He caressed my cheek, and then he pressed his lips to mine. "Always."

"Ahem." Micah and I parted, and looked toward a slightly peeved Corporal Rawson. "The kiss comes *after* her vows."

"My apologies," Micah said, stepping back from me. "Please. Continue."

Rawson huffed a bit, then he turned to me. "Your vows, please."

I looked at Micah, searching his guise of Mike Silver, wondering what I could possibly say that would explain how I felt. Then I saw the glint in his silver eyes, and I realized that I didn't need to explain anything. Micah had always known that I loved him, and that I always would.

"I love you," I murmured, lacing my fingers with his. "I'm yours."

Rawson cleared his throat again; these were not Peacekeeper-approved vows. Rather than berate us for not being properly prepared, he decided to hurry us along. "The rings?"

With that, I squeezed my hand around the pennies. A moment later, I slipped a copper band that mimicked an oak leaf onto his finger. Micah smiled, then took my breath away as he produced a silver ring shaped like two twisted silver vines, crowned with a deep green emerald. If we ever get this elemental royalty business sorted out, Micah and I have a definite future in jewelry design.

"May I kiss her now?" Micah asked, once the ring was on my finger.

"I now pronounce you husband and wife," intoned Corporal Rawson, while Sadie cried and Mom beamed. Even Max looked happy. "You may kiss the bride."

Micah swept me into his arms. "Bride," he murmured as he kissed me. "My bride."

That journey back to the manor was as joyous as the last had been somber. I'd never been so happy, knowing that I was going to spend the rest of my life with such a wonderful, amazing man. Never, not once as a kid, and definitely not during my less than perfect adulthood, had I ever thought I'd find someone to love me, never mind marry me. I was, without a doubt, the luckiest person in the world, Mundane or otherwise.

"I will challenge you for that position," Micah murmured when I shared my feelings.

Even though I was, without a doubt, happier than I'd ever been, a few less than awesome thoughts kept nagging at me. First and foremost, we needed to resume our search for Dad and figure out what was really going on with all those copper gifts in the atrium. And, there was the fact that I owed the crone…something. Man, Micah was going to freak when he found out.

"What are you thinking, love?" Micah murmured. I decided to shelve all of those niggling concerns for now and just enjoy my wedding day.

"Nothing," I demurred. "Just about how much I like being married to you."

Micah brought my hand to his mouth and kissed it. "I was thinking exactly the same thing."

When we reached the manor, we learned that while we were off in the Mundane realm, the silverkin had put together quite an impressive feast, and a whole new heap of gifts from the Whispering Dell was piled before the entrance. Word sure travelled fast in the Otherworld.

Just as I suggested that we invite those from the village to the feast, because we had plenty of food, and weren't weddings supposed to be big and loud and boisterous, the silverkin suddenly swarmed Micah, chirruping and chittering away. Mom and Sadie looked thoroughly confused, but I'd learned quite a bit of their birdlike language. Someone was coming up the main walkway, someone unknown and...powerful.

"But, who could it be?" Micah asked, while Mom demanded to know what was wrong with the silverkin now and didn't we regret putting them back together again? I looked down the walkway and saw a form approach, a man's form. He walked with a purposeful swagger, almost cocky, his bright hair flashing in the sunlight. Recognition flared, and I threw open the door.

"Dad!" I cried, and I leapt into my father's arms.

ACKNOWLEDGEMENTS

For all of you who remember *Copper Girl's* acknowledgements (riveting reading, that), you know that the process of creating this little stack of pages is arduous at best, and at worst... Well, let's not go there.

Anyway, what I declined to mention is that all of those little straws that pile up on the author's back are multiplied a hundredfold when one is working on a series. Plot holes? Multiply them times four. Worldbuilding? Better remember all those awesome details. And, while you're plotting the next few installments, please try not to stray from the over-arching theme of the whole thing.

Sheesh.

But, you know what makes it all worthwhile? You, the readers. For every one of you that left a positive review of *Copper Girl*, thank you! As for those reviews that weren't so positive, I took them all to heart and tried to learn from my mistakes to make *Copper Ravens* the best story it could be. And, for the woman who came up to me at New York Comic Con (Rachel!) bearing a slightly worn *Copper Girl* and demanding my autograph, you not only made my day, but my year.

Without all of you, the readers, this would be all for naught. Thank you, from the bottom of my heart.

The 400lb Gorilla

Matt Danmor thinks he's lucky. Not many people survive a near-death accident with nothing more than a bout of amnesia, a touch of clumsiness and the conviction that the technician who did the MRI had grey skin and hooves.

DC FARMER

the 400lb gorilla

SOMETIMES YOU HAVE TO MAKE YOUR OWN LUCK, OR DIE TRYING

Still, it takes time to recover from trauma like that, especially when the girl who was in the accident with you disappears into thin air. Especially when the shrinks keep telling you she's just a figment of your imagination.

IT IS MARCH 32ND, THE DAY
THAT DOESN'T EXIST...

...and Death, the agent of nightmares,
has been demoted and exiled to live
among mortals for the rest of his
unnaturally long life. Everyone knows
They don't look lightly on important
items getting lost or an agent falling in
love.

Call of the

Jersey Devil

By Aurelio Voltaire

Four Goth teens and a washed up musician get stranded in the Pine Barrens and discover that New Jersey really is a gate to Hell—and if they don't do something, being banned from the mall is the least of their worries.

THE OTHER TREE

DK MOK

*A grad student and a
disillusioned priest race a
greedy mage-corporation
in a search for the Biblical
Tree of Life.*

*A werewolf must find the murderer of
a child in Boston while coping with
frightening memory loss and the rest
of the supernatural community.*

What if YOU let someone precious slip away?

LISA AMOWITZ

BREAKING GLASS

When the girl Jeremy loves disappears, he tries to call her back from beyond the grave to solve her murder.

How far would YOU go to get them back?

Book A Trip To The Bermuda Triangle

A cruise ship. A beautiful island. Two sexy guys.
What could possibly go wrong?

In the Bermuda Triangle—a lot.

SPENCER HILL PRESS · spencerhillpress.com

ABOUT THE AUTHOR

Jennifer Allis Provost writes stories about faeries, orcs, elves, and the occasional zombie. She's a native New Englander who lives in a sprawling colonial along with her beautiful and precocious twins, a dog, two cats, a maroon-bellied conure, and a wonderful husband who never forgets to buy ice cream. As a child, she read anything and everything she could get her hands on, including a set of encyclopedias, but fantasy was always her favorite. She spends her days drinking vast amounts of coffee, arguing with her computer, and avoiding any and all domestic behavior.

Find her on the web at jenniferallisprovost.com.